# KINGZ OF THE GAME 2

Lock Down Publications and Ca$h
Presents
# Kingz of the Game 2
A Novel by *Playa Ray*

**Lock Down Publications**
P.O. Box 870494
Mesquite, Tx 75187

**Visit our website @**
www.lockdownpublications.com

Copyright 2019 Kingz of the Game 2

*This is a work of fiction. Names, characters, places, and incidents either are products of the author's imagination or are used fictitiously. Any similarity to actual events or locales or persons, living or dead, is entirely coincidental.*

**Lock Down Publications**
**Like our page on Facebook: Lock Down Publications @**
www.facebook.com/lockdownpublications.ldp
Cover design and layout by: **Dynasty Cover Me**
Book interior design by: **Shawn Walker**
Edited by: **Lashonda Johnson**

# Stay Connected with Us!

Text **LOCKDOWN** to 22828 to stay up-to-date with new releases, sneak peaks, contests and more…

Thank you.

# Submission Guideline.

Submit the first three chapters of your completed manuscript to ldpsubmissions@gmail.com, subject line: Your book's title. The manuscript must be in a .doc file and sent as an attachment. Document should be in Times New Roman, double spaced and in size 12 font. Also, provide your synopsis and full contact information. If sending multiple submissions, they must each be in a separate email.

Have a story but no way to send it electronically? You can still submit to LDP/Ca$h Presents. Send in the first three chapters, written or typed, of your completed manuscript to:

LDP: Submissions Dept
Po Box 870494
Mesquite, Tx 75187

*DO NOT send original manuscript. Must be a duplicate.*

Provide your synopsis and a cover letter containing your full contact information.

Thanks for considering LDP and Ca$h Presents.

# Acknowledgments

*Y'all know I always start off by showing my gratitude to my Lord and Savior. I mean where else did my wisdom and extraordinary talents come from? To the whole staff at Lock Down Publications & Ghostwriter Inc Literary Services, I appreciate the hard work and dedication you all put into this project to bring it to fruition. Hell, I even appreciate you all for getting on me about using 'Big' words in my writing, telling me that this is not a college exam and that people shouldn't have to stop reading the book to refer to Google in order to understand what I'm trying to convey to them. It's constructive criticism, in which I gladly accept.*

*I'm always thankful for my family and true friends who've been with me every step of the way. You know who you are. Other people who've supported me are Latasha Michelle Brooks, Dartanya 'Bravo' Brooks, Jessee 'J.J' James, Joseph 'Platinum Slim' Wright, Tony 'Bubble' White, Marcus 'Money' Morris, Kevon 'Number One' Thomas, Jaime 'Serio' Lopez, Oscar 'Nino' Reyes, Jonny 'Kuico' Deleon, Ruben 'Oso' Almaguer, Alexander 'Peso Loso' Moreno, Alonzo 'Dada' Pierce, Donta Green and everybody who've purchased the first installment of the King Of The Game Series. Much Love! Also, make sure to shop Drogueclothing.com for an assortment of some of the most fly gear on the market.*

*Thank You*
*Playa Ray*

*"When you're a King, there are no set rules in the game, because it's played by niggas who you Lord over. So, to be the King, means to never lose, because you set the rules and only a fool loses at his own game!"*

Randal 'Big Ru' Jones
CEO of FTP Records
Facebook: Randal Jones

Playa Ray

# CHAPTER 1

"What the fuck is all this!" James exclaimed as he neared Felicia's house, where an ambulance and several police cruisers were parked. He also noticed officers searching Black's BMW, which was parked behind Felicia's car.

"Man, I hope this shit ain't just popped off like this," Ray said as he observed the scene from the front passenger seat.

After James received the call from Black and explained everything to Ray, they apologized to the family and quickly made their exit. All the while, Ray was hoping Black was exaggerating, but, as he observed the scene, reality struck him like a slap in the face. But who would kidnap Felicia and Kevin?

Ray wanted to blame Drop Squad, but, for some reason, it didn't make sense to him. *It's not that they wouldn't pull such a stunt, because they would. But if they wanted to do something to me and my crew, they would have taken advantage of that chance outside Club Strokers last night,* Ray thought.

"Somebody was waiting on him, James said as he drove past the crime scene.

"Huh?" Ray broke from his thoughts, not hearing what his brother said.

"Somebody was waiting on him," James repeated.

"How you figure that?"

James told Ray about the sounds he'd heard in the background that concluded Black's call. Black was in mid-sentence when someone struck him. There was a short cry of pain, and the sound of both body and phone crashing to the floor. James listened for another two minutes as the culprits moved about the house. After all movement had ceased, James hung up.

"Why you ain't tell me that shit earlier?" Ray asked, after hearing the shocking news.

"Because, I ain't want you to panic and ask me all kinds of questions while I'm trying to figure this shit out."

"So, what we do?"

"Right now, we don't have any options," James answered.

"So, I guess we head back to grandma's house and try to have a Merry Christmas? Hopefully, we'll hear something by the time we get up with, Fred."

# CHAPTER 2

"It's too early for assumptions," Fred told James and Ray.

They were all assembled in the living room of James' house still known as *The Palace*. They had the television turned to the news to see if their friend had made the headlines, but the '*Top Story*' was about a male and female who were murdered in a car parked on Catheryn Street, last night. According to the reporter, the female, who was a known prostitute, was performing oral sex on the male at the time the car was riddled with bullets.

"So, you don't think he was kidnapped?" Ray asked.

"It's possible," Fred answered. "But if it was done for a ransom, we would have gotten a call by now. Like I said, it's too early."

"So, we just sit around and do nothing?"

"Nope," James cut in. "We continue conducting business as usual. If I'm not mistaken, you have a package to drop off at twelve-thirty."

"Yeah I do," Ray confirmed looking at his watch, seeing that it was eleven twenty-three.

"You gon' be aight?" Fred kept a wary eye on him as he stood, donning his large, black leather coat.

"Yeah, I'm good," he answered not making eye contact.

Fred and James exchanged glances. James was about to ask him if he needed someone to ride with him, but he was already headed out the door, closing it behind him.

"Man, this shit can't be happening," James said, taking a sip of his beer that was sitting on the coffee table. "And where the fuck is Curt with our money?"

"Ain't no telling," Fred picked up his cell phone. "I'll hit him up after I inform E' on this situation."

Eric answered almost immediately. "I was just about to call you, lil' bruh."

"What's up?" Fred asked.

"Somebody got at Curt, last night."

"He was robbed?"

"Nah, he got wet up. It's all over the news."

At that instance, Fred shifted his attention to the T.V., where they were still showing footage of the silver Acura with multiple bullet holes that grazed the sides.

"Damn!" he exclaimed in a low tone.

"What?" James asked, hoping he was not about to receive news he was not ready to accept.

"That's Curt," Fred asserted not taking his eyes off the screen.

It didn't take James long to discern what Fred was talking about. He, along with Ray and Fred, had been watching the news since it came on at eleven o'clock, waiting to hear something on Black, but neither of them had paid any attention to the familiar Acura.

"He was out there tricking off," Fred said almost to himself.

"I told that nigga 'bout that shit." Eric sounded somber.

"Well, I don't mean to change the subject, but we have another problem on our hands."

"What's that?"

Fred gave him the full run-down on Black, from what James and Ray told him.

"Man, what y'all done got into?" Eric asked after listening, and apparently reflecting both tragedies.

Fred thought back to the last heist that claimed the life of a member of the Drop Squad. He trusted his brother, but the Kingz made a royal oath not to mention anything about the robbery to anybody. No matter what.

"We're trying to sort this shit out now," Fred answered.

"I'll hit you back once we come up with something."

"Yeah, make sure you do that," Eric told him. "And y'all boys be careful!"

Fred ended his call and looked over at James, who had re-lit his blunt, and was staring at the ceiling as he slowly exhaled the weed smoke. Fred didn't smoke, but how he was feeling at the moment, he wanted to tell his friend to pass the blunt. But that would only cloud his mind, and he needed his mind completely clear as he tried to figure things out.

"It's them," James asserted, still staring at the ceiling. "They know."

"Yeah. I think so too," Fred agreed.

"But I had to do them, niggas!" James was now looking at Fred. "You know that!"

"We all know that, Jay," said Fred. "Right now, you, need to call Ray and tell him to retreat. We gotta shut down shop until we find out what's going on."

James was already dialing Ray's number. He was all for saving his brother's life, but shutting down shop was not part of his plans. The ball was rolling, and they were just starting to make progress and connect with the right people. Perhaps Fred was just speaking out of fear, but James had never known Fred to fear anything or anybody. Hell, he didn't think Fred feared God.

"Yeah?" Ray answered.

"Where you at?" James asked.

"I'm on the expressway," he answered. "Why?"

"Retreat."

"Do what?"

"Retreat," James repeated. "Come on back to The Palace."

"Is something wrong?"

"Um—" James lingered, debating if he should tell him now, or when he returned.

"Man come on with it," Ray prompted.

James lingered for another brief moment before telling him about Curt.

"So, y'all figure Drop Squad got their hands in all this?" Ray asked.

"Pretty much," James answered. "Just come on back."

"A'ight."

"He's on his way back," James said after concluding the call. "Now, what were you saying about shutting down shop?"

**\*\*\*\***

*Man, this is too much*! Ray thought to himself.

He was scared when he was informed about Black's situation. Obviously, Drop Squad had found out about them and linked them to the home invasion where one of their comrades was murdered. Now, they were out for revenge.

As soon as that thought entered his mind, bright lights flashed through the back window of his BMW. Looking through his rearview, he couldn't make out the make or model of the car that was flashing its lights, apparently trying to get his attention, but he could tell there were four occupants. He didn't know who they were, or why they were trying to flag him down, but he pretty much had a clue.

He didn't have to buy a vowel. The lights flashed again, putting Ray in the mind of a gun when it's being fired. That's when he realized that his right hand was rested on his gun in his lap.

"I ain't going out like this," he said to himself. "Not tonight."

Ray accelerated, pushing his speed from 55 mph to 65 mph. His pursuer must have done the same because his car was still within seven feet of the BMW. Not wanting to cause a stir or kill himself, Ray initiated his right turn signal, and casually eased into the next lane. That's when he finally caught a glimpse of the vehicle through the left-wing mirror. It appeared to be an old, light rusty-colored Dodge. Ray was not familiar with this car.

As he moved along the right side of a tractor-trailer, he glanced into the rearview to see the Dodge move into his lane, attempting to close the gap between them. Ray lightly pushed down on the gas pedal to clear the truck. Once that task was complete, he veered left, cutting in front of the truck, barely missing the bumper of another car.

As if his nerves weren't already bad, the blaring of the truck's horn didn't make it any better. It did, however, cause him to nudge the gas pedal, lest he be forced into a fishtail by this huge road hog, which made him wonder which would be less painful, a car wreck, or a barrage of bullets?

At the moment, he was not trying to find out. Hearing the truck's horn again, caused him to peer into the mirror to see that his pursuer had cut in front of the truck and was gaining on him.

Now, Ray was starting to weigh his options. He could take the next exit, then use traffic lights and back streets to make an escape. Or he could ride Interstate 285 until someone ran out of gas. They were not such bright options, but it was all he could come up with at a time like this.

He opted for the latter, being that he'd filled his tank before leaving his grandmother's house, and he was one hundred percent sure the Dodge was a gas guzzler. Besides, it would be way too easy for them to catch him on the city streets.

His pursuer had other plans. He shifted into the left lane and attempted to employ every horse that his car was equipped with. Ray's radio was off, so he could hear the roar of this four-wheeled metal beast as it neared the left side of his car. Undoubtedly, these guys were ready to get this over with. No more cat-and-mouse games.

Ray wanted to accelerate perhaps to remit the inevitable, but there was a van in front of him and another car to his right. Now, the Dodge which he now noticed was a two-door Charger with dark tinted windows had pulled alongside him. His first thought was to ease off the gas and toy with the brakes, but a mental picture of the tractor-trailer behind him ceased that thought.

Ray thought he must've had the heat turned up high because he was perspiring and extremely hot. He could feel the moisture on his hands as his left stayed glued to the steering wheel, and his right rested on some hard object in his lap— his gun! Keeping his eyes on the road and the Dodge, he fumbled around with his gun until he attained a firm grip, and his index finger touched the trigger. He cast another glance at the Dodge and saw that the passenger side window had started to roll down. Shit had just gotten serious!

# Playa Ray

# CHAPTER 3

"I can't agree to that one," James told Fred. "Ain't no way in hell!"

James had been pacing back and forth in front of the T.V., trying to convince Fred that shutting down shop would be a bad move, right now.

"I'm looking out for our best interest," Fred spoke in his usual composed tone.

"Our best interest is to get this money!"

"What about Drop Squad?"

"Man, fuck Drop Squad!" He faced Fred. "Them niggas better respect our hustle! They better respect the Kingz period! And if I find out they had anything to do with Black, I'ma buss every nigga I see with that chain on!"

"Now, suppose they were thinking the same thing," Fred stated ready to make his point. "Suppose they found out we had something to do with the death of their homeboy, and plan on knocking *us* off." James just stared at Fred. "That's what's happening," Fred continued. "At least that's what it looks like. Until we find out what we gotta shut down. Pull all workers off the streets. Stick close and keep a close eye on our families. That means I'll have to let E' know everything so he'll know what we're up against."

James thought about that for a moment, then stated, "You and Ray do what y'all feel is best. I organized this shit, so I'll follow through with the plans."

"Why the fuck are you being so difficult?" Fred was pissed off, but not at all surprised at James' behavior.

"I came too far to back down."

"It's not about backing down, Jay," Fred countered. "It's about making the right decision."

"And how do you know that shutting down shop would be the right decision?"

"I don't know," Fred confessed. "But that's all I can see, right now."

"Well, I can't see it," said James. "And we really don't know how Ray feels about it."

At the mentioning of Ray's name, Fred looked at his watch and saw that it was twelve minutes until one. James had spoken to Ray almost an hour ago.

Thinking the same thing, James grabbed his cell phone off the coffee table and speed-dialed Ray's number to no avail. Pressing *End*, he tried again, getting the same result.

"He ain't answering," James snarled.

They just stared at each other. They both had a strong premonition of shit being ugly.

**** 

"That shit ain't that damn funny!" Ray told B.J. and Moe, another one of their friends they'd grown up with, who was still laughing at the fact that they had inadvertently scared the daylights out of their friend.

They were on their way to have a nightcap with two girls who were now seated at a table across from them when B.J. spotted Ray's car and told Moe to flag him down. Being that Moe's horn didn't work, he had to activate his headlights. After pulling alongside Ray, and he identified them. He motioned for them to make the next exit where they assembled at the nearest gas station.

There, he told them about Curt, but withheld the news on Black, knowing that all kinds of questions would follow. Questions he was not allowed, nor able to answer. Ray knew James wanted him to retreat back to The Palace for fear of his safety. He didn't think Ray was competent enough to withstand or handle any street drama.

Thinking of that angered him a little. So, without making it seem like something was wrong, Ray asked B.J. and Moe to accompany him to East Point, where he was to make his drop. On the drive there, he was hoping to run into Drop Squad, or whoever was behind this chaos, but the drop had gone smooth as usual.

Now, he, B.J., Moe, and the girls were seated at a local barbecue joint in East Point.

"Boy, your scary ass hit the gas on our ass!" B.J. said, gaining control of his laughter. "That shit was too funny!"

"How's your mom?" Moe asked changing subjects.

"Better," Ray answered. "She has a boyfriend now."

"Y'all niggas let her have a boyfriend?"

"He seems like a nice dude," Ray admitted. "But you know how that goes."

"Yeah."

"We'll be closing in five minutes," the pot-bellied owner said before retreating through the door which he'd come.

"What you 'bout to get into?" B.J. asked Ray.

"I'm 'bout to head to the crib," he answered. "It's been a rough day."

"They say pussy soothes the savage beast," B.J. joked.

"It can also kill the savage beast," Ray said not meaning to sound comical although he laughed along with his friends.

"You got somewhere to go in the morning?" Moe asked Ray. "Nah."

"Shit, you might as well roll with us," Moe told him. "We already got a room. These girls are down for whatever."

Ray pondered that as he glanced over at the two girls who were done eating, and apparently ready to go. They were highly eye-catching. Ray considered the fact that he had not had sex in over a month, and he somewhat found it strange he was thinking of sex at a time like this.

"Aight. I guess I can chill for tonight." He gave in.

After gathering their coats, they all exited the restaurant, heading for their cars. Ray used his remote to start his.

"Can I ride with you?" one of the girls asked Ray.

Ray eyed the caramel-skinned female, who was looking at him with a warm smile, despite the thirty-degree weather. Then, he shifted his gaze to B.J. and Moe, who were giving him parallel confirming looks.

"Yeah, you can roll," Ray asserted, making eye contact with the girl for a brief moment before they climbed into the BMW.

"What movie is this?" she asked looking at the screen mounted above the radio.

"New Jack City," Ray answered, checking his cell phone for missed calls and messages.

There were ten missed calls, seven from James, and one each from his mother, sister, and Fred. If he didn't return anyone's call tonight, he knew he would have to call James.

"Man, where the fuck you at?" James demanded through the phone.

"I'm in East Point," Ray answered in a composed tone.

"What the fuck you doing out there?"

"I handled that," Ray told him. "I'll get up with y'all later."

Ray ended the call by shutting his phone off and shoved it into the glove compartment.

# CHAPTER 4

"Hey, my son!" Fred's mother beamed at him as he exited his room, clad in gray sweatpants and shirt. She was coming out of the bathroom, which was right across from his bedroom.

"Hey, Ma'" he mumbled, still not fully awake.

"Do you have any plans for the afternoon?" she asked.

"Not that I know of. Why?"

"I was hoping to be treated to some fish."

"I can do that."

It was the least he could do, after breaking her heart while they were having Christmas dinner with Eric and Sharonda. He had to tell her the child Tee was having was not his. He liked Tee, but not enough to take care of another man's responsibilities. After showering and getting dressed, Fred took his mother, who had donned the full-length fur coat she'd gotten for Christmas, to Captain D's, where they ate and reminisced about the past.

Fred was enjoying his mother's company, but it was hard to give her his undivided attention as he constantly thought about Black and Curt. During those times, he would periodically survey the restaurant for any potential threat.

"Fred, I have something to ask you," his mother spoke in a more serious tone. Fred just stared at her. He knew every time she spoke in this tone, something was amiss. "Are you in any kind of trouble?" she asked.

"Why would you ask me that?" He was hoping she hadn't noticed how strange he was acting.

"I um—" she hesitated. "I had a disturbing dream last night."

**** 

Awakening, James rolled over and squinted at the clock on top of the nightstand. He wasn't a bit surprised to see that it was almost one-thirty in the afternoon. After Fred left The Palace around one o'clock that morning. James called Brenda and told her that he was stressing, and in need of some therapy.

"As soon as this nigga takes his ass to sleep," she'd told him. "I'm on my way."

Hell, that took almost an hour, but James was too upset to sleep. Therefore, he was wide awake when she arrived. His therapeutic healing had taken place on the living room sofa, where Brenda let her mouth do all the work. She allowed him to ejaculate into her mouth, and she didn't let up until she was certain she had sucked every drop of semen from his swollen penis.

Feeling better afterward and being that it was still considered Christmas Night, he gave her a thousand dollars for her services, sent her on her way, then finally got some sleep. Now, he got out of bed, fired up the half of blunt that was in the ashtray, and made for the bathroom to take a shower so he could get ready for the Kingz meeting at five.

The meeting was early because there were packages to be dropped off and money to be made. The first drop of today was at six, so whether the Kingz decide to close shop, or continue, they would have enough time to make calls and convey the verdict to their clients.

****

"So, what's on ya mind, lil homie?" Ray asked Moe, who'd volunteered to walk him to his car, leaving B.J. and the girls in the motel room.

"I got a child on the way," Moe told him.

"Yeah?" Ray regarded his friend with admiration.

"Hell yeah!" Moe smiled back. "My girl is two months pregnant."

"Congratulations!"

"Thanks!"

"Do I know her?"

"I doubt it," Moe answered. "She's seventeen, stays in Cobb County with her parents. They're Christians."

"Uh-oh!" Ray asserted, shaking his head.

Moe chuckled. "Yeah, I know, I ain't even met them yet."

When they'd made it to Ray's car that was already running, Ray turned to face his friend, who looked like he wanted to say something.

"What's on ya mind?" Ray tried again.

"I need to get my paper right," Moe acknowledged. "I was hoping y'all would put me down."

"Nope," Ray answered sternly. "Ain't no way in hell, it's too dangerous."

"I know how dangerous it is," Moe admitted.

"Nah, Ray countered. "You *think* you, know how dangerous it is! This ain't no movie. Niggas are really losing their lives in this shit!"

"That's one of the consequences of being in the game, Ray," Moe stated. "It's called taking chances. Right now, I have a child on the way. I want to be established by the time my baby arrives. I'm willing to take a chance. Can you help me or not?"

"Of course, I can," Ray answered. "But if something happens to you, I would be responsible, and that's one responsibility I'm not ready for." With that said, Ray got into his car and drove away.

He had already figured Moe was going to come at him like that. He didn't mind helping his friend out, but things were a bit complicated right now, and Moe didn't need to get caught up in something he didn't know anything about. At that moment, Ray thought about his cell phone he'd left in his glove compartment all night. As he pulled it out, he saw that there was a message from James.

"The Palace, five p.m.," James' voice played through the phone.

Ray wanted to call him to see if he'd heard anything on Black but thought against it. He would find out everything at the meeting. Right now, he just wanted to eat, shower, and relax a little. He pulled into Maple Creek Apartments and saw Precious standing on the porch in her overcoat. To see her standing there alone in this cold weather, struck him as odd.

"You be missing all kinds of customers," she said as he approached.

"Yeah, I know," Ray said sticking his key into the lock of the burglar bar door.

"One of 'em told me to give you this," she said, producing a small, white envelope. "Some girl."

"What'd she look like?" Ray inquired, receiving the envelope that had his name in pink ink.

"Like she was twelve months pregnant," Precious answered, smiling.

That could either be Sylvia or Kim, Ray thought as he unlocked the next door and entered his apartment, almost forgetting about Precious.

"Can I come in?" she asked.

"Yeah," he answered, disregarding her as he tore open the envelope and pulled out the short note that was also written in pink.

It read: *I know you're still mad at me, and you have every right to be, but we need to talk. If you can find it in your heart to put the past behind us for a few minutes, I'll be at Petro, in the dining area of Iron Skillet. 9 p.m.*

Now, Ray just stared at the letter, trying to discern the handwriting. He wasn't all too familiar with Kim's handwriting, but he could clearly tell that it wasn't Sylvia's. Perhaps he should ask Precious for a better description. That's when he looked back and realized that the front door had been shut, and there was no sign of Precious.

'*Did she leave?*' he thought.

Dismissing the thought, he headed for his bedroom, but upon entering the living room, he stopped in his tracks, surprised to see Precious sitting on the sofa. He was even more surprised to see that she'd shed her coat and was staring at him with those hazel eyes he found extremely seductive.

"Is everything okay?" she asked.

"Yeah," he managed. "Everything a'ight. So, how can I help you?"

"By letting me help you."

"Come again."

"You be missing out on a lot of money," she told him. "I work from home, so I'm always here. Need I say more?"

"Not really," he answered staring at her as if he was trying to decide.

"I don't have any intentions of stealing from you," she stated. "But it's up to you to trust my word. That's all I have."

"Let me get back to you on that," Ray asserted, looking at his watch.

"When can I expect a reply?"

"Probably tonight."

Playa Ray

## CHAPTER 5

"We have two issues at hand," James told Ray and Fred, who accompanied him at the conference table. "First off, no one has heard anything on, Black. So, we'll have to notify his aunt, so she can file a missing person's report. Second, we have to come to some kind of agreement on what we're going to do about this business. Do we shut it down, or push forward? Now, before you offer your opinions, I want you to consider the consequences of both options. King Fred?"

"I believe we should shut it down for a while," Fred answered. "At least until we find out whose after us, and why."

"Your decision is highly respected," said James. "What's your decision, King Ray?"

"Well, we really don't know if anybody's after us," Ray answered, looking from James to Fred. "Black was a King, true enough, but no one knew that Curt was affiliated with us, except for the few customers he dropped off to."

"So, you feel we should continue?" James asked, feeling exuberant that his brother was in his favor.

"Yeah," Ray answered. "But we'll have to proceed with caution. Every drop should be made with all Kingz present, plus armed Kingzmen."

"I like that!" James admitted. "We can do this shit like the Italians and Columbians! I like that shit, King Ray! What you think about it, King Fred?"

"I like it," Fred answered. "I still think we should shut down for a while, for at least two weeks. That should give us enough time to find out if we're being targeted or not."

"We'll miss out on a lot of money in two weeks," James said. "And probably lose customers."

"We can make up for all that," Fred assured. "Right now, it's about our safety. We got our money right, so we can afford two weeks and a few customers."

Before James could convey his thoughts, his cell phone vibrated on the table. Being that this was a Kingz meeting, he was not allowed to answer it, but he did glance down at the screen. The number was unfamiliar, but what had him confounded, were the words.

'*Who the hell is calling me from Grady Hospital?*' he thought.

He figured it to be Kim, but why was she calling him? The baby wasn't due until February, but James had already concluded that he was not the baby's father. So, he just watched the phone until it stopped vibrating.

"What were you saying?" James asked Fred.

"We can make up for the loses," Fred repeated. "Right now, we have to—"

"Think about our safety," James finished for him. "The game ain't never been safe, King Fred. Shit, these days, it ain't even safe to go out and check ya mailbox, but if you feel like—"

The ring from the Kingz Distribution phone that sat in the middle of the table, grabbed his attention. Sliding the phone towards him, he noticed that the number on the screen was the same number that had just shown up on his cellular screen.

"Kingz," James answered the phone, refusing to say Distribution, being that he didn't know who was on the other end.

"May I speak to Jay?" came a female's voice.

This struck him as odd because the only female that referred to him as *Jay* was Kim. This was not Kim!

"Who is this?" he asked.

"I'm, ah—" she hesitated. "I'm Officer Singleton from the Atlanta Police Department."

James did not want to believe what he'd just heard. '*This has to be some kind of prank*', he thought.

The caller ID indicated that the call was coming from Grady Memorial Hospital, but the caller identified herself as an officer from the Atlanta Police Department.

Maybe Kim had been harmed or was in some kind of trouble. Then, at that moment, realization kicked in, Kim did not have the number to this phone. To her, this phone didn't even exist. James was just about to hang up when the female asserted.

"I'm at the hospital with your friend."

"You got the wrong number," James told her, not willing to proceed with this game, or whatever she had going on.

"He said you would say that."

"Look, I don't—"

"Keith Daniels," she announced, cutting him off.

Hearing her speak Black's government name, sent chills down his spine. He didn't know what to make of this, but his thoughts of hanging up quickly evaporated.

"What about him?" James asked sagely, being careful not to say anything that would incriminate himself, just in case this bitch had something up her sleeves.

"He wanted me to let you know that he's okay," she told him. "Right now, he's in recovery unit of Grady Hospital. Once they clear him, he will be transferred to the Pretrial Detention Center, where he'll be booked for breaking and entering, and vandalism.

"What happened?"

"I don't know," she answered. "He said he would call once he gets to Pretrial. I guess he'll explain everything then." She hung up.

James placed the receiver back into its cradle, then looked at Ray and Fred who were giving him similar inquisitive looks.

"What's up?" Fred asked.

"Long live the Kingz!" James exclaimed with a broad smile on his face.

\*\*\*

James pulled his BMW into the parking lot of Kroger City on Cleveland Avenue and spotted the white Lexus parked further away from the other cars. After the call from the officer that confirmed Black was alright. The Kingz all agreed they would continue with business, but all drops would be made with all Kingz present. Plus, four heavily armed Kingzmen, which was why Ray and Fred were also seated in the car with James, and four Kingzmen trailed behind them in a black Chevy Suburban.

James cut his lights and pulled in front of the Lexus as the Suburban parked further down. After they surveyed the area for any potential threat, Ray, who was seated in the back seat, got out and approached the Lexus. Looking around once more, he climbed into the back seat and produced a small paper bag.

"That truck with y'all?" the passenger known as Poppo, asked.

"Yeah," Ray answered.

"Y'all ain't bullshittin'!" Poppo exclaimed, laughing.

This was Ray's fourth time dealing with Poppo. Each time Ray made a drop to him, they'd kick it like they'd known each other for years. It was alright because Ray had always enjoyed his company. Tonight, Ray was going to have to take a rain check, it was already eight-thirty, and he had a rendezvous at nine. Plus, they were awaiting a call from Black, so they could get his bail fee in order.

"We're just being careful," Ray said, handing him the paper bag.

"Ain't nothing wrong with that," Poppo assured, nodding at the red-bone chick in the driver seat, who handed Ray a similar bag.

"You ain't gon' check it?" Ray asked Poppo.

"I'm a good judge of character," Poppo said, now looking back at him. "A person couldn't really judge you by your appearance, but I can tell you're not the type that would pull some bullshit. So, if something's wrong with the product, I'll view it as a mistake, and count it as a loss." Poppo placed the bag into the glove compartment, and, as if it was her cue, the girl started the engine. "I can see you're in a rush, so I won't hold you up," said Poppo.

"Yeah, I am."

"But you know where I'm at," Poppo told him. "I run Cleveland Avenue and half of Stuart Avenue. These niggas don't eat without my permission! And I'm still trying to find out who killed them folks on Catheryn Street, a couple days ago. Them niggas gon' pay!"

The mentioning of Curt's murder had Ray's full attention. He was ready to leave, but he couldn't depart without acquiring whatever piece of information he could.

"You knew the dude who was killed?" Ray tested.

"Nah," he answered. "I knew the girl. She was my girl's cousin. Although she smoked dope and sold her body, I had much love and respect for her."

"Honey ain't never hurt nobody," the girl finally spoke.

"Well, if you find out somethin', let me know," Ray said. "You know the number."

"I'll do that," Poppo assured.

****

It was twelve minutes after nine when Ray entered Petro and entered the dining area of Iron Skillet. He scanned the small dining area but didn't see Sylvia, Kim, or any familiar face amidst the small crowd. Then, at that very moment, he noticed someone waving at him from the back of the diner. *Sylvia!*

"Who wrote that letter?" he asked as soon as he sat down across from her. "That wasn't your handwriting."

Now looking at her, he realized he didn't recognize her at first, because her hair was cut low to her scalp, and not only did her stomach get bigger, but her face was looking a bit plump.

"I had to get somebody to write it for me," she said holding her hands out for him to see them. "My hands and ankles are swollen, which hinders me from doing too much. I can't even work."

"How's the baby?" Ray asked.

"She's killing me!" Sylvia answered with a broad smile. "But she's okay, thanks for asking."

"This meeting is about the baby, right?"

"Pretty much."

"I'm listening."

"First, let me ask you something," she started. "I know you hate me for what I've done, but did that change the way you feel about the baby?"

Ray tried his best not to think about the day he caught Sylvia sucking off the dude she claimed to be her cousin, but there was nothing he could do to parry the thoughts as they came rushing back to him. Now, he could feel the hatred for her building up inside him again. He knew he had to contain it because whatever decision he made would affect the child.

"I can't fault the baby for what you've done," he stated calmly. "It's not her fault, but I still plan on taking a paternity test."

"I concur with you on that," she professed. "And there's no doubt in my mind that you would make a great father."

As they stared at each other, some of the hatred Ray was feeling towards her, started to abate.

"Are you done?" Ray broke eye contact to check his watch, and to also maintain the new barrier he'd placed over his heart.

"Not really," she answered, sounding a bit uncomfortable.

"What else?"

She lingered for a moment before saying, "Right now, I'm unable to work. I was hoping you would help me out until the baby is born, and I'm able to do for myself. I'll pay you back, someday."

"Help you out with what?"

"Utilities," she answered. "My aunt helps me out from time to time, but she's barely making it herself."

"I can feel that," he said. "I guess I could help you out. What you need right now?"

"Two-fifty."

Ray pulled out a wad of folded bills, handing them to her.

"Is this two-fifty?" she asked, receiving the bills with an incredulous look on her face.

"It should be close to eight."

"Oh, thank you."

Ray nodded.

"So, how do I get in touch with you besides leaving notes on your door, or with your neighbor?" she asked.

After inserting his number into her cellular, Ray made his exit. Getting home, before he could park his car, Precious emerged from her apartment and stood on the porch, waiting for him.

'*This girl is persistent*', Ray thought as he approached.

"Is this a wrong time?" she asked.

"Not really," he answered. "I've had enough time to think everything through. You can work for me, but I have to know one thing."

"What's that?"

"How do you feel about guns?"

# CHAPTER 6

James was awakened by the sounds of someone knocking on his front door. Immediately, he glanced over at the clock. It was ten thirty-seven. He was kind of suspicious because whoever this was, they were knocking instead of using the doorbell.

"I'm coming, whoever the fuck you is!" he shouted, donning a pair of shorts, and tucking his gun at the small of his back.

Approaching the front door, he peered through the window. "Oh, shit!" he exclaimed, smiling as he pulled the door open. "What up, boy!"

"What it do!" Black returned his friend's greeting with a smile and hug.

"How the hell did you get out?"

"My baby came and got me," Black said, nodding at Connie, who was standing behind him.

"Hey, James," she spoke.

"What's up!" he regarded her, then stepped aside allowing them entrance. "Y'all come on in out the cold! Why you ain't use the doorbell?"

"Shit, it don't work," Black answered as he entered, followed by Connie.

"I gotta get it fixed," James asserted, taking his friend's word for it. He closed the door and joined his company in the living. "Y'all have a seat. I'm 'bout to go and freshen up. When I get back, I wanna hear the whole story."

James made for the bathroom, where he brushed his teeth and washed his face. After taking and depositing the gun in his bedroom, he re-entered the living room, where Black and Connie were seated on the sofa.

"Man, what the fuck happened?" James asked, taking a seat in the recliner.

Black told him everything about his arrival and everything he'd encountered at Felicia's house that Christmas day.

"What happened when we were on the phone?" James was anxious to know.

"Somebody came from behind me," Black asserted, rubbing the back of his head where he sustained the blow. The same spot where four staples resided. "I remember getting hit. When I woke up, I was in the back of an ambulance, on my way to the hospital."

"What about Felicia and Kevin?"

"I ain't heard nothin'."

"You ain't try her cell phone before you called me?"

"Nah," Black answered. "She'd already gotten the number changed, and I ain't had a chance to get it from her."

"This shit ain't adding up," James said almost to himself.

****

"Will you be long?" Connie asked as she pulled the Ford Focus in front of Felicia's house.

"I shouldn't," he kissed her lips, then exited the car.

As he slowly approached the front door, flashbacks of that tragic Christmas morning, played in his mind, which had him wondering why he'd even come out here knowing that Kevin and Felicia were missing. As he got within six feet away from the door, it swung open, causing him to stop dead in his tracks.

"Nigga, I know you ain't coming over here to burglarize my house again!" Felicia, clad in a gray sweatsuit, stepped out on the porch making her accusation.

"Do what?" Black was taken aback.

"Don't play dumb nigga!" she persisted. "The police told me they arrested Keith Daniels for breaking in and sabotaging my shit. You doin' that bad you gotta steal from me, and who that bitch is? Ya get-away driver?"

"Man, I came over here to drop off Kevin's gifts," Black explained. "When I got to the door, I saw that it was open."

She crossed her arms, giving him a skeptical look.

"Come on, Felicia!" Black stood his ground. "You know damn well, I wouldn't pull no bullshit like that!"

"Why'd they lock you up for it?" She was more composed now.

Black took a deep breath and flipped the collar of his coat up to shield his neck from the cutting wind as he explained everything to her.

"We were at Becky's house," she asserted when he was done. "We left around ten-thirty, let me see your head."

Black closed the gap between them and turned so she could see the staples in his head.

"Damn!" she exclaimed. "It took me almost five hours to clean your blood out of my carpet."

"Where's Kevin?"

"Still sleeping, they stole my baby's Christmas. I'll have to buy him some more shit."

"The gifts I bought him should still be in my car," Black said. "I can't get it back until Monday."

"How's Nikki and the kids?" Felicia asked, changing the subject.

Black just stared at her. That's when he realized that Felicia was unaware of the separation.

"They a'ight," he answered, not yet ready to tell her of his mishap.

****

"Now that all Kingz are back on their thrones," James started after Black had relayed his story to the other Kingz. "We can finish our discussion on the future of this business. Anybody still thinks we should shut it down?"

"Shut it down?" Black asked, not willing to believe what he was hearing. "For what?"

James didn't answer. He just looked across the table at Fred, who was already looking in his direction.

"We'd already decided to make all drops with all Kingz present, and armed Kingzmen," Fred reminded him.

"I've thought about that also," James said. "Traveling like that could be too conspicuous. If we're in any kind of danger, it's because the dope game is dangerous anyway, but I don't think somebody is actually trying to do us in."

"I agree," Ray chimed in.

"Me, too," said Black.

Fred didn't agree at all, but said, "So I guess we continue with business as usual. Tonight, we have two drops and seven pickups. I make one drop and pick up in Herdon Homes and Carver Homes."

"I'm supposed to make the other drop, right?" Black asked.

"Yeah," James answered. "Flat Shoals, plus, you got pick-ups in Perry Homes and Summer Hill. King Ray, you pick up in Thomasville Heights. I got the last two pickups. It's all chump change. That's why we need to expand. We also need a small warehouse building. So, if anybody see one for lease, let me know. Anything from my fellow Kingz before we dismiss?"

"Let's get this money!" Black asserted, glad to be back with his crew.

# CHAPTER 7

Everything was going well for the Kingz all transactions were made with no complications. Black picked up his car from the impound and saw that all of Kevin's gifts were gone, so he gave Felicia fifteen hundred to take him shopping.

"You must've found a rich bitch?" she'd asked, indicating the money and the BMW she'd seen for the first time.

Precious was doing a good job of holding down Ray's spot, which left him with a lot of free time. He could stay out as long as he wanted, and not have to worry about losing out on any money, knowing that she was not going to leave until he returned. He had also gotten a call from Sylvia on Sunday night.

"Do you still want me to name her, Rachel?" she asked.

"Unless you got something better," he told her.

"No," she answered. "I like Rachel, I hope she has your eyes."

"Why?"

"I don't know. maybe I miss looking into your eyes."

Ray didn't tell her that he missed looking into her eyes as well. He'd also enjoyed their conversation that lasted almost two hours. He was in a good mood. Maybe it was because he was about to be a father.

Fred, who still believed that his crew was being targeted, moved with extreme caution as he conducted transactions, or even visited Michelle in Edgewood. Poncho had informed him Sunday, that Drop Squad was still riding through looking for Lil' Al and Dre, but Fred knew better than to believe that Lil' Al and Dre were the only ones on the mob's list. He was surprised that they hadn't declared war on Edgewood and Kirkwood projects for the shit they'd done. In fact, Fred made a mental note to not revisit Edgewood or Michelle.

James had preached the need of expanding to the rest of the Kingz, but after checking the product, he realized they were running low and was in dire need of a re-up. They had enough money to keep from hitting up drug houses, so their only result was to find a supplier. He turned to Eric.

"What about Carlos in Hollywood Courts?" Eric asked.

"Nah," James answered. "He ain't got what we're trying to get."

"Shit, what y'all trying to get?"

"Twenty."

"Straight up?" Eric asked, surprised. "Twenty kilos?"

"At least," said James.

"Damn!" Eric exclaimed. "Y'all niggas ain't bullshittin'! Let me make a few calls and see what I come up with."

While Eric worked on that, James worked on the next part of his plan. He without consulting the other Kingz rounded up their six Kingzmen and showed them all the trap spots they were going to take over after the new year. He'd also leased a warehouse on Fulton Industrial, where they would be conducting business in the near future.

Now, it was Wednesday *New Year's Eve* and the Kingz were all seated in the back of a stretched Hummer, on their way to a New Year's Eve party at Club Strokers. Ray had insisted that since they were businessmen they should start dressing the part, which is why they were all clad in three-piece suits. Earlier, James had surprised them with golden crowns he'd paid a jeweler to make, and royal blue robes he'd helped design.

"Man, we look like *Coming to America*," Ray joked indicating the crowns and robes.

"Nah," James countered. "We look like we *own* America!"

"We definitely look like we *own* this bitch!" Black said, relishing his new look.

The outside of Strokers was packed. For it to be a strip club, it seemed that there were more women than men waiting outside to get in. Once the truck made it to the entrance, three of the Kingzmen that occupied the SUV behind them, approached the Hummer. One of the Kingzmen opened the door, and the Kingz dismounted. As always, the crowd was gawking at them to see if their favorite celebrity was amidst the entourage, but their visages showed that they were not at all disappointed. In fact, they seemed to be awed by the Kingz display.

"Aww shit, muhfuckas and muhfuckettes!" D.J. Spenz voiced over the music once the Kingz made their entrance. "Y'all know we can't start the new year off without the royal family. Ladies, be on ya best behavior, cause these guys may be looking for a few concubines to take back to the kingdom. Y'all give it up for The Kingz!"

The large crowd erupted with cheers and applause as four scantily clothed dancers approached, each wrapping an arm around a Kingz' arm, leading them to the VIP booth where there were four thrones. Now, it was the Kingz turn to be awed, well except James, who'd set it all up. As they entered the booth, the three Kingzmen positioned themselves right outside the booth, the other three were to remain outside the club.

Between the thrones that were made of red oak, were small tables that contained bottles of wine in buckets of ice, and large porcelain drinking cups, in which the girls had poured the Kingz wine. Fred and Ray didn't drink but they accepted their cups and sipped for the occasion as the girls began to dance.

"I want y'all to enjoy this shit!" James told his comrades. "Y'all earned it, this is our year. We're the new kings of the game."

"Cheers!" Fred asserted, holding up his cup, his friends doing likewise.

The girls were well into their third song when Eric, Twon, Big O' and Dexter approached the booth.

"They cool," Fred told the Kingzmen, who'd already formed a semi-circle around the big homies.

"Damn, y'all got it like *that*?" Eric asked, amusement in his voice as he entered the booth, followed by the others.

"Just being careful," Fred replied as both groups greeted each other with hugs.

"Y'all hoes get lost!" Black told the naked strippers. They shot him contradictive looks like they'd never been referred to as garden tools before, but held their tongues as they picked up their G-strings and scattered bills off the floor and made their exit.

"I see you still got a way with the ladies," Dexter jokingly commended Black.

"Man, where the fuck you been hiding at?" James interjected.

"Shit, here and there," Dexter answered. "Pushing crumbs, trying to reach y'all status. In a minute, y'all might have to give *me* a job!"

"Bullshit!" said Fred.

Big O' said, "Shit, y'all might have to give me a job *too*."

"Y'all know that ain't no problem," James insisted. "That's if y'all serious," he added, wisely eyeing them both seeing that they were serious.

They chatted for about fifteen more minutes before the big homies left to mingle with the other party-goers, but before they'd departed, Eric told James that he hadn't heard anything yet. After they left, James glanced down at the tall, light-skinned woman by the bar, who he'd noticed amongst a lot of other party-goers had been watching them from the moment they'd entered the booth. She was about 6'1", clad in dark, snug-fitted jeans, a black waist-length leather coat, and six-inch heeled boots. She was accompanied by a few other girls, but as she conversed with them and sipped from her cup, her eyes were fixed on the VIP booth.

"What up, fellas!"

James broke his attention away from the girl, to see D.J. Spenz and some other guy who looked too young to be at anybody's club, held up at the entrance by the KMs.

"Let them in," he said, pouring himself another glass of wine.

"You got the D.J. booth on auto-pilot?" Ray joked as Spenz entered followed by the kid.

"I got a back-up D.J.," he answered, shaking hands with The Kingz. "He ain't no D.J. Goldfinger, but he's tight on the boards."

"Drop Squad ain't here?" James wanted to know.

"Nah," he answered. "Y'all copped the club before they could. I guess they got their two-step on somewhere else."

"So, what's on ya mind?" he asked Spenz.

"First, I came to compliment y'all," he answered. "Man, y'all gotta be the flyest niggas on this side of the planet, right now! Straight up!"

"And we appreciate the compliment," James said. "What else?"

"I wanna introduce y'all to my lil cousin," he said, positioning the kid in front of him. "He got skills."

"What kind of skills?" Ray asked, ready to tell them that The Kingz was not going to put drugs in the hands of any kids.

"I'm the best lyricist in the south!" The kid boasted, tilting his head as if he defied anyone to say otherwise.

"Says who?" Ray asked, relishing the kid's arrogance, and doing his best not to smile.

"Says me!" The kid stood his ground. "Yung J-Bo!"

"Yung J-Bo?"

"Yeah."

"Never heard of him," Ray was enjoying this.

The kid shot Ray the meanest look he'd ever seen. If looks could kill, Ray would have keeled over the instant the look was activated.

"Yung Jay got raw skills, fa' real," Spenz prompted. "Just in case y'all get bored and decide to buy Atlantic or Universal Records and want some real lyrics, he gotcha."

"How old are you?" Black wanted to know.

"Fifteen."

"Spit somethin'!" Fred asserted, grinning wanting to see what all the hype was about.

"Yeah, spit that shit!" James said standing. "I'll have to take a rain check. My bladder is filled to the rim."

"Go ahead," Fred prompted once James had left.

J-Bo cleared his throat and ranted off. "I come hard like I'm chewing on the blue pills/Outta sight like a Mack truck on two wheels/You can say what you want, you just poppin' off/Hit the switch, have ya whole team droppin off/I don't know how you—"

James, who told the KMs he didn't need anyone to escort him to the restroom, was walking towards the bar, passing people who were drinking, eating, dancing, or watching strippers dance.

"King James?" The manager Clyde stopped him several feet away from his target. "Should I have the table brought up?"

At first, James was ready to slap the piss out of Clyde for breaking his stride, but the mentioning of the table changed that.

"Yeah," James answered. "As a matter of fact, we'll need four more chairs for our company. Make sure my Kingzmen are fed, also, there's three more outside.

"They'll come in and grab a plate?"

"Nope."

"Why not? I can't send half-naked women out in the cold like that!"

Now James was ready to slap this clown. His expression must have betrayed him, because Clyde quickly agreed to deliver the food himself, then disappeared through the crowd.

*'Now, where was I?'* James thought, now looking at the woman who was regarding him with expectant eyes. Wasting no more time, he approached her, brushing one of her friends in the process.

"Bring in the new year with me," he whispered in her ear.

"I'm bringing in the new year with my girls," she said, now looking to the ceiling as if she wasn't interested.

"Your invitation includes them too."

"I'll join you," she said loud enough for her friends to hear her. "But if my girls don't want to, you'll have to find somebody else to bring in the new year with."

"We don't know them!" one of the girls blurted out.

James turned to face the girl, who stood about 5'5"-5;7", and was giving him a disgusted look, with a cup in one hand, and the other hand poised on her hip.

"We're just out having a good time," the feisty one asserted.

"We ain't looking for nobody, and we damn sho' ain't trying to be nobody's sex toys!"

"Sheila!" One of the girls nudged her. "Girl calm down!"

44

Ignoring Sheila, James turned to the red bone and said, "If you change your mind, you know where I'm at."

There was a long line for the restroom. James spotted Dexter in line and joined him.

"A King shouldn't have to wait in line," Dexter told him.

"Yeah, I know," James answered. "Next time, I'll make sure they leave one stall reserved for us."

Dexter laughed. "Now that's some space-age ballin' type of shit right there!"

"True that," James said. "So, how's the wife and kids?"

"They good."

James hesitated, but asked, "Were you serious about what you said earlier?"

"What's that?"

"A job, you need some work fa' real?"

"I mean, it's ugly for a nigga," Dexter answered. "But you know I like to get my own money."

"I feel that, but ain't nothing wrong with asking for a lil help. You know we got you."

Dexter nodded his head. "I can dig that."

About fifteen minutes later, James exited the restroom and passed the girls without looking in their direction. He had already made up in his mind that he was going to fuck that red bitch, to-night. Fuck, Sheila! Getting back to the booth, James saw that the table and four extra chairs were already set up, and the other Kingz had taken off their robes and hung them on the back of their thrones as James had done before leaving. He re-took his seat.

"Who are the extra chairs for?" Black asked.

"Them," James answered, spotting the girls, who were mak-ing their way to the booth. He motioned for the KMs to let them through.

"Y'all can have a seat," James told them. "Thanks for joining us. The food should be here, shortly."

There was a moment of hesitation, then the red-bone took off her coat, hung it on the back of a chair and sat down across from James. Reluctantly, the other girls followed suit. Sheila James noticed still acted like she didn't want to be there, so she was the last to be seated, taking a seat by the entrance, which was right across from Ray. She didn't take her coat off.

Disregarding her, James said," I'm King James, and this is King Black, King Fred, and my brotha, King Ray."

The Kingz all nodded.

"I'm Shonda." The red-bone took the initiative. "And this is Ebony, Theresa, and my cousin, Sheila."

"Nice to meet y'all," said James. "I hope y'all brought appetites, cause here comes the food."

Everybody looked to see a line of half-naked dancers, carrying various size trays of food, led by the manager, Clyde. The women entered the booth, one at a time, placing their trays on the large table. There were bottles of champagne on ice, trays of hot wings, barbecue wings, chicken fingers, shrimp, crab legs, thin slices of ham and cheese, salad, various salad dressings and dips, and a white-iced cake with *The World Is Ours Kingz* in blue icing.

While the girls were doing their 'jobs,' Ray cast a glance across the table at Sheila, who wrinkled her nose up at every girl that entered. One of the girls noticed it and returned the look as she exited. Ray found that funny.

"What, you don't like women?" Ray asked her.

"I don't get down like that!" Sheila snapped.

"Well, how do you get down?"

"I like men."

"I can't tell."

"Just because I don't like you, doesn't mean I don't like men."

"Y'all enjoy," Clyde said once the last girl had cleared the booth. "We got about fifteen more minutes til' countdown.

"Feed my men!" James told him.

"I'm on it," Clyde answered.

*'I can't tell,'* James wanted to say, but he'd promised himself that he was going to keep his cool tonight. "Black, where the dope at?" he asked.

46

Black pulled from the inside of his blazer, a Ziploc bag containing eight blunts that were already rolled up.

"Y'all gone and dig in," James said. "Get' cha' grub on."

Black blazed up a blunt while everybody except Sheila got their grub on. Ray was about to dig in when his phone vibrated.

"Yeah?" he answered.

"What y'all boys up to?" B.J. asked.

"Man, James done threw a party at Strokers," Ray answered, then told him about the crowns, robes, and thrones.

"So, y'all threw a Halloween party on New Year's Eve?" B.J. laughed. "Well, I hope I get invited to the Christmas party on Valentine's Day."

Ray couldn't help but laugh. "Nigga, you're a real late-night comedian! And what you doin' for the new-new?"

"Watching the peach drop."

"Bullshit!"

"Nah, straight up," said B.J. "Me, Krystal and T-Roc."

"That's what's up. However, we made it through another one."

"Fa' sho'."

"But I'ma get up wit 'cha," Ray said. "Y'all be easy out there."

"Aight, one!"

"One!"

Ray concluded his call as James was pouring everybody a glass of wine. Sheila just stared at the glass in front of her like it was poison.

"Anybody got any New Year's resolutions?" Fred asked.

"I'ma just concentrate on being happy," Theresa, who was sitting across from Fred, asserted.

"Shit, that should be *her* resolution," Fred said, nodding at Sheila.

"Don't worry about my resolution!" Sheila snapped, rolling her head. "Whatever it is don't include you!"

Fred laughed. "I hope not."

"Man, I got one," Black spoke up, passing James the blunt. "We don't celebrate our birthdays. I think we should start."

"If you want us to take you to Chuck E. Cheese, just say it," Ray told him.

"If we did take him, you couldn't go," Fred told Ray.

"Why not?"

"Cause, you're scared of rats."

"Hell, Chuck E. Cheese ain't no rat," Ray protested. "That's a nigga!"

Everybody laughed hard at the statement, including Sheila.

"A'ight pimps, playas, gangstas, hoes, bitches, and bitch-niggas!" D.J. Spenz yelled into the mike after killing the music. "I know y'all got on y'all's expensive ass Movado and Rolexes 'n shit, but that don't mean shit. It's 'bout time for the countdown, and we're going off my cheap ass watch tonight. Now, when we count this thing down, I wanna hear y'all get live in this bitch. Act like y'all glad to see another year, cause somma y'all ugly muhfuckas should've *been* dead! Hell, somma y'all ugly muhfuckas should've never been born! A'ight, let's get it!" he regarded his watch. Ten—nine—eight—seven—six—five—four—three—two—one—"

The whole club screamed. "Happy New Year!"

The music started back up, and the crowd seemed to party harder. After the Kingz hugged and told each other Happy New Year, they sat down to eat and converse with the girls. As soon as Black fired up another blunt, his cell phone vibrated on his hip. He passed the blunt across the table to Ebony and answered his phone.

'Yeah?"

"Happy New Year, baby!" Connie asserted through the phone over the loud music in her background. They'd both decided to bring in the new year with their friends, at separate clubs.

"Happy New Year!" he returned. "How's everything going?"

"Good,' she answered. "We're having a good time. Even Sylvia brought her extra-large pregnant ass out tonight."

The mentioning of Sylvia's name caused him to glance over at Ray, who was helping himself to some shrimp and sauce.

"Well, y'all be careful," he told her. "And, if anything happens—"

"Nothing's going to happen, baby." She cut him off. "Stop talking like that."

"I'm just saying."

"I know what you're saying," she said. "Everything's alright. Enjoy yourself, and I'll see you when you get home, okay?"

"A'ight."

"I love you!"

"I love you, too!" He ended the call.

Over an hour later, the food was almost consumed, and the last blunt was in rotation. Like Fred and Ray, Sheila didn't smoke, and she'd only nibbled on a few slices of ham and cheese, chasing it with small gulps of champagne. While everyone else was engaged in conversation, she had slightly turned in her chair and directed her attention on the other activities going on in the club as she bobbed her head to the music.

At times, Ray found himself staring at her. He couldn't help but notice how cute she was. Even in the dimness of the club's lights, he could tell there were no blemishes on her caramel-colored skin.

"So, what y'all doing after the club?" James asked Shonda, who was sitting in his lap with his crown on her head.

"I don't know," she answered, then asked her girls. "What y'all doing after the club?"

"I ain't in no rush to get home," Ebony declared.

"I'm waiting on the after-party," Theresa asserted, looking Fred in his eyes.

"Shit let's get a room," said James."

"I'm in," Shonda said.

"Me, too," said Theresa.

"Me, three," came Ebony.

Then, almost simultaneously, everybody looked over at Sheila, who had a skeptical look on her face.

"I can't believe y'all!" she snapped. "Y'all don't know them— all they want is sex!"

"Girl, ain't nothin' wrong with a lil bump-n-grind," Ebony joked. "It's the New Year.

"Well, if you catch AIDS, you won't live to see the *next* New Year!" Sheila persisted, making direct eye contact with her cousin, Shonda.

"Man, what's up with y'all girl?" Black asked, already sick of this bitch's shit.

"She just broke up with her boyfriend," Ebony stated.

"Don't be telling them my business!" Sheila almost leaped from her chair.

"Damn, shawty," Fred asserted. "You ran ya, nigga, off?"

"I ain't run *nobody* off!" she insisted. "He was a dog, like all men!"

"I find that hard to believe," Ray pitched in.

"I don't care what you believe, you don't know me!"

"So, I guess y'all ain't going, huh?" James said to Shonda.

"Man, we can drop Drama Queen off!" Black insisted.

"You can't drop me off nowhere!" Sheila protested. "I got my own car. They rode with *me*!"

"Sheila, we're trying to hang out, tonight," Ebony told her.

"Yeah, girl," Theresa joined in. "You don't have to go if you don't want to."

"You don't mind driving home by yourself, do you baby?" asked Shonda.

All Sheila could say was, "No."

"I'ma have to take a rain check myself," Ray announced.

James asked, "Are you sure?"

"Yeah."

"You want us to drop you off?"

"Nah," Ray answered. "I'ma hit Spenz up."

Ray dialed D.J. Spenz's cell number.

"What's up, Ray?" he answered.

"If somebody stole your car, how would you get home?" Ray asked.

"With my foot in somebody's ass!" Spenz remarked.

Ray laughed. "Well, it's a good thing I'm asking for it.

"You need the whip?"

"Yeah, Ray answered. "You gotta stop by the crib, tomorrow, right?"

"Yeah."

"Pick it up then."

"A'ight."

Ray promised to pick the keys up on his way out, then ended the call.

"You good?" James asked.

"Yeah, I'm straight."

"Do we need to send one of the Kingzmen with you?" asked Fred.

Ray declined. After saying goodnight to Eric, Big O', Twon, and Dexter, who were at the stage tipping dancers, Ray copped the keys from Spenz, and the Kingz and the girls left the club.

Playa Ray

# CHAPTER 8

It was Saturday, and the Kingz all vowed to attend Curt's funeral. There weren't many people at the service, and there were even less people at the burial site, where they were now standing afar off watching as the casket was slowly lowered into the earth.

"I told that nigga 'bout that shit," Eric who was standing with the Kingz, said for the umpteenth time.

"That's the choice he made," said Fred, who'd been vigilant the whole day, and was still surveying the area for potential danger.

The only thing he'd noticed out of the ordinary was a black H-2 Hummer with tinted windows that rode through at a casual pace, almost ten minutes ago.

"That's true," Eric agreed. "Sometimes, we make choices we have to live with."

"Or *die* with," Ray stated. He'd sat at the back of the church, refusing to look at Curt's body, being that he wasn't too fond of funerals.

"Y'all ready?" James asked.

"Yeah," Eric answered. "I gotta get to the barber shop."

They all headed for their vehicles.

"Look," Eric started. "Y'all be careful when y'all meet with dude. I ain't never met the nigga, but I heard he's straight up. He was in the Army, fought in Desert Storm, plus, he got some goons that don't play the radio. Drop Squad won't even fuck wit' 'em."

\*\*\*\*

Their meeting was at five o'clock in Lithonia, Georgia, in which they'd rented a Lincoln Town car for the occasion. Making the exit, it took them seven minutes to find the deserted dirt road where they were to meet their supplier, who'd agreed to ten key's instead of twenty, stating that he'd never heard of the Kingz, and didn't trust any newcomers.

Ray put the car in park but left it running and looked over at James, who was seated in the passenger seat with a briefcase in his lap.

"Are you sure we're at the right spot?" Ray asked.

Before James could answer, they heard the sound of dirt crunching under tires, and saw two white Cadillac Escalades approach, and park fifteen feet away from the right side of the Lincoln. No one got out.

"Let's do this," said James.

They all exited the Lincoln, clad in dress suits and trench coats. Ray and Black walked around to the right side, so they were all standing together. Seconds later, all four doors opened on both trucks, and from the back seat of the first one, came the supplier. A white man looking to be in his mid-fifties, with a crew cut full of gray hair. Despite his age, he looked to be physically fit underneath his dark-green three-piece. His goons all seven of them looked like he'd recruited them right off the military base. They were all clad in fatigue pants, coats, and hats. They were also armed with AK-47s and M-16s.

"Anytime today, comrade," the supplier, whose name was Franco, said impatiently.

"In and out, Jay," Fred mumbled to James, hoping like hell James didn't do or say anything to rouse the infantry.

As if he didn't hear Fred, James proceeded towards the entourage at an even pace. As he approached, one of the soldiers stepped forward, frisked him, seized his handgun, and showed it to Franco, who nodded, opened the rear passenger door, and gestured for James to get in. Once James climbed into the truck, Franco got in behind him, closing the door.

The Kingz couldn't see through the tinted windows, so they just stood there, staring at the infantrymen, who were staring back at them. Almost ten minutes later, the rear door opened, and Franco got out, followed by James, who was still carrying the briefcase. Once they'd shook hands, and the soldier returned his gun, James tucked it and made it back to the Lincoln.

"I wanna be like that nigga when I grow up!" James told his crew, smiling.

****

After leaving Lithonia, Fred and James tended to the cooking and weighing of the product, and Ray journeyed out to Eric's house, where he picked up six pounds of weed for he and Precious to break down into ounces and half ounces. Black headed home.

"Baby, can we move?" Connie asked Black over dinner.

"Where you wanna move to?"

"It really doesn't matter," she answered. "As long as we're far away from this dump. Besides, you're making a lot of money now, and these niggas know it."

It didn't take long for Black to actualize what she was telling him. It was bad enough he'd moved to Chapel Forest and pretty much invaded with his nickels and dimes. Now, he was part of a notorious group and was making more money in a week, than these niggas would make in six months, and that was just his share, alone. So, it was indisputable that these niggas envied him and wouldn't hesitate to group up and make a move on him.

"We'll look for a house Monday," he told her.

Connie was stunned. "A house?"

"Ain't that what I said?"

"Okay." Her eyes were wide and she was smiling like a child who'd been promised a trip to Disney World.

Playa Ray

# CHAPTER 9

"Yeah?" Ray answered his cell phone.

It was Sunday, and he was at the gas station pumping gas into the tank of his Delta Eighty-Eight. Although he didn't have to be at his mother's house until five for dinner. He took it upon himself to head out early so he could spend more time with April, before she headed back to Massachusetts.

"How are you doing?" Sylvia asked.

"I'm decent," he answered, screwing the gas cap on and placing the nozzle back into place. "How you doing?"

"Terrible!" she answered with a giggle. "Your daughter is kicking my ass! I just hope like hell she doesn't have your head.

"Why not?" Ray asked, now back in his car.

"Cause, you got a big ass head!" she joked. "That could be real painful!"

"No, you didn't!"

Sylvia was laughing hysterically now.

"You just better hope she don't inherit those eagle claws of yours," Ray shot back.

"Eagle claws!" she exclaimed. "I have beautiful feet."

"Beauty is in the eye of the beholder."

"So, I don't have beautiful feet, Ray?"

"To be honest, I've never paid too much attention to your feet," Ray admitted.

"Why not?" she sounded disappointed.

"Because, I'm not a foot person," he answered. "I don't have a foot fetish."

"Ouch!" she cried out. "I'll be glad when I deliver this heifer! And speaking of heifers, how's, Kim?"

"I don't know," Ray answered, feeling the hatred for Kim stirring inside of him.

"You don't talk to her?"

"I don't have a reason to."

"Oh."

Either Sylvia was pretending, or she really had no knowledge of Kim's infidelity.

'*Bitches ain't shit,*' he thought. "Look, hit me up later, a'ight?"

"What time?" she asked.

"Sometime around eight or eight-thirty."

"Okay."

Ray concluded the call and headed for his mother's house. Seeing that his mother's, Robert's and James' cars had taken over the soil-distant driveway. Ray parked across the street, behind a green Buick Lesabre. He exited his car, but as he approached the house, he cast a glance at the Buick that was now familiar to him.

Knowing that the front door was unlocked, Ray entered the house and immediately lost his appetite, which was replaced with anger. His eyes instantly locked on Mark, who was confined to a wheelchair in the middle of the living room, although he was aware of his dad and his dad's wife.

"Hey, twin!" April, who was sitting on the sofa beside Raymond, beamed.

But Ray absently disregarded his sister.

"Boy, it ain't summertime!" he heard his mother say and didn't realize she was talking to him until she rushed over to close the door, he'd absently left open.

At that time, James exited the kitchen and leaned against the threshold with an amused smirk on his face.

"You ain't gon' speak to nobody?" Mary asked.

"You invited them over?" he asked, now facing her.

"No," she answered. "They stopped by to see me and asked how you were doing. They can stay for dinner if they want to."

"No, that's alright," Victoria, Mark's mother, said. "I'm cooking tonight."

"Girl, what you whipping up?" Mary inquired.

Ray sighed as Victoria ran down her list, and Mary ran down hers. Not in the mood to be rational, Ray swaggered through the living room and made for the bedroom, he and James shared when they were kids. Closing the door behind him, he sat on his old bed that sat opposite of James'. Seconds later, James entered, locked the door, and sat on his bed across from Ray.

"You should've let me put that nigga in the ground," James spoke in a low tone.

Ray just stared at his brother.

"It's not too late," James assured. "I can send a few Kingzmen to their crib tonight, and wet 'em all up."

"They ain't no issue," Ray finally spoke.

"I can't tell!"

"What'd you mean?"

"Look at how you just acted," James pointed out. "Your whole demeanor changed when you hit that door and saw them sitting in the living room. Nigga, you had the look of a stone-cold killer! You hate them with a passion!"

Ray took off his coat and laid it across the bed before responding. "I hate a lot of people with a passion, but—"

"Like who?" James cut him off. "You don't even hate Sylvia for what she did to you. Hell, you hate Mark more than you do, Trina."

"How you figure that?"

"Cause, I know my lil' brotha," James answered sternly. "Don't nobody know you like I do. Now, should I make the call or what?"

****

Fred was sitting on his bed, counting large bills from a shoe box when someone tapped on the bedroom door.

"It's me, lil bruh," Eric announced before entering and closing the door back. "You sure you don't want to go?"

"Nah, I'm good," Fred answered. "Y'all have fun."

It was Eric's turn to treat their mother to Sunday dinner. Fred wouldn't have minded tagging along, but he'd already made plans to get up with Theresa, the girl from the New Year Eve's party at Strokers. He figured he, James and Black were going to run through her and her friends, but Shonda made it clear that it wasn't that type of party. Therefore, they ended up getting three separate rooms, but that was fine with Fred because Theresa had proved to be a worthy opponent in bed.

"I hope y'all plan on putting that money to good use," said Eric, eyeing the neatly stacked bills on the bed.

"In due time," Fred admitted. "Right now, we're still organizing."

Eric smiled. "I'm proud of y'all boys. Just don't let that shit come between y'all."

Eric left, leaving Fred to ponder that last statement. For some odd reason, it had caught him off guard and sent chills up his spine. Was Eric insinuating something?

He couldn't help but think of James at this time and come to think of it, James had been acting a bit strange since they'd been getting to the money. Like he had some kind of ulterior motives.

****

Dinner was over and to Ray's surprise, everything had gone well. During the course of the conversation, there was no talk of Kim, Trina, Mark or anything that was known to spark a fuse. Hell, James and Robert had taken over the conversation, talking about cars and sports. They'd even laughed and given each other dap across the table. At first, Ray thought it was all a ploy. Then he realized his brother was really enjoying himself.

"Y'all excuse me," April said, getting up from the table. "It's quite hot in here, I need some air."

"You're going outside?" Raymond asked like he couldn't believe she was leaving without him.

"Just for a few minutes," she answered. "You can join me if you want."

She exited the kitchen without waiting on his response. As if she knew he would trail behind her like an obedient dog, and her perception was right. Raymond quickly excused himself and hurried after her. James watched the scene in disgust but didn't let it show. Ray, Robert, and Mary exchanged glances.

"Mama, you ain't thought about moving out of this raggedy house?" James asked, slicing his piece of chocolate chip pound cake with his fork.

"Robert asked me to move in with him," she answered.

"What you got, a mansion?" James asked Robert.

"Not quite," Robert answered. "But it's in better condition than this one."

"Sold!" Ray piped up, banging his fist on the table. "We'll have her packed up and ready to leave in twenty minutes!"

"Hold on," Mary mustered through her laughter. "Y'all act like my house is the raggediest house in Bland Town!" Ray shot her an *are-you-serious* look. "It ain't!" she protested.

Ray begged to differ. "Mama, this house is, indeed, raggedy!"

"How raggedy?" James prompted, knowing Ray was about to steal the show.

"Man, this house is so raggedy," Ray started. "When you ring the doorbell, the toilet flush." This sparked laughter, but he wasn't finished. "And don't make me talk about how small it is."

"How small is it?" James urged.

"It's so small." Ray went on. "That when you walk through the front door, you walk right out the back door."

"Boy, you oughta stop!" Mary barely got out through her laughter.

This went on for another moment before James excused himself and entered their old bedroom for his coat.

"Thanks for the dinner mama," he said, re-entering the kitchen, kissing her on the cheek and shaking Robert's hand.

"You're welcome, baby," she answered. "Be careful out there."

"I'm always careful." He dapped Ray, then made his exit.

James saw that it hadn't gotten dark yet. He also saw April and Raymond standing in the parking lot of a small furniture warehouse, a few yards up. They were hugged up and were probably kissing before he walked out.

"I can't get a hug before you leave?" April yelled out to him.

He wanted to be sarcastic, but, instead, he told her to meet him halfway. She complied, with Raymond tagging along.

"Make sure you have your ass on that bus tonight," he told her.

"Why would I not be on the bus?" she asked.

James darted his eyes from Raymond to April.

April caught the hint. "Don't even go there! You know me better than that!"

"I hope so."

He hugged his sister, said goodnight, and made for his car. As he drove away, he glanced at them in the rearview mirror. He didn't like this picture at all, but then again, maybe ol' Raymond would come in handy someday.

****

"So, what you and Raymond got going on?" Ray asked April as they traveled Northside Drive to the Greyhound Station.

"Huh?" she said as if she'd been daydreaming.

"Honda?" Ray shot back, which is something he'd always say whenever someone says *huh*.

"He's a nice guy, Ray."

"That's not what I asked," he reminded her. "Y'all act like we can't see what y'all up to."

"I don't think we were trying to be subtle." She took offense. "I mean, why should we? We're grown, I like him and he likes me."

Ray glanced over at his baby sister, who was almost nineteen. He knew he and James were being selfish by treating her like she was still a child. He also knew one day, they were going to have to back up and let her breath. Let her live her life how she sees fit.

"Don't get too big for ya britches over there!" Ray said with a look that caused her to laugh. "You may be grown, but I'm still big bruh!"

"You'll always be, my big brother," she stated in a more composed tone. "You and James but I'm eighteen now. Y'all have to let me make my own decisions and face my own consequences. Experience is the best teacher."

"And we're trying to keep you from experiencing a lot of things you shouldn't have to."

"Like love?" she asked.

"What you know about love?" Ray was not expecting this one.

As far as he knew, April had never had sex, but to hear her speak the '*L-word*' pertaining to anybody outside of family, struck a huge nerve.

"Ray, I'm eighteen," she reminded him.

"Wow, that says a lot!" he joked. "You got muhfuckas out there that's way older than you and me, both and still don't know a damn thing about love! Just because you like a person, doesn't mean you're in love with them."

"I didn't say I was in love with Raymond," April protested. "But I do like him a lot."

Ray was shaking his head. "I can't believe I'm having this conversation with you."

"So, you don't agree with me dating, Raymond?"

"I don't agree with you dating period!" he answered. "But I don't run your life— you do." There, he'd finally admitted it.

He'd finally got it off his chest. Now, he felt relieved. He could tell that she was feeling the same way because she was smiling from ear to ear.

"So, does that mean you will be open-minded about it, and be more supportive?" she wanted to know.

"I'll be open-minded," he agreed. "But the only thing I'm supporting is you finishing school and becoming successful. No kids until you turn forty."

"Forty!"

"Okay, thirty-five and a half."

He and April laughed and joked all the way to the bus station. After dropping her off, he set off to his apartment, where he found Precious sitting on the sofa, and her perfume lingering in the air. Although he'd never known her to smell like anything other than soap.

"What's up," he greeted her.

"Hey! How was dinner?"

"Pretty good."

"Well, you see what I had to consume," she said, indicating the two Wendy's bags and two drinking cups on the coffee table.

Now, he could understand two bags, but why would she need two— the sound of the bathroom door interrupted his thought. For as long as Ray had been staying in Maple Creek, he'd never known or seen Precious with a man besides her cousin, whatever his name was. Nor had he ever heard her mention anything about a boyfriend. Now, he knew that was about to change. He was finally about to meet this—

"What's up!" the intruder greeted him with a hand extended. "You must be Ray?"

# CHAPTER 10

"Ooh, baby, that's it!" Connie exclaimed from the passenger side of Black's BMW, as they pulled up in front of the white and greenhouse, they'd selected from a Home Shopping catalog.

"Now, where's that damn realtor?" Black was already mad that this dude had chosen to meet them at one o'clock, and not earlier, being that he had rounds to make before the Kingz meeting, tonight.

"He'll be here, baby, calm down," Connie cooed, rubbing the back of her hand along his jaw, which always seemed to work.

"It's already twelve after," he told her. "I got things to do."

"I know baby, but I don't think—" She stopped to gander at the champagne-colored Cadillac that pulled into the driveway.

Black was watching too. "I hope that's him."

At that time, a white man in a gray suit exited the car.

"That's gotta be him," Connie said.

"Good, let's get this over with." Black cut the engine, and he and Connie got out and approached the realtor.

He greeted them with a broad smile. "Good afternoon! I'm Calvin Bevel, the one you spoke to on the phone. Sorry, I'm late, I had to play taxi driver for one buyer because her husband drove their only car to work, but everything worked out. Now, shall we begin?"

After touring the house, Black paid the forty thousand deposit, dropped Connie off in Chapel Forest, where she would use her car to go furniture shopping, then headed out to do his rounds.

His first stop was Perry Homes, where he was to pick up some money from one of his workers who'd been recently hired. Parking in front of the apartment, Black pulled his gun from his holster under his coat, checked it, then reholstered it. Getting out, he headed for the apartment, looking around. He wasn't scared, he just had to be on point, because niggas be on some real bullshit when an outsider enters their projects. They should know who he is because his coat was open, and his *Kingz* medallion was prominently on display, but that didn't mean they were going to respect it.

"Who is it?" a female answered his knock.

"King Black," he said loud enough for the inquisitive spectators to hear.

The door swung open, and the female who stood about 5'4", shot Black a disapproving look like she was actually expecting a *king* to be standing on her doorsteps.

"Where Greg at?"

"I ain't seen, Greg," she answered curtly.

He eyed her for a second. She looked to be in her mid-thirties. Black wasn't a junkieologist, but he could spot a female drug addict from a mile away, and this woman was, indeed, an addict.

"Do you know when he'll be back?"

"I ain't seen, Greg," she reiterated, this time with a shrug of her shoulders, or was it a twitch!

"Well, when he gets home, can you—" Seeing her twitch again, made him reconsider. "Never mind."

Black turned and made for his car, hearing the door slam behind him. He hadn't memorized Greg's number, being that this was his second time dealing with him. But like the other workers, Greg was instructed to stay at the designated drop spot until the transaction was made.

As Black approached his car, something inside him urged him to look back. He did and saw the curtains flutter in an upstairs window as if someone had been watching him, and quickly backed away to avoid being seen. He figured it had to be Greg. He just hoped Greg knew what he was getting himself into.

****

Ray's new house had three bedrooms, one and a half bathrooms, and a hardwood deck that overlooked a fenced in backyard. After making his deposit and doing the necessary paperwork, he left Riverdale, Georgia and headed for Cleveland Avenue, where he was to make a drop off to Poppo.

As he drove, he thought about the room he'd picked out for his daughter in his house. He felt a bit silly thinking this when he didn't know for sure if the baby was his. That's why he was going to remit decorating the room until the DNA test results. Deep down inside, he didn't have the slightest doubt that the baby was his. He pondered this all the way to Cleveland Avenue until he found a parking spot in Kroger City's parking lot. Being that it was daytime, he parked amongst other cars so not to draw attention to him and what was about to take place. Then, he dialed Poppo's number.

"Yo," Poppo answered, his voice bearing his up-north accent.

"Can I speak to, Romeo?" Ray asked.

"You got the wrong number."

"So, I guess Juliet ain't there either, huh?"

"Man find somebody to play with!"

Poppo hung up, concluding the code call they'd concocted. Ray glanced over at the entrance of Kroger, wondering if he should go in and grab something from the deli, being that he was hungry and hadn't had time to stop and grab something to eat. Instead, he called Tasha.

"I hope you're on your way," Tasha boomed through the earpiece.

"Pretty much," he told her. "You're my next stop."

"And how long would that be?"

"I can't say."

She smacked her lips.

"You cooked?"

"No," she said with a bit more attitude. "Why?"

"Cause, I'm hungry."

"I'll fix you something. You just better hurry up before I change my mind."

'*Like that'll make me move any faster*,' he thought, but said, "Yes ma'am."

"I ain't playin', Ray!"

"I'll see you when I get there, Tasha."

Ray concluded the call. This would be Tasha's last time doing his hair because she was moving back to Chicago this weekend. He couldn't deny he was going to miss her, although she'd promised to keep in touch.

At that moment, Poppo's Lexus pulled into the parking lot and found a spot in the next row behind him. Ray watched through his rearview mirror as Poppo got out and pretended to stretch as he surveyed the parking lot. Seeing that it was clear, he made his way to the BMW and climbed in beside Ray.

"What up homie!" Poppo greeted with a broad smile, and his hand extended.

"I can't call it," Ray answered, shaking Poppo's hand, once again relishing the guy's energy. "How you been holding up?"

"Man, you know me." He pulled out a wad of folded bills, handing them to Ray. "I do what I do."

"No doubt," Ray agreed, accepting the money and pulling a small paper bag from the console between the seats, handing it to him. "You ain't heard nothing on that murder?"

"Nah," Poppo answered, placing the product in his coat pocket. "If niggas know something, they ain't talking, but I did have one smoker say he heard the shots, but by the time he got to the window, he caught the taillights of a black army truck."

"Army truck?"

"That's what he said," Poppo confirmed. "But keep in mind that I have a fifteen-hundred dollar reward out for accurate information on that shit."

"Oh okay," Ray said, realizing that the smoker was probably trying to collect the reward money, so he could smoke himself into oblivion. "Can't knock him for trying."

"I don't," Poppo told him. "So, what you got going on with the fro? You going to a seventies party?"

Ray lightly patted his afro. "Nah man. I gotta hit my stylist up when I leave here."

"That's what's up," said Poppo. "Well, whenever you ain't doing too much, you're welcome to stop by the crib and kick it."

"I'll remember that," Ray assured.

****

James exited his house with Shonda in tow. She'd called him last night wanting to hook up. Being that she didn't have a car, and James didn't feel like driving out to Stone Mountain, he had her take a cab and paid the fare when she arrived.

Now, as they headed to the car, James stopped to check his mailbox. There were three pieces of mail two bills and a letter from Boss. When they climbed into the car that was already running, he tossed the two bills on the back seat and opened Boss' letter which was brief, telling him that he had a trial date in March and that he'd placed James and Ray on his visitation list.

'*I wonder why he ain't called me yet,*' James thought as he placed the letter in the glove compartment.

"Is everything, okay?" Shonda asked.

"Huh?" James snapped out of his reverie. "Oh yeah. I was just thinking about some shit, that's all. We doing lunch?"

"Don't you mean brunch?"

"Yeah, that too. Where you wanna go?" Before she could answer, his cell phone rang. "Yeah."

"Did I wake you?" Fred asked.

"Nah," James answered. "I was on my way to grab some brunch. "What's up?"

"I'm out here with dude," Fred explained. "He ordered the merchandise you wanted, but it don't come in until after five, with some other shit he ordered for himself."

"So, we gotta wait until after five?"

"He said he'll deliver them to The Palace himself."

"You didn't give him the address, did you?" James hoped like hell Fred hadn't done an irresponsible thing like that.

"Of course not!" Fred took offense. Besides, he'd never known the address to the warehouse that was now The Palace.

"Good!" James said relieved. "We can't take that gamble. Cancel the order."

"You sure?"

"Positive."

"I'll do that."

Ending the call, James pondered for a moment. He was cool with the guy that Fred sold, traded, and bought guns from, but he didn't trust him to make drops or be anywhere near The Palace. He wanted the merchandise he'd ordered, being that they were requisite, but he couldn't take that chance.

'*Besides*,' he thought, '*There's more than one way to skin a cat.*'

**\*\*\*\***

Fred didn't know what to make of James' decision to cancel the order of guns and ammunition he'd ordered. All he could tell the puzzled gun shop owner was that he didn't know the reason for the change of plans.

Leaving the gun shop, he headed for Hair Masters, the barbershop that was now owned by Eric. As he exited off on West Lake, en route to Bankhead Highway, his cellular rang.

"Yeah?" he answered.

"What's up ol' high-yellow, glow in the dark ass nigga!" Ray teased.

"Ol' earthworm Jim lookin'ass nigga!" Fred countered, laughing.

"What's up wit 'cha?"

"Not too much," Ray answered. "You suppose to holla at E today?"

"I'm on my way now."

"Could you grab that for me?"

"I can," Fred told him. "But what am I supposed to do with it?"

"Bring it to the meeting," Ray said. "If you don't mind."

"You know I don't mind, but why can't you do it?"

"I'm getting my hair braided."

"Aight," Fred gave in. "I might charge a trafficking fee though."

"How much?"

"Nigga, I'm bullshittin'! I'll bring that through."

"Aight, thanks."

Fred entered the barber shop that adjoined a beauty shop and saw that it wasn't crowded. There were six stations and only four men were getting haircuts. Eric was cleaning his station as he bobbed his head to *Nelly's 'Air Force Ones'* playing from the stereo.

"What up, lil nigga!" Eric smiled at his brother through the large mirror.

"What it is?" Fred hugged his brother and verbally greeted the other barbers.

"Man, you might as well gone and catch this chair," Eric told Fred, swiveling the chair around. "You look rough."

"Yeah, I kinda noticed that this mornin'," Fred admitted, hanging up his coat before taking a seat.

That's when he noticed that Eric was wearing his double-gun holster under his light-weight jacket. It was comprehensible because you never knew what was on a person's mind. Eric was not one of those fake gangsters who carried guns and wouldn't use them when it was time to use them. There may not be a law for it, but he definitely believed in self-defense.

## CHAPTER 11

"This is the shooting range," James told his comrades as they entered another room of the warehouse that was constructed by carpenters, and God knows who else. But the room was, indeed, a shooting range with five booths and targets hanging from mechanical cranes that moved them back and forth at a distance that looked to be about eighty yards to the backdrop of stacked sandbags. There were even protection goggles and headphones hanging up in all stations. "This is where the Kingzmen will be training."

"Training?" Fred inquired.

"Of course," James said, now facing his fellow Kingz, who were all dressed in suits and ties, the appropriate dress code for a Kingz meeting. "Anybody can shoot a gun. Being that the KMS are our bodyguards. They need to know how to do more than just shoot a gun. I want accuracy! I put Grip in charge of them, being that he was in the Navy and is more experienced. He'll be teaching them hand to hand combat, also."

"I feel safe already," Ray joked.

"You should," James uttered as if he'd missed the punchline.

"So, we can't use the shooting range?" Black wanted to know.

"This is The Palace," James told him. "If a King can't use it, nobody can." James exited the room, heading for the next one.

As they followed him, Fred noted how James had been acting since he'd arrived. As if he was agitated or worried. '*I'll have to pull him to the side later*,' he thought. '*And find out what's what.*'

"This is the conference slash courtroom," James said throwing double doors back, stepping aside so they could peer inside. "This is where we'll sit on our respectable thrones and conduct business with our workers. If anyone violates, this is where they'll face judgment and execution."

"So, the workers will have to come here for transactions?" Fred asked, surveying the room that displayed their thrones from the New Years Eve's party at Club Strokers, sitting at the head of the room, facing metal folding chairs lined up in five rows of six.

"That hasn't been decided yet," James answered. "That's one of the things we'll discuss at the meeting."

As they made for the office, they passed another door that was closed and secured with a padlock.

'*Knowing James, it might be a torcher chamber*,' Ray thought humoring himself.

Entering the office, they all took a seat in their black soft leather chairs that surrounded a black oak table, where a telephone sat in the middle.

"Okay," James started. "Our first issue is, should we conduct business with our workers here at The Palace, and why?"

"I think we should," Ray took the initiative. "It'll keep us out of harm's way and under the radar."

Black nodded his consent.

"He pretty much summed it up," Fred agreed. "That way, we can play the background like we're supposed to. It limits the risk."

"Does it?" James asked, looking around at his comrades for an answer, which he did not receive. "Let's say one of our workers are under surveillance. If he's not careful, they'll follow him all the way to The Palace. We won't know until the doors are kicked in, and them folks hollin' *Freeze, you're under arrest!*" James could clearly see that his fellow Kingz was really considering his statement.

Ray decided to test the waters. "So, what if one of our workers are under surveillance, and one of us catch the heat while making a drop? Either way, it goes, we're taking penitentiary chances."

"That's true," James agreed. "But we're too cautious to be tailed and not know it. I can't say the same for them."

"Okay," Ray persisted, feeling like he hadn't validated his point. "What if they decide to move in once the drop is made, and jam a King in the process?"

"That would mean that the worker was an informant," James offered. "And if that shall happen, the remaining three Kingz will bond that one King out. If they raid The Palace, that brings down the whole deck. Plus, the charges would be more severe, and the bonds would be extremely high. I don't mean to sound harsh, but

I believe one King is expendable, considering the circumstances. Any comments?"

Before anyone could comment, there was a knock at the door. They all looked up to see Grip, the head Kingzmen, who was dark-skinned, stood 6'3", and weighed about two hundred and thirty pounds of pure muscle. James waved him in, and he entered clad in a black cargo pants suit and boots, which was the required attire for the active Kingzmen.

"What's up?" James asked him.

"You got company," he told James. "Some dude in a tow truck."

"Aight," James said, standing. "I'll be right back Kingz."

"Expendable?" Black said as soon as James had left the office. "What the fuck does that mean?"

"Sacrificial," Fred answered.

"And what you think about that?" Black asked Fred.

"It's logical," Fred admitted. "One King down is better than all Kingz down. If I was that one King down, I could rest easy, knowing that y'all would do whatever it takes to get me out. Y'all should feel the same way."

"Yeah, I feel that," said Black.

"What about you, King Ray?" Fred asked.

"No doubt," Ray said, slowly nodding his head.

They all sat in silence, each thinking about the possibilities and consequences of this thing called *the game*, in which they were already knee-deep.

Moments later, James re-entered carrying a 6x9 manila envelope. He stepped aside as Raymond entered, pushing a hand-truck that carried a box-shaped object hidden under a cloth, and strapped to the hand-truck for leveling.

"Over there, Ray," James told Raymond, pointing to a corner.

"What's up, Ray!" Raymond acknowledged Ray as he wheeled the box past him to the corner.

"What's up wit 'cha?" Ray returned.

"Nothing much, just making a delivery."

"I thought you delivered cars," Ray said accusingly, eyeing Raymond, wondering about his presence, and what he and James had going on.

"I do," Raymond admitted, unstrapping the box but not uncovering it. "But I'll make an exception from time to time for some extra cash."

"Raymond," James intercepted the conversation. "That's King Fred and King Black."

Once the greetings were made, James quickly ushered Raymond out of the office. Moments later, he returned, still carrying the envelope. Closing the door, he approached and uncovered the box. What they were looking at was a boxed artifact made of wood, with a smooth surface, and images, such as trees, crowns, dollar signs, and naked women carved in on each side.

"Somebody get the blinds," said James.

Black and Ray tended to the blinds in the three windows. Once they'd returned to their seats, James pressed a hidden button on the side that caused the front part to snap open, revealing a steel safe with four keyholes trimmed in different colors. Tearing open the envelop, James, emptied the contents on the table, which were four vending machine-looking keys that were each outline in the same colors of the locks, indicating where each key was to be inserted.

"One key per King," James told them, taking the initiative and selecting the key that was outlined in red, which was the one that fitted the top lock. After his comrades had selected their keys, he continued. "This is where we'll keep the Kingz' Account from now on. All locks have to be unlocked to open it. If one King is absent— hell, y'all understand." He snapped the wooden door shut and re-took his seat. "So, what y'all come up with on the first issue?"

"We scratched it," Fred spoke up. "At least for now."

"Y'all got my vote on that," James said. "Any other issues?"

"Yeah!" Black took the initiative. "I did my rounds and picked up at three spots."

"I thought you had four spots today," said James.

"I did," Black replied. "One came up M-I-A."

"Who?" James demanded, leaning forward in his chair.

He had been anticipating the day when one of these crumb snatchers came up short. Or didn't come up at all with their money. So, he could make an example for the next nigga that even thought about crossing the Kingz and what they stood for.

"Greg," Black answered.

"That name doesn't ring a bell," James said.

"We just hired him," Ray acknowledged. "Perry Homes."

"So, he wasn't at the drop spot?" James asked Black.

"The drop spot is his apartment," Black explained. "His girlfriend said he wasn't there. I ain't know his number off the bat, so I had to stop by the crib and snatch it up. I called him twice, he ain't answer. I left a message and he still ain't hit back."

"I'll put the troops on it," James promised. "Anything else?"

"Yeah," Fred spoke up. "You bought the safe from the Kingz Account, right?"

"Right," James admitted.

"You also paid the construction people from the same account?"

"Yeah."

"Okay," Fred leaned forward, rested his arms on the table, and looked James directly in the eyes. "Correct me if I'm wrong, but being that the Kingz Account is a joint account, all Kingz have to agree on where, when, and how the money is spent, right?"

"Are you insinuating something?" James countered.

"Right, or wrong?" Fred pressed, not wavering.

James sighed, leaning back in his chair. "You're right."

"King Ray, have you agreed to any of this?" Fred asked.

Ray shook his head.

"What about you, King Black?"

Black did likewise.

"At least y'all know where the money went," James protested. "Y'all make it seem as if I'm stealing."

"Where's the books?" Fred wanted to know.

"At the house," James answered. "Where it's always been. Why?"

"It should be here where we can view it," Fred told him. "As a matter of fact, I'm calling a Kingz meeting, tomorrow. Six p.m., King Black and King Ray, bring notepads. We'll each make our own copies of the books and bring them to every meeting. Plus, bring every penny that belongs to the Kingz Account. Once we have everything in order, we'll do business the way we agreed to. Any objections?"

****

Ray tried not to think about James and his habitual spending habits of the Kingz Account money as he left The Palace. He just hoped that once they went through the books, tomorrow, everything checked out, but, knowing James, it wouldn't. There was no telling what James had spent their money on. Being that Ray had a date with Sylvia at eight, he excused himself, copped the six pounds of weed from Fred, and made his exit.

"Are you ready to order, sir?"

Ray looked up at the Iron Skillet waitress, who he'd told ten minutes ago that he wasn't ready to order. Since Sylvia hadn't arrived yet, he went on and ordered a Philly Cheesesteak and fries. Seconds after the waitress left to tend to his order, Sylvia wobbled into the restaurant, looking like she was ready to burst through her waist-length coat.

"Sorry, I'm late," she apologized as she approached the table, dropped her purse in the seat across from him, and began taking off her coat. She noticed that Ray was watching her smiling. "What?"

"Nothing," he lied, knowing he was amused by her having to suck in her stomach to take the strain off the zipper.

"Yeah, I had to squeeze into my coat," she admitted as if reading his thoughts. After laying her coat over her purse, she took a seat across from him. "So, how did it go?"

"What?"

"The house," she reminded him. "Did you get it?"

"Yeah, I got it."

"How many rooms?"

"Three."

"Here you go, sir," the waitress placed Ray's order in front of him. "Would you like anything, ma'am?"

"Just a glass of unsweet tea," Sylvia answered.

"Unsweet tea?" Ray inquired after the waitress retreated. "That has to be the second nastiest drink on earth!"

"And what's the first one?"

"Castor Oil."

"Boy, Castor Oil ain't no drink!" Sylvia stated, laughing.

"It may not be a soda," Ray pressed. "But it's definitely in the alcohol section. Hell, my mama had us taking shots at a young age."

"Castor Oil is a laxative."

"Could've fooled me," Ray told her. "I thought she was trying to kill us, so she wouldn't have to buy us no school clothes."

Sylvia cackled so loud, everyone in the restaurant was looking in their direction. She sheepishly apologized and they continued to enjoy each other's company. Ray consumed his meal as Sylvia casually sipped her tea. After checking his watch, Ray realized they'd been conversating for little over an hour.

"I've held you up too long, huh?" Sylvia asked, taking notice.

"Not really," he answered. "But I do have some business to tend to."

"I understand. I want to ask you something that I keep forgetting to ask you when we talk."

"What's that?"

"Will you be there when I have the baby?"

"I should."

"In the delivery room?"

"Huh?"

"Honda?"

Ray smiled at the fact that he'd been hit with his own comical reply. At that point, he realized how much he missed being with her. If it wasn't for the fact that he'd actually caught her mouth around another man's rod. He probably would have forgiven her, but in the back of his mind, he knew, he wasn't the only one. Hell, the girl was too sexually active.

"Do I have to be right there in the delivery room while it's going down?" Ray now asked.

"You don't wanna see your baby come into the world?"

"I guess I should want to," he stated calmly. "I just don't think I can take the sight of it."

"Yeah, you would probably faint," she insisted. "My dad fainted when I was born."

"I don't know," Ray said as he stood and donned his black leather trench coat. "I'll just have to prepare myself for it. Did you drive?"

"Somebody brought me," she answered quickly, then glanced out at the parking lot. "They're still out there."

"Okay," Ray gave her the twelve hundred dollars he'd brought for her, hugged her, then made his exit. Curious, as he made for his car, he looked around to see who Sylvia had waiting on her for over an hour. It didn't take him long to spot the SUV parked in the far corner of the parking lot with the exhaust fumes blowing visibly from the exhaust pipes.

'*It might be his baby*,' Ray thought as he climbed into his car and drove away. He had one more person to deal with tonight, and that was Precious.

Thinking about her, made him wonder how he'd not discerned that she was a lesbian. Not that he paid that much attention to her, but he could have a least suspected it. Was that what he was doing now? Suspecting her of being a lesbian? It was obvious, although she introduced the girl, he'd encountered in his apartment last night, as Bree, her girlfriend. Bree favored Da Brat, with her long plaits, brown complexion, nose ring, and loose fitted clothes. Plus, she looked like she would win a pussy-eating contest against a giraffe.

"Did I wake you?" Ray asked as he entered the living room, where Precious was stretched out on the sofa with her shoes off.

"I guess I dozed off for a minute," she said, sitting up.

"Sleeping on the job!" Ray teased, making her laugh. He placed the large paper bag on the coffee table. "We can break these down, but I need to shower and change first."

"Okay," she said, yawning. "I'll set everything up."

Ray set off to conduct his freshening up which took about forty minutes. Now, in a pair of jogging pants, a t-shirt, and house shoes, he was sitting at the kitchen table with Precious, where she'd set up the digital scale and bags. V-103's Quiet Storm was playing slow jams on the stereo in the living room.

"I ain't never smoked this purple stuff," Precious admitted. She was bagging the weed after Ray weighed it.

"He said that's what everybody's smoking now," Ray told her. He didn't know too much about the purple weed, which was why he'd only purchased two pounds of it and four pounds of regular.

"That's what I hear. So, you ain't never smoked?"

"When I was thirteen," he answered, looking into her eyes for the umpteenth time, relishing the fact that she was extremely sexy when she was high. "I stopped before I turned seventeen."

"Why?"

Ray sensed the disappointment in her voice. "Cause, at the time, I was stealing cars and constantly running from the police. It was kinda hard trying to out-think the police while under the influence."

"Well, why didn't you just smoke on the days you weren't stealing people's cars?" She was smiling.

"And what day was that?"

"You stole cars every day?" Her chinky eyes were now beaming.

"That was my hustle," he told her. "After I stopped smoking weed, I started selling it."

"Well, I think that was a good change of profession," she complimented.

"Yeah, me too," he agreed. Now, he was ready to confirm his suspicion of her sexuality. "So, when did you decide to become a lesbian?"

She giggled at the question. "What makes you think I'm a lesbian?"

"Because, I've never seen you with a man," he pointed out. "Plus, Stevie Wonder could see that Bree don't want nothing to do with a man, sexually."

"And that makes me a lesbian?" she asked, smiling.

"Does it?" Now Ray was studying her with arched eyebrows, anticipating her answer.

"No, it doesn't," she answered. "That's not enough evidence to convict any woman of lesbianism, but I am bi-sexual."

"Hell, I buy sex, too," Ray joked. "But being bi-sexual means, you have sex with men *and* women."

"I do," she admitted. "Well, actually, I haven't been with a man in almost two years."

"Two years!" Ray exclaimed.

"Almost," she corrected.

"Almost doesn't count," he countered. "If it's been that long, then, by popular belief, you're a certified lesbian."

"I doubt that," she protested. "I still crave a hard dick from time to time. I'm just stubborn with my pussy. I won't open my legs for just any man. I have to really like him and know that he respects me."

"So, what kind of men do you like?"

"Looks are not all that important," she answered. "But I like a sensitive man with a great sense of humor."

"Sensitive?"

"With a great sense of humor."

"So, you want a man who cries when he watches movies like Roots and Titanic?" Ray stated.

She could not hold back her laughter. "That's not what I'm saying, silly!"

"I mean, ain't nothing wrong with that," he persisted. "Sometimes, I just cry for the hell of it."

"Yeah, whatever."

After they'd converted the six pounds into twenties and ounces and stored everything in the stash room which was the second room of the two-bedroom apartment. Precious donned her turtle-neck sweater and waited at the door for Ray to let her out.

"What time?" she asked when he approached.

"I should be leaving out around two, but if something comes up before then, I'll let you know."

"Okay, goodnight."

Goodnight."

He let her out and waited until she was in her apartment before securing his door. Feeling the crave for chocolate, he grabbed the last four, Star Crunch pies from atop the refrigerator, turned off the stereo in the living room, and retired to his room. Where he dove on top of his bed and used the remote to surf the channels on his T.V. until he came across an episode of The Jamie Foxx Show.

"See what that boy Foxx talkin' bout," he said, tossing the remote on the bed and starting on his pies. He had just finished his third pie when his cell phone vibrated atop the nightstand. He answered without checking the caller I.D. "Yeah?"

"Are you in bed?" Precious asked.

"Nah," he answered. "What's up?

"Can you come over here for a minute? I need your assistance. It won't take long."

"A'ight."

Ray downed his last pie, slipped back into his house shoes, grabbed his keys, and headed for the door. Precious was already standing in her door waiting for him. She stepped aside and locked the door once he'd entered.

"What you need help with?"

"This," she said, letting the robe she had on fall to the kitchen floor, revealing her nude and petite frame.

Wasting no time, she closed the gap between them, pressing her body against his body and her lips against his lips. Ray was a bit surprised, but he returned her kiss, wrapping his arms around her small waist to fully embrace her. His manhood responded immediately, feeling like it was about to burst through his sweatpants. Breaking the kiss, Precious then regarded him with a look in her eyes he'd never seen before— *Lust*!

## CHAPTER 12

It took less than an hour to access the money, drugs and drug sales. Then line everything up with everything James had purchased. Fred did the calculating, while he, Ray and Black copied down their own notes on their notepads to corroborate the original books.

While they were doing that, James just sat back in his chair, twirling a blunt through his fingers that he'd been ready to fire up since they arrived. It wasn't like he was nervous. He knew he'd spent way more money than he'd professed and that the books were way off, being that he didn't record anything he'd done personally. But he didn't notice it until he checked the books last night, after rushing home from the meeting. He discovered that the books were off by almost two hundred thousand dollars.

James knew he couldn't show up at the meeting with that kind of money unaccounted for. Therefore, he took seventy thousand from his stash leaving him with three, made a few phone calls, and managed to borrow one hundred and twenty thousand from an ex-drug kingpin, who now secretly operated as a loan shark for known drug dealers that find themselves in little binds and needs assistance.

Well, James was, indeed, in a bind, and needed some assistance. When he contacted the loan shark, introduced himself, and stated how much he needed. He immediately agreed to meet with James, saying it would be an honor to do business with the Notorious Kingz.

"How many bricks are we short of, King Black?" Fred asked, making sure that they had the same addition.

"One," Black answered.

"How much money are we short of, King Ray?" Fred asked.

"Eleven-fifteen."

"That's the one we split between Big O' and Dexter," James admitted.

"It's not in the books," Fred pointed out. "Do they owe us?"

"That was something we agreed on, remember?"

"You said you were gonna look out for them, but you didn't say how much."

"Okay," James leaned forward. "That's lack of communication on my part, and I forgot to put it in the books. No, they don't owe us."

Simultaneously, Fred, Ray, and Black scribbled on their notepads. Fred looked up at James. "What about the eleven-fifty?"

"That's the money I was supposed to pick up, yesterday," Black intervened.

"He still M-I-A?" James wanted to know.

"Yeah, pretty much."

"I'll handle that," James promised. "What about the weed campaign? How we looking on that end?"

Ray and Fred exchanged glances.

Fred answered, "We don't have any ties to it."

"What'd you mean!" James wasn't hearing this. "That weed came from a heist we all hit. The hell if we don't have no ties to it!"

"Every penny King Ray made from the weed," Fred explained. "He put into the Kingz Account. The weed he'd been buying lately, is from his own pockets. Which is something he'd been doing since he was seventeen."

"You're right," James conceded. "So, how you looking on that, King Ray?"

"I'm good," Ray answered. "I got somebody holding down the spot when I'm not there."

Ray did his best not to think about Precious, all day. However, the mentioning of somebody holding down his spot, brought back memories of her and the breath-taking sex she'd bestowed upon him last night, and this morning before he could even awake and realize he'd fallen asleep in her bed. Before he could open his eyes, she already had his early morning hard as a brick penis in her mouth, with the tip of it palpating her tonsil.

The very thought of it almost sparked an erection, but he mentally fought it off. Then, instantly, his mind switched over to Sylvia, who he'd actually been thinking about all day, ever since the dream he'd had about her. Although he was sleeping beside Precious, the dream was a bit disturbing to him, because Sylvia appeared to be a spirit, and he clearly noticed she wasn't pregnant. He didn't know if he should take that as a sign that something was wrong, or that the baby wasn't his, or both.

\*\*\*\*

All James could think about was how he was going to make enough money to pay back the loan shark, fill his stash spot back up, and buy the other stuff he'd planned to buy. Now, he was regretting that he'd bought the safe, but he knew it had to be done because he had become too reckless with the Kingz Account. Plus, he didn't want his stupidity to cause him to fall out with his cronies.

He had to pick up money from three spots. He'd called the two workers in Carver Homes and told them he was on the way, so they were already standing by the mailboxes when he arrived. Transactions were made inside the car. After leaving there, James headed for Summer Hill.

"He's in the living room," Tek's girlfriend, who always answered the door, said when she let him in.

The living room was where they always conducted business. It was always just him and Tek, but when James entered the living room, there was another guy present. This dude was extremely black, with long dreads. He looked like he'd had his share of street brawls growing up.

"This my nigga, Barlow," Tek said, catching James' inquisitive look. "We grew up together. He just got out yesterday. He's cool, but if you don't wanna do business in front of him, I can respect that."

Reluctantly, James took a seat on the sofa beside Tek, being that Barlow occupied the recliner. There were two stacks of bills on the table. Tek handed one to James, who counted it, put it in his coat pocket and produced a small paper bag.

"This should be the last one," Tek said, accepting the package. The next time you drop by I should have enough clout to cop my own shit."

"That's what's up," James told him. "You gon' shop with us?"

"I don't see a reason not to. Y'all ain't beefing with Drop Squad, are ya?"

"Nah. Why?"

"Cause, they be supplying the rest of these niggas in Summer Hill," Tek mentioned. "I just don't wanna get caught up in some bullshit that ain't got shit to do with me."

"Yeah, I feel that." James knew how easy a drug war could ignite when it came to territories.

He was waiting for Drop Squad to cross that line, so he could send his small brigade Kingzmen into battle, which is why he had Grip training them in every form of combat he knew. Drop Squad is a large mob, but they were just average street niggas with guns. When Grip gets finished with the Kingzmen, they are going to be an average street nigga's worst nightmare. Fuck Drop Squad!

"My nigga Barlow wanna holla at you, 'bout some business, tho," Tek stated.

"What's up?" James asked, to him Barlow didn't look like he could be trusted to go to the store to buy a box of blunts.

"Shit, I'm fucked up," Barlow said. "I ain't never sold for no-body, but I got a daughter to take care of."

"What you trying to get?"

"It don't matter," he answered. "I trap right here in Summer Hill, and University Homes where my sister stays. So, I'ma get off whatever you drop on me."

James looked over at Tek.

"The nigga got major trap skills," Tek confirmed.

"I can put you on," James said, standing. "But I'll have to get with the other Kingz first."

James left Summer Hill, still trying to sort everything out in his mind. For some reason, he kept thinking about using the rest of the money from his stash to cop a few ounces and put some niggas down. Hell, maybe he could use Barlow being that he had trap skills.

James pulled into Deerfield Apartments on Campbellton Road and parked. After checking his gun, he got out and approached Steve's door. Before he could knock, Steve opened the door letting him in.

"I thought you had forgot," Steve said, locking the door. "I was just about to call you."

"Shit just took longer than it should," James asserted, taking a seat on the living room sofa. "What, you got somewhere to go?"

"Nah. I just got a few homies coming through. We ain't finna do shit but smoke weed and talk shit."

James just looked at Brother Steve his ex-cellmate, who used to always talk about the Bible and doing God's will. James didn't trip, because he was eminently conversant with the type: Thug in the streets, Christian behind bars.

After the exchange, they made small conversations for a good twenty minutes. Right as James stood to leave, someone knocked on the door, causing him to reach for his Glock.

"That might be my niggas," Steve said, heading for the door.

James still kept his hand on his gun, not willing to trust anything or anybody. He was definitely not going to trust a nigga who would turn his back on The Man Above.

Steve opened the door, and three men entered. The first man introduced the other two. James was busy studying their movements, so he wasn't looking at their faces until the introducer introduced one of the men as Moe. That's when James locked eyes with Moe, who'd grown up with him and Ray, although he was a few years younger.

"What up boy!" James greeted, removing his hand from his gun.

"What up, my nigga!" Moe beamed. "Y'all don't fuck with the hood no more."

"Shit, we still swing through from time to time," James said, embracing his friend. "What you been up to?"

"Man, I've been trying to get up with y'all."

"Straight up?"

"Hell yeah."

"Shit, I'm 'bout to bounce," James told him. "Walk me to the car."

James dapped Steve, then he and Moe exited and climbed into the BMW that was already running with the heat permeating the interior.

"You *and* Ray got Beamers," Moe pointed out.

"Shit, the whole squad got Beamers," James told him.

"That's what's up."

"So, what you trying to do?"

"I'm trying to get paid," Moe answered. "I got a baby on the way, and I need to get my—"

"Say no more," James interrupted. "Gimme ya cell number."

Moe wrote his number down and gave it to him.

"I'ma hit you up in two days," James promised.

"That's a bet."

They dapped and Moe made his exit. As James rode off, he finally made up his mind. He was going to conduce the money in his stash to the game and produce his own workers. So far, he had two volunteers.

**\*\*\*\***

Ray made a good point when he said they needed at least four tractor-trailers to sit in front of The Palace. To keep down suspicion, which was why Fred had driven through Bland Town, telling anyone he'd encountered that if they saw Bobby, to tell him to get at him.

"I've been up all night," Fred's mother told him as she sat in her favorite recliner, picking over the soft tacos he'd brought her from Taco Bell.

"Why?" he asked.

"Because, I had that dream again," she answered. "I woke up in a cold sweat and haven't been back to sleep since."

"Mama, you're not ready to move out of this house?" Fred was hoping to change the subject because he was not in the mood to go through this with her again.

"This house doesn't have anything to do with my dreams, Fred." She was now looking at him with those dark eyes he'd inherited from her.

"I'm not saying that mama," he challenged. "I was just hoping you were ready to move into a better place than this. A better neighborhood."

"I'm not," she admitted. "I have too many memories of this place and this neighborhood. I can't just leave."

Fred still didn't want to leave his mother in this house, but he had to do something. Because he had guns, jewelry, and over three hundred thousand dollars stashed in his room, which was accessible to a burglar. Being that the front and back doors could not be locked due to termite-infested wood. This also made it feasible for him to be roused from his sleep by masked men with guns waving in his face. It also put his mother in danger, but Fred knew that if something like that ever occurred, it wouldn't be by the hands of anyone from Bland Town or Knight Park. His mother was well respected. Plus, he and Eric had proven they were not to be fucked with.

"I understand, mama," Fred told her.

"I was hoping you would," she insisted. "And how's the Get Along Gang?"

"They cool," he answered, knowing she was talking about James, Ray, and Black.

"They haven't been by lately."

"I'll make sure I tell them to stop by."

"I miss Ray, with his silly self," she said, giggling. "Do you have plans for tonight?"

"Not that I know of. What's up?"

"We haven't played poker in a while," she told him. "The cards are on my dresser."

"You gonna eat first?"

"Yeah, I'ma eat," she answered. "Go and get the cards."

While she tended to her tacos, Fred retrieved the cards and a chair from the kitchen. He had to position the coffee table in front of her, and his chair across from hers. After an hour and a half of playing poker, Fred's cell phone rang.

"What's up?" he answered.

"That's what I called to find out," Theresa purred. "What 'cha doing?"

"Chillin' with moms."

"What 'cha doing afterward?"

"Jumping in the bed."

"Your bed's not big enough for the both of us?"

Fred laughed. Then seeing his mother's disappointing look, he told Theresa he'd call her back. After two more games, his mother retired to her room. Fred tucked her in, made for his room and flopped down on his bed, lying on his back. He thought about the Kingz meeting today. James had shown him up because he just knew that the Kingz Account was going to be way off. Now, he was feeling kind of bad for doubting his long-time friend.

"Let me call, my nigga," he said to himself, but before he could dial James' number, his phone vibrated. "Yeah?"

"You wanna see your daughter?"

**\*\*\*\***

Upon leaving The Palace, Ray decided to drive home, but after receiving a call from B.J., who playfully accused him of disowning him. He detoured to East Lake Meadows, where B.J. shared an apartment with his girlfriend, Krystal. T-Roc and three of Krystal's friends were present. They had been drinking and smoking. Ray was sitting on the couch between two girls who were unsubtly vying for his attention.

"Y'all crazy!" Krystal would tell them when one tried to out talk or debunk the other in order to impress him.

"Man, you remember when we stole that ice cream van?" B.J. asked.

"Hell yeah!" said Ray. "We probably sold three ice creams, ate ten, and gave the rest away. Then, you got on my last nerves, ringing that damn bell all day!"

"Shit, the radio didn't work," B.J. countered, laughing. "I had to make some kind of music."

"Remember that fox we found?" Ray asked.

"Fox!" Krystal exclaimed. "A real fox?"

"Hell yeah!" B.J. answered. "We thought it was a dog."

"It didn't look like a fox?" one of the girls sitting beside Ray asked.

"It did," Ray answered. "But we still thought it was a dog. We were young."

"Old man Smokey used to tell us it was a fox," B.J. explained. "But he stayed drunk so much. We ain't pay dude no attention. So, by the time we figured out he was telling the truth, somebody had stolen the fox."

They reminisced for another forty-five minutes before Ray announced he was ready to turn in. He bid everyone good night and allowed B.J. to walk him to his car.

"You strapped?" Ray asked once they'd exited the apartment.

"Man, you know I keep that tool by the waist," B.J. boasted. "I grew up out here, and I still don't trust these niggas."

"Smart man!" Ray commended. "I see you just done adopted, T-Roc."

"Yeah, pretty much," said B.J. "His mom ain't doing shit for him. All she wanna do is smoke dope and smoke more dope. He ain't trying to be around no shit."

Ray had met T-Roc's mother, who favored Gabrielle Union. A person wouldn't know she was a smoker unless they knew her, or she admitted it. Then, they still wouldn't believe it.

"You wouldn't make father-figure of the year," Ray joked. "But you do keep the lil' homie fresh, and some money in his pockets."

"Shit, we may have to find us a new gig," said B.J. "We ain't even found another chop shop yet. Plus, we got a couple of cars we can't even get off."

"What y'all got in mind?" Ray asked, already knowing the answer.

"We don't have but two options," B.J. answered. "Either sell dope or rob."

"Three options," Ray insisted, starting his car by remote.

"What's the third one?"

"Get a job."

"Where— McDonald's?"

"It wouldn't kill you."

"Don't that make you a hypocrite?"

"I'm not telling you *not* to sell dope or rob," Ray countered. "I'm just letting you know that those are not the only options you have."

After sermonizing his friend, Ray was en route to his apartment, wondering why he hadn't received a call from Sylvia yet. In fact, B.J. was the only person he'd received a call from today. He checked his phone to make sure he didn't inadvertently deactivate it. It was still activated. After entering Maple Creek Apartments, Ray parked retrieved his tarpaulin from the trunk and covered the BMW. He'd decided he was going to drive his Oldsmobile for a few days. Upon entering his apartment, he heard *Tracie Spencer's 'Tender Kisses'* playing at a low volume from the living room.

"Damn, I wish I knew you had Tracie Spencer," Ray said as he entered the living room, where Precious was lounging on the sofa.

"It's a mix CD," she said, sitting up. "It got *Patti Labelle, Regina Bell, Lisa Fisher, Stephanie Mills, Toni Braxton—*"

"What song by *Toni Braxton?*" Ray asked, not able to hide his excitement, being that he was crazy about *Toni Braxton.*

"*I Love Me Some Him,*" she answered, smiling.

"That's my shit! What you know 'bout that?"

"Trust me," she stated, sexually eyeing him. "I know a lot about loving me some him."

"I just bet you do," Ray told her, with a smirk on his face, causing her to laugh. He sat on the other end of the sofa. "So, how's business?"

"Pretty good," she answered. "Four ounces of purp, two ounces of mid, and seven dubs."

"So, niggas are on that purple stuff, huh?"

"A few of 'em said it was about time you got some."

"I'll take that as a compliment," he said. "If you wanna go ahead and turn in, I'll take it from here."

"I'm good," she told him. "Unless you're kicking me out."

"Nah," he said, standing. "You can chill all you want. I'm 'bout to hop in the shower and kick back myself."

"I'll be right here," Precious said as Ray exited, then continued listening to the stereo, and watching the muted T.V., where the news was still talking about a woman found dead on Bankhead Highway.

Ray had been in the shower for about ten minutes when he heard the stereo's volume increase, and *Toni Braxton's 'I Love Me Some Him* filled the apartment.

"Okay!" he exclaimed, closing his eyes and snapping his fingers to the rhythm. The music was so loud, he didn't notice the bathroom door open and close quickly.

His eyes were still closed, so he didn't see Precious ease into the shower behind him, wearing nothing but a smile on her face.

"Oh shit!" Ray exclaimed, upon opening his eyes when he sensed her behind him. "Girl, you scared the—"

She silenced him interlocking her mouth with his, and her body pressed into his body. Somehow, she managed to worm one of her hands between them and grab his penis, inducing an instant erection.

Yes, she definitely knew how to love her some him!

****

Greg hadn't driven his car since yesterday since Black came looking for the Kingz' money. He also didn't hang out in Perry

Homes in the daytime, just in case Black, or the other Kingz returned. He also told Fanaye not to open the door for anybody or answer her phone if the caller I.D. didn't show the call was coming from a payphone. It was true that he was a smoker, and he, Fanaye and a few other smokers had smoked up most of the Kingz product.

He'd managed to sell two twenty sacks in 2000, the small, and shabby apartments that were pretty much next door to Perry Homes, where he hung out during the day. He used thirty dollars of the sale and bought groceries, cigarettes, and beer, in which he carried in two grocery bags, with the case of beer tucked under his arm as he cautiously made his way to his apartment, looking around for any potential threat. He didn't notice anything out of the ordinary.

As he approached the door, he sat one bag down, so he could initiate his code knock that Fanaye would recognize.

His hand never touched the door. Greg didn't hear the footsteps of the three Kingzmen as they silently rushed up from behind. He did see a sudden flash of an arm before it wrapped around his neck. He tried to yell, but it was nothing more than a gasp as the arm tightened around his neck, cutting off circulation. He tried to struggle, but it was futile. He'd never been in this kind of position before, so he felt like he was about to die as his lungs burned from the lack of air. Then, darkness befell him. The last thing he heard was his groceries and beer crashing to the ground.

# CHAPTER 13

James woke up at 11:28 a.m., thinking about the call he'd gotten from Grip, last night. He'd been expecting the call, because, not once did he doubt that Grip would catch and abduct Greg before the break of dawn. Well, Grip proved to be a man of his word.

Getting out of bed, James tended to his washings, got dressed and ate breakfast. After eating, he called his fellow Kingz and told them they had court at six, and to dress like Kingz. Then he grabbed his log book and called all of their workers, giving them directions to The Palace, informing them to be there no later than 5:50 p.m.

Once this was done, James retrieved the three thousand dollars from his stash, donned his coat, tucked his pistol and headed out the door to make his appointment for today. He pulled into Hollywood Courts at 2:19 p.m. Apparently, Carlos had seen James pull up because he opened the door as James approached.

"Come on in, Your Highness," Carlos bantered, smiling.

"You mean to tell me you didn't roll out the carpet?" James joked back as he entered the apartment.

"I would have," Carlos said. "But the dog done chewed, pissed and shitted all over the muhfucka." That statement caused the black pit bull lying beside the sofa, to stand up like it was ready to attack, James. "At ease, bitch!" The dog obediently re-took its position. "Have a seat, my nigga."

James didn't hesitate, but he sagely took a seat on the other end of the sofa, keeping a wary eye on the dog, who was doing likewise.

"You want a beer?" Carlos asked.

"Yeah."

As soon as Carlos exited the living room, the dog raised his head to watch James. "At ease, bitch!" James said in a low tone, and the dog obeyed. This made James laugh to himself.

"I hope you're not too superior for a Miller," Carlos said, returning with two beers.

"Never that."

Carlos handed him a beer, then sat down. James met Carlos in Bland Town, seven years ago, when Carlos started coming out to kick it with Twon, Big O' and the other big homies. At the time, Carlos was just a rookie to the weight game, being that he'd just started dealing with a bigger scale. He didn't supply Bland Town, nor Knight Park, because dudes were already dealing with Norris, another big homie, who'd gotten his money right and moved out of Bland Town at a young age.

James wanted to do business with Norris, en lieu of Carlos, but Norris had gotten a whiff of how good the Kingz was doing and was quite pleased. He sent his commendations through his sister, Kris. Out of all people, James didn't want Norris to think the Kingz were already failing.

"So, what can I do for you?" Carlos asked, sipping his beer.

"I need you to front me two bricks," James told him. "I got you three thousand in advance, right now."

Carlos laughed so hard, he spilled beer in his lap. "Nigga, you full of shit! Ain't no way in hell! If anything, y'all niggas should be fronting *me* a couple bricks! Man, you—"

Carlos stopped mid-sentence when James began dumping bills from a Ziploc bag onto the coffee table.

"You're dead-ass serious, huh?" Carlos concluded.

"You can count it if you want." James sat back and downed the rest of his beer.

It was clear that Carlos wasn't studying the money because he was still regarding James with an incredulous look.

"When do you need 'em?" Carlos finally asked.

"As soon as possible."

Carlos lingered a few seconds before placing his beer on the table and standing. After a few more seconds of eyeing James. He walked over to the wall and did something James didn't catch, causing a hidden door to open in the wall that led to the adjacent apartment. Saying nothing, Carlos entered the other apartment, closing the door behind him.

After scoring the bricks from Carlos, James was on his way to Herdon Homes to see Kado the neighborhood's chemist. He was going to ask Kado if he would cook the dope and accept pay later, but since Carlos didn't take the three thousand, James could make proper payment. He just hoped Kado would accept him with no appointment.

"Man, you know I work by appointment," Kado reminded James through the cracked door that was held in place by the security chain.

"I'll pay you extra for the inconvenience," James promised. "Unless you're already working on another client."

"Not at the moment."

Kado removed the chain and opened the door. Entering, James noticed that Kado was holding an Uzi.

"What 'cha got?" Kado asked.

"Two birds."

"Take 'em to the kitchen."

Kado followed James to the kitchen, where James took the kilos out of the grocery bag and placed them on the table.

"A person would expect more than two bricks from the legendary Kingz," Kado insisted.

"This some personal shit," James said, disregarding the signification of the statement. "I got a meeting at six. How long will this take?"

"I'm expecting a customer."

"I'm paying extra," James pointed out. "Reschedule that, nigga!"

****

Black had been up since receiving the call from James about the Kingz having court at six tonight. Connie had gone to work. He didn't remember her climbing into bed last night. Just that she'd been up waiting on Sylvia to call back.

Now, dressed, Black exited the apartment, starting his car by remote. He climbed in and grabbed the already rolled blunt from his ashtray. He lit the blunt while letting the car warm up, thinking about this long day of his. It was his turn to tend to the new house.

He had to buy a washer and dryer, cut or pay someone to cut the grass and be there when the three bedroom and living room suites Connie bought were delivered.

Black wasn't sure about who he was going to get to cut the grass because he and Connie had agreed to be very cautious about who they let know where they stayed. So, he pushed that thought to the back of his mind. After grabbing something to eat at Checker's, he hit the expressway en route to Covington, Georgia. As soon as he made the exit his cell phone vibrated in his pocket.

"Yeah?" he answered.

"Hey!" Nikki's voice boomed through the earpiece.

"What's up?"

"Not too much," she answered. "Will you be busy this weekend?"

"I'm moving into my new house Saturday," he told her. "Why?"

"I was gonna let the kids spend the weekend with you."

Black was ecstatic. "We can make that happen. You gotta let me know what time you're bringing them."

"I don't know the exact time," she admitted. "I'll let you know something tomorrow night."

"A'ight."

"Your son is trying to walk, with his badass!" Nikki giggled.

"Yeah?" Black found himself smiling.

"Yeah," she answered. "His lil' badass would crawl to the coffee table, pull himself up and walk around the table, holding on to it and his lil devil-ass just be laughing up a storm too."

A mental picture of his son holding on to the table as he walked around it laughing like a devilish child caused Black to laugh. "Man, I miss y'all. I really mean that, Nikki."

"We miss you too, Keith," Nikki asserted in a more composed tone. "I hate it had to end like it did, but things happen."

"Only if we let them happen," Black countered. "That was minor. We could've talked that shit out."

"Keith, you know my daddy used to beat on my mama," she reminded him. "How can I consider that as minor? This is something I had to endure growing up."

"Yeah, I know," Black admitted silently cursing himself for the trillionth time for letting his anger cause him to put his hands on her.

"I'll call you tomorrow night," she said with recognizable pain in her voice.

She hung up before Black could say anything. Although he didn't have anything to say, he'd heard the pain in her voice, which had to be equivalent to how he was feeling at the moment. He still loved Nikki and couldn't help but think she still loved him.

**** 

Fred had already showered and cooked him and his mother breakfast when he got the call from James. But his mind was mostly preoccupied with the call he'd gotten from Tee last night telling him to meet her at her parent's house to see *his* daughter. His first thought was to hang up, but after thinking about the dreams his mother had been having about him. He figured it would be best to see what he would be leaving behind, just in case his mother's dreams were more than just dreams.

Fred had just tied the shoestrings on his Nikes, when his mother called from the living room, informing him that he had company. When he entered the living room, he saw Bobby, who he'd been expecting.

"You must've got my message?" Fred asked Bobby once they'd entered his room.

"Ms. Eva flagged me down in Bland Town a few minutes ago," Bobby told him. "Said you were looking for me."

"Yeah. You still be fucking with them trucks?"

"Shit, that's all I do!"

"Well, we need four of 'em."

"Damn!" Bobby exclaimed. "Y'all moving that much?"

"How much are you gonna charge us for four and four trailers?" Fred asked, not in the mood for small talk, being that he had to get going so he could handle other affairs, starting with meeting Tee at her parent's house in Decatur, Georgia.

"I don't know," answered Bobby. "I gotta get 'em first. I don't even know how long that's gonna take."

"I feel ya." Fred jotted his number down. "Just hit me up when you get 'em."

"Aight," Bobby agreed. "Does it matter what kind of trucks I get?"

"Not really," Fred answered, not knowing a thing about trucks.

Once Bobby left, Fred gathered the suit, robe and crown he was going to wear to The Palace and headed for the front door with everything in a gym bag.

"I assume you're staying somewhere else tonight," his mother asked when he entered the living room.

"Not that I know of," he told her. "You need anything before I leave?"

"I'm okay. What time will you be back?"

"I have no idea."

"You don't ever have an idea," she joked smiling.

Fred wanted to tell his mother about the call he'd gotten from Tee and that he was on his way to see the baby, but he didn't want to get her hopes up again. He was going to find out if the baby was his first.

**** 

"Who is it?"

Fred had never met Tee's mother, but he was sure it was her who'd answered the door sounding like it was an enormity for anyone to show up at their house.

"Fred," he answered.

There was a moment of silence before the door swung open. As soon as she laid eyes on him, her visage quickly took on a look of disappointment. Or was it disgust?

"Did you say, Fred?"' she asked like she didn't believe him to be who he claimed to be.

"Yes, ma'am.'

She just stood there giving him that suspicious look.

"Let him in mama!" Tee, who happened to materialize, demanded. "That's Fantasia's daddy."

"Hmph!" Tee's mother reluctantly stepped aside.

"Come on, Fred," Tee gestured. "Your daughter's in my old room, sleep."

Fred followed Tee to her old room, where she eased the already ajar door open. Fantasia was asleep in the middle of the huge bed, swathed in baby blankets. Fred walked over to the bed and peered down at the infant, immediately apprehending Tee's mother's behavior towards him. This was not his baby!

Fred didn't know much about babies, but he was sure that a high-yellow-ass nigga like himself, was incapable of producing such a dark child as this one. Hell, he had always used protection with Tee. The only reason he took the initiative to come out to see the baby, was because a condom had burst on him, once right when he was at the peak of his climax and he didn't pull out. Plus, he learned in *Sex Education* that one insemination was sufficient to prompt impregnation.

"So, what're you gonna do about your baby?" Tee pulled him from his reverie.

He faced Tee, who was standing akimbo, a few feet away from him.

'*Either this bitch is really dumb*,' he thought. '*Or she hellbent on putting another man's baby off on me.*'

Clearly, Tee's mother couldn't miss out of the action, because she was leaning against the threshold of the door, with her arms folded over her chest. Fred didn't feel right talking to Tee in front of her and she must've sensed it because she mumbled something incoherent then strutted off.

"Shawty, you know we gotta take a DNA test," Fred finally spoke.

"*A DNA, test!*" Tee snapped. "You must've forgot about the day that rubber burst, and you nutted in me?"

'*This bitch is really going to try and use that to her advantage*', Fred thought. "I remember that," he said. "That's the only reason I came, but that lil' girl don't look nothing like me."

"Why? Because she's darker than you?" Tee insisted. "A baby don't always take on its father's complexion when they're first born."

"Says who?"

"The doctor."

"Look," Fred was ready to end this frivolous quarrel. "Call and make an appointment for a DNA test. We'll let them prove it. You know my number."

"I don't believe you!" Tee exclaimed as Fred was leaving the room.

Fred ignored her as he exited, making for the front door. He thought Tee was going to trail him but she didn't. He thought Tee's mother was going to magically appear, with that same disgusted look on her face but she didn't. He made it out of the house unscathed. The wintry breeze added to his relief, although the sky was dark.

****

"What are you gonna do with the apartment when you move?" Precious, who was sitting on the edge of the bed, asked Ray, who was filling a second box full of clothes that he was going to drop off at his house in Riverdale, before going to The Palace.

Precious had awakened him up with breakfast in bed, washed the dishes, cleaned the apartment and taken the used sheets to the community's laundromat. Now, Ray was looking at her in a whole new light. He'd also noticed how comfortable she'd become with him since they'd been having sex, which, he figured, was the result of not being with a man for almost two years.

"If you wanna continue doing business," Ray answered, "I'll keep the apartment. I'm sure you wouldn't wanna use your apartment."

"Of course, I wanna continue doing business," Precious asserted. "Unless I find another job that'll pay me five hundred a week."

After filling the second box with clothes and taping it shut, Ray shed his pajamas and donned his blue two-piece suit and matching Mauri shoes while Precious watched attentively. As soon as he grabbed his tie, Precious leaped from the bed.

"Let me do that." She playfully snatched the tie from his hand and began tying it.

"Don't be trying to choke me."

"I wouldn't hurt you, baby," she swore, drilling those seductive, hazel eyes into his. "I promise."

Once again, Ray was mesmerized by her seductive eyes. She had not smoked today, so Ray could see her full pupils. Her breath smelled of Colgate toothpaste, and her body of Zest soap, which made him think about the Zest commercial's motto: *"You're not fully clean unless you're Zest-fully clean."*

"There you go, boo." Precious had tied the tie, then kissed him on the jaw. "Now, all you need is a stick."

"A stick?"

"Yeah," she answered. "To fight off them other chicken heads, with your fine ass."

Ray laughed as he went to his closet and retrieved his robe and crown, placing them on the bed. Precious couldn't help herself. She grabbed the crown, placed it atop her head and posed in the dresser's mirror with her arms folded over her chest.

"Yeah," she took on a deep voice. "I'm, King Ray. How dare thou disrespect my Lordship! Off with his head!"

Ray could not contain his laughter. "Girl, you smoke too much weed, and watch way too many cartoons!"

"I make a good King Ray impersonation, huh?"

"You really want me to answer that?"

"Yes."

"Okay," he gave in. "You make a good King Ray impersonation."

"Aww, that's so sweet!"

"What?"

"You lied to keep from hurting my feelings," she assumed, smiling. "That's real considerate of you. I think it's cute." She moved in to kiss him, but he leaned out of her way.

"What?"

"I wouldn't feel right kissing a King," Ray told her. "That would disrespect my royal oath."

"Oh! I'm sorry, Your Majesty!" Precious removed the crown and gently placed it atop Ray's head. "Guess what?"

"What?"

"I've always wanted to kiss a King." She moved, wrapped her arms about his neck and inserted her tongue into his mouth, which Ray did not resist as he returned the kiss and gripped her butt with both hands.

Ray was hesitant to break the kiss, but he did, telling Precious he had to get going.

"You got an umbrella?" she asked. "They said it was gonna rain today. It was drizzling when I went to the laundromat."

"Yeah, I got one."

But the rain was pouring as Ray loaded the two boxes of clothes and the garbage bag with his crown and robe, into his Delta. He was just about to slide into the driver's seat when Precious called out to him. She was standing on the porch, holding a small wooden box that resembled a pirate's treasure chest. It contained his Kingz necklace.

"You don't need this?" she asked.

He retrieved the box, thanked her and bustled back to the car, being that he'd already folded the umbrella and left it in the car. As he pulled off, Precious waved and mouthed something that was too distinguishable for interpretation.

*'Maybe, she was saying that in a joking matter'*, he thought. Then again, she hadn't been with a man in almost two years. Plus, when they had sex, it was done passionately and Ray was quite sure Bree couldn't make her feel like he could. So, perhaps Precious was really expressing her true feelings.

Ray wanted to push the thought of Precious to the back of his mind, so he injected one of his DJ Goldfinger CD's, and turned it up as he cruised the highway. Getting to Riverdale, his first stop was at a gas station, where he encountered, Joe who was exiting the store, accompanied by a female who was much taller than him.

"Damn! What up, my nigga?" Joe greeted him.

"What the move is?" Ray dapped him up.

"On a paper chase, like always," Joe answered, then introduced his company as his wife, Valerie. "Baby, you can go on to the truck," he told his wife, who obeyed and said that she would pump the gas. When she left, Joe asked, "You live in Riverdale?"

"Not yet," Ray answered. "I bought a house out here that I'll move into Saturday. I thought you stayed in Douglasville?"

"I do. I told you, I fuck with credit cards and checks."

"Yeah, you did," Ray remembered. "That's what you up to?"

"Shit, we got one more check to cash," Joe said. "I wanna buy a few ounces of weed, but y'all don't sell weed, right?"

"It's on deck," Ray told him. "How many?"

"Bout three, or four."

"I can handle that," Ray assured him, then jotted Joe's number down. "I'll hit you up when I get back to the crib."

"That's a bet."

As if on cue, Valerie pulled up on them in a champagne colored Infiniti truck on chrome wheels. They dapped, and Joe climbed into the passenger's seat. Just as Ray had suspected, Joe was getting to the money.

It was five fifty-five, and the rain had let up almost an hour ago when Ray pulled up to the front gate of The Palace, where two Kingzmen occupied the small security booth.

"State your business!" one of the KMs demanded, once Ray had rolled his window down.

Ray just stared at him, trying to discern if he was joking, but he should know better than to do something like that, which was disrespectful.

"Nigga, that's King Ray!" the other KM acknowledged.

"Oh shit!" The first KMs eyes enlarged and he had a look on his face like he'd disrespected God Himself. "Sorry 'bout that, King Ray. I ain't never seen you in that car before."

"I'll let it slide this time," Ray told him. "Don't let it happen again!"

"Yes, sir!"

Ray rolled his window up, and when the electrical gate was wide enough, he drove through. As he approached the building, he looked over the cars he supposed belonged to their workers, but James didn't mention anything about them being here.

Ray parked in his reserved spot, grabbed his bag containing his regalia, and a large portrait of Mona Lisa in a gold frame, then headed for the entrance.

"R.T. sir," a KM standing just inside the door, said.

"What?" Ray noticed the Tech-9 strapped to his shoulder.

"They're at the Round Table."

"A'ight." Ray moved on, wondering why the Kingzmen was referring to him as sir. He knew it was James' doing. Perhaps he'd increased their pay.

"Come on in, Christmas!" James said as soon as Ray entered the office.

He, Fred and Black was already seated with their robes on the back of their chairs, and their crowns on the table. There were also four two-way radios on the table. Once Ray placed the portrait on the shell of the safe, behind two-way radio battery charger, hung his robe on his chair, placed his crown on the table, and folded the bag, he took his seat.

"So, what the word is?" Ray asked.

"What's with the Mona Lisa?" Fred wanted to know.

"It's to decorate the safe, so it doesn't look too obvious," Ray explained.

All Kingz nodded their consent.

"We were discussing the re-up," James told Ray. "I'ma hit Franco up later and set something up. Plus, we got these two-way radios we'll be using at The Palace. Our code names are our initials: K.J., K.R., K.B., and K.F. The Kingzmen are K.M. One to Six, with Grip being K.M. One." James looked at his watch, then grabbed his radio. "K.J. to K.M.—One."

"Go head for K.M. One, "Grip sounded through all radios.

"It's time," James told him.

"Ten-four," Grip responded, then said, "K.M. – One to all K.M.'s. Twenty-five to Headquarters. All K. M's, twenty-five to Headquarters. Over."

Ray was impressed. He could tell that Fred and Black were also.

"Shit let's have court!" James said as he stood, donning his robe.

After the Kingz donned their crowns, robes, and clipped their radios to their belts, they exited the office, where Grip and three other KMs were waiting.

"Where are the other two?" James asked.

Grip answered, "They gotta lock the fence and let the dogs out. They should be on the way in." As soon as he said it, the last two from the security booth entered the building. "We're ten-four?" Grip asked them.

"Yes sir," they answered in unison.

"Let's get this over with," James said, leading the way.

When they approached the double-doors, two of the Kingzmen held them open as the Kingz entered. Most of the chairs were filled with their workers, who were in awe, being that they'd never seen the Kingz 'dressed up.'

The Kingz made it to their respective thrones, sat down and looked out at their small audience.

"Roll out the tarp and bring in the criminal," James spouted.

They watched as Grip interacted with the KMs. Three of them rolled out a clear tarpaulin in the space between The Kingz and the audience, and the two standing by the door left the room with Grip.

"Good evening men!" James spoke. "I wanna thank y'all for coming out. What we're about to do is have court. One of our workers has violated the Crown and must face judgment. Mike, would you please step forward?"

"Huh!" Mike looked as if he was about to shit bricks.

"Step forward!" James reiterated.

Mike reluctantly stood and stepped forward, stopping several feet away from them on the tarp. At this time, Fred, Black, and Ray were trying to figure out in their minds what Mike had done to violate the Kingz, but it was confirmed the second Greg was escorted through the double-doors by Grip and the other two KMs, shackled and hands cuffed behind him.

Mike had introduced Greg to the Kingz.

## CHAPTER 14

'*James has really lost his mind*', Fred thought.

He was actually going to kill Greg and possibly Mike in front of their other workers. Fred understood that his friend wanted to prove a point by making an example but doing it in front of people was too risky.

"Mike, do you know this man standing beside you?" James asked.

Mike looked at Greg for a moment, like he was wondering what his fate would be by admitting that he knew the guy who stood beside him, restrained looking like he'd been in the ring with Mike Tyson.

"Yeah," Mike finally answered.

"You were the one who'd introduced him to The Kingz, right?"

"Yeah."

"Did you know that he ran off with the Kingz' merchandise?"

"Nah," Mike answered, giving Greg a look of disdain. "I ain't know that."

"That makes you guilty by association, Mike."

"Hold on!" Mike protested. "I ain't have no part in that!"

"That's why it's guilt by association," James explained. "You brought this piece of shit to our organization. You know what they say about birds of a feather."

"We're not birds of a feather," Mike contradicted. "I've been holding up my end."

"The Kingz are not to be violated, or disrespected," James addressed the congregation. "Greg violated the Kingz by stealing, and he should be punished. Does any King disagree?" James looked to his crew and seeing that neither one spoke, he continued. "Greg, you have been found guilty of stealing and sentenced to death. Mike, you have been found guilty by association. You have a choice of being co-defendant, or executioner."

At that time, Grip handed Mike a .38 revolver, and one of the Kingzmen kicked Greg in the back of his leg, forcing him to his knees. The one with the Tech-9 aimed it at Mike, who was just staring at the gun in his hand.

"Any last words, Greg?" James asked.

"Suck my dick!" Greg said in a groggy voice.

"It's on you Mike," James said, not wanting Greg to live another second for that statement. "You got sixty seconds."

Mike was still looking at the gun in his hand. Greg dropped his head, accepting his fate. Grip was looking at his watch. Ray was thinking about the two teenagers who were murdered in front of him. Fred was hoping Mike made the right decision. Black's cell phone vibrated in his pocket. He pulled it out to see Connie's number on the screen but didn't answer it.

"Time!" Grip announced.

James nodded at him.

"K.M. Three execute!" Grip barked, and the one with the Tech-9 squeezed the trigger, sending slugs through Mike, killing him instantly.

Grip picked up the revolver and shot Greg in the back of his head. There were gasps from the other workers as they gawked at the cadavers that lay on the tarp which was now coated with blood, mucus and brain matter.

James stood. "The Kingz wanna thank you all for coming out. Let this be a lesson for the disloyal niggas. The Kingz put y'all on to help y'all put money in your pockets. You're not just workers. You all have the Kingz stamp. That means you have the Kingz protection. If anybody has any problems they need to discuss, stop by the office on your way out. Grip cut that nigga's dick off, and stuff it in his mouth!"

"Yes, sir."

The Kingz sagely walked over the tarp and were escorted to the office by the two Kingzmen from the security booth.

"Put the dogs up and get back on post," James ordered them.

"Yes sir," they both responded.

"What dogs?" Ray asked once they were all seated at the Round Table.

"Grip got us two Rottweilers," James answered. "They look mean, but they wouldn't hurt a fly."

Black's phone vibrated for the third time. He pulled it out, seeing Connie's number again. Sensing something was wrong, he wanted to answer, but that was not allowed at meetings. Therefore, he returned the phone to his pocket.

"I guess nobody had any problems," James asserted.

"They might be a lil' traumatized by what just happened," said Black.

"Let's just hope nobody reports that shit," Fred pitched in.

"Was I wrong for doing it like that King Fred?" James asked.

"A King is never wrong in another Kingz' eyes," Fred recited. "King Ray?"

"I agree."

"King Black?"

"Kingz for life!" Black answered, pulling out his vibrating phone, seeing Connie's number again. "I gotta take this call, y'all."

"Go ahead," Fred granted.

"Yeah?" Black answered his phone.

"Why haven't you been answering your phone?"

There was no mistaking the tone of Connie's voice. She was crying.

"What's wrong, baby?" Black asked, hoping like hell that a nigga hadn't tried her up in Chapel Forest.

"You need to come home, right now!"

Whatever was wrong, Black knew it was something extremely bad, for her to be crying. "Y'all gotta excuse me," he told his crew.

"What's wrong?" asked Fred.

"I don't know yet. I gotta get to the crib, *asap!*"

"Be careful," Fred told him. "Hit us up if you need us."

"A'ight."

Black gathered his things, left his radio on the table, and rushed out of the office. He wished Connie would have told him what was wrong over the phone, so he wouldn't have a million thoughts running through his mind, but whoever had made Connie cry, may God have mercy on their soul!

\*\*\*\*

After Black left, James, Ray, and Fred made small talk for a while, then made their exits. James stayed back for a meeting with the Kingzmen. Fred pulled off while Ray was having problems with starting his car. Once he'd gotten it started, he dialed Sylvia's number. She didn't answer. He wanted to leave a message, but instead, dialed Precious number.

"Hello?" She answered.

"What 'cha doing?" he asked.

"Serving a customer."

"You had dinner?"

"No."

"What'd you want?"

"Whatever you choose."

Ray got them something from Burger King on Fulton Industrial, and headed home, which was about fifteen minutes away. Precious must've been looking out the window before Ray could park, she was already standing in the doorway. That made him smile because Precious who was four years older than him seemed like a teenager, who was helplessly in love. Maybe she was.

"Hey, baby," she greeted him, smiling.

"Grab this," he told her.

She grabbed the food and drinks, and Ray went back to the car to retrieve his regalia. Once he'd put his things away, he joined Precious in the living room, where she'd laid the food out on the coffee table.

"What did we do?" he asked her.

"Seven ounces and eleven dubs."

"That's nothing," Ray told her. "I need another spot."

"Where would you open another spot at?"

"I don't know," he answered. I got a dude in Douglasville who wanna cop four ounces. Let me go ahead and hit him up."

Ray dialed Joe's number.

"Yeah?" Joe answered.

"It's me. You still want them?"

"Hell yeah!"

"Four?"

"Yeah."

"You know where Maple Creek at?"

"Nah," Joe answered. "But I can't pick 'em up now. It'll have to be tomorrow."

"That's cool." He gave Joe directions and told him that someone would be there if he wasn't.

"A'ight," Joe agreed.

**** 

Black turned his BMW into Chapel Forest Apartments, expecting to see police cars and ambulance, but everything seemed normal. The local drug dealers were out and about as always. As he drove towards his apartment, he eyed all of them, wondering which one of them he was going to empty the clip on.

Black pulled up in front of the apartment and saw Star's car, so he knew Sylvia was there. He wanted to sit in the car for a while to get himself prepared for whatever bomb Connie was about to drop on him, but he couldn't. He had to get it over with.

Using his key, he entered the apartment and encountered Meeka, Star and some older, dark-skin woman, sitting in the living room. The woman was clad in the same uniform as Connie and Star, indicating that she also worked at the Mark Inn.

All four women regarded him with red, teary eyes. Black didn't know what to say, or if he should say anything. Well, he didn't have to ask what happened, because the T.V. was on the news station, and the male reporter caught his attention, saying something about a body being found on Bankhead Highway, behind a dumpster at Auto Zone. Then, they showed the victim's picture.

"Damn!"

# CHAPTER 15

After briefing the Kingzmen on what to do with the bodies of Mike and Greg. James retreated to the office and slumped down in his chair, contemplating whether he should go ahead and call Franco and place their order. Instead, he called Shonda and told her to catch a cab to his place, in which she gladly agreed to.

James lounged around the office for another fifteen minutes, then grabbed his things and exited the building. The dogs spotted him going to his car and charged at him, barking fiercely.

James was scared, but he knew better than to show it. So, he nonchalantly placed his regalia on the back seat, climbed behind the wheel and drove up to the booth that was occupied by one KM.

"You can lock it up and head on home," James told him, then drove towards the expressway.

He was traveling the highway, listening to *Fat Joe's 'Who Got Gunz,'* when his cell rang. He muted the music before answering. "What up?"

"Y'all still at The Palace?" Black asked.

"Man, Ray, and Fred left like thirty minutes after you," James told him. "I'm on my way to the crib now. What's up?"

"Man, this shit's ugly."

"What?"

After taking in everything Black told him, he asked, "Why you call me and not him?"

"Cause, I ain't good at this shit."

James understood and knew what he had to do, but first, he had to head to the house and intercept Shonda. Who should be halfway there by now. He thought the cab would be sitting in front of his house when he pulled up, but it wasn't. Therefore, he took the initiative to take his regalia into the house and take a piss. When he finished, he went and peered out the window, only seeing his car that was still running.

"Where the fuck you at?" he said to himself, dialing Shonda's number.

"Hello?"

"Have you left the house yet?"

"I'm getting off the expressway now."

James concluded the call, donned his trench coat, stepped out on the porch and fired up a blunt, thinking about how he was going to break the bad news to his brother. He didn't want to do it, knowing that Ray was going to be crushed, but it had to be done and James knew it had to be him who did it.

Halfway through his blunt, James watched a red Kia Sportage pull up and park behind his car. His coat was unbuttoned, so the gun in his shoulder holster was easily accessible, but he didn't have to go for his gun because seconds after the truck came to a halt, Shonda emerged from the passenger side, carrying a tote bag. James figured to be her overnight clothes and cosmetics.

James locked the house up, then walked out towards the truck. That's when he realized that Sheila was the driver of the Kia. She rolled the window down when he approached.

"How much do I owe you?" James asked her, bracing himself for whatever sarcastic remark she was about to hit him with.

"Nothing," she answered calmly. "I was at home, bored and felt like driving."

"You gon be alright, baby?" Shonda, who was now standing beside James, asked Sheila.

"I'll be fine," Sheila responded. "Y'all have fun. Well, not too much fun."

Shonda leaned in the window, hugging her cousin. Then, they watched her drive off.

"I hate leaving my cousin at home, alone," Shonda said.

"I'm surprised she didn't cuss me out," said James.

Shonda laughed. "She ain't really like that. When y'all met us, she had just broken up with her boyfriend."

"Look, you mind chilling here til' I get back?" James asked, almost forgetting about his mission. "I gotta stop by my brotha's crib for a minute.

"Yes, I do mind!" she answered, now standing akimbo. "I didn't come out here to be alone! I could've stayed at home for that!"

James had no choice. The rain had started back drizzling by the time James had made it to Ray's apartment.

"I gotta stay in the car?" Shonda asked once James had parked.

"That's on you."

They got out and headed for the door. James knocked and seconds later, an unfamiliar female opened the door and looked out at them like she was expecting them to assert a password or show some sign of acknowledgment.

"Oh!" she exclaimed as if recognizing James. "Come on in. Ray just got out of the shower." She let them in, then locked the door back. "Y'all can have a seat."

"Who're you talking to?" Ray asked from the bedroom.

"Um, one of your King-friends," Precious answered hesitantly.

That's when James realized she'd recognized him by his KINGZ symbol, being that his trench was still unbuttoned.

"*One of my King-friends?*" Ray sounded puzzled.

"It's me lil' bruh." James took over. "You got on some clothes?"

"Yeah," Ray answered. "Come on in."

"I'll be back," James told Shonda, then headed for Ray's room.

Ray, in a pair of Sean Jean pajama pants, was standing at the dresser's mirror, applying deodorant under his arms when James entered, closing the door.

"What the move is?" Ray asked, donning his pajama top.

"Not too much. You a'ight?"

"Yeah, I'm good."

James was stalling. He thought he could do this. He thought he was going to breeze through this like he'd done over and over again in his mind. He thought—

"What's on ya mind?" Ray asked, apparently sensing that something was wrong.

James knew he had to do this, so he took a deep breath and let it flow. "They found Sylvia's body yesterday morning, behind Auto Zone. She was raped and strangled to death."

Ray just stared at James. On the surface, Ray appeared to be unfazed by the news, but James knew his brother. Ray had always been good at harboring his true feelings.

"Did they catch the person that did it?" Ray asked in an even tone.

"Not yet. At least that's what Black told me. He's the one who called me about it."

Ray sat on the bed, looking like he was in deep thought. James didn't know if he should embrace his brother or say something because Ray wasn't displaying any kind of emotions to act on.

"I'm 'bout to head to the crib," James finally spoke. "You gon' be a'ight?"

"Yeah," Ray answered, not making eye contact.

"Call me if you feel like you need to talk." Ray nodded. Fighting the urge to hug his brother, James left the room.

Ray was crushed. He felt like his heart had been snatched from his chest. His breathing was normal, but to his mind, it was complicated. The tears that welled up in his eyes, threatened to cascade down his face, but he kept them at bay.

He didn't want to believe someone had just violated Sylvia like that. It didn't matter if she was caught red-handed performing fellatio on a dog, she didn't deserve death.

"Baby, you okay?"

All Ray could do was stare at Precious, who'd stuck her head in the door. The tears in his eyes had to be noticeable because she rushed in and dropped to her knees in front of him with her hands resting on his thighs.

What's wrong, boo?" she asked, looking into his eyes with concern. "You can talk to me."

But he couldn't. He didn't know what to say. He couldn't stand to look into her eyes any longer, lest he lost his composure. So, he turned his head and closed his eyes. All Precious could do was wrap her arms around him and lay her head on his chest. That did it! The floodgates opened, and the tears, uncontrollably, streamed down his face. He cried, he cried for Sylvia, he cried for his unborn child. He cried so hard he didn't notice Precious was also crying— *for him.*

Playa Ray

# CHAPTER 16

Ray awakened the next morning with an extreme headache, feeling like he had a hangover. He didn't remember falling asleep last night. He definitely didn't remember climbing into bed and covering himself with the bedspreads. He looked around the room to make sure he was in the right room. He saw that the door was closed, and the apartment was quiet, perhaps too quiet.

The clock on the nightstand read 10:28 a.m. Ray's stomach growled, pretty much letting him know he needed to put something in it, but first, he had to do something about his headache. He did a full stretch, extending his arms and legs, but as soon as he was about to get up, he heard a noise coming from the other end of the apartment. It sounded like a door opening and closing.

Not believing what he'd heard, Ray lied still, to see if any other sound would ensue. Seconds later, he heard a soft thud that sounded like it came from the kitchen. That was enough to make him reach under his pillow for his gun, but it wasn't there. Ray wasn't hearing this! His gun was always under his pillow if it wasn't on his hip. He clearly remembered putting it there before taking a shower last night. Maybe it was under the other pillow. He checked—zilch. That's when the bedroom door opened, startling him.

Precious peered in, seeing him awake, she entered. "You feeling better, baby?" she asked, standing over him.

"I got a headache," he managed dryly.

"You got some Tylenol Three in the medicine cabinet," she told him. "You want some?"

He nodded. Precious left the room, returning moments later, with a glass of water and two Tylenol tablets in her hand. Ray sat up to take the pills. Precious took the glass from him, sat it on the dresser, then sat down beside him.

"I know what happened," she spoke.

Ray just looked at her.

"It was on the news," she explained. "But I didn't know who it was until your brotha called last night and told me to keep an eye on you. He was calling to check on you, but I told him you were asleep. Also, B.J., Fred, and Black called last night. Your sister called this morning.

Ray nodded, then stood up. "I gotta go.'

"Go where?" she stood to block his path.

"I need some fresh air."

"At least eat first," she told him. "You're not hungry?"

Damn! He'd forgotten about his stomach, but his stomach could wait. He felt like Precious was smuggling him, and he just needed to be alone for a few days.

"I'll grab something while I'm out," he told her, then headed for the bathroom. Where he brushed his teeth and washed his face.

Precious was sitting on the bed when he re-entered the room. She didn't say a word as he got dressed and donned his coat. She pulled his phone from her pocket, handing it to him.

"You seen my gun?" he asked.

"I moved it."

"Why?"

She just looked at him. Ray was no fool. He knew exactly what she was thinking. Sylvia's death had a great impact on him, but suicide? No way!

"Can I have my gun?" he asked, not feeling what she was thinking, but respecting the fact that she was considerate enough to think it.

"Do you really need it?" she asked, looking up at him.

"I wouldn't know until that time comes," he told her.

She lingered a moment before pulling out one of the bottom drawers and removing the gun from under his folded pants. Ray holstered it and, "I'm gone," was all he said as he exited the apartment.

**** 

James awakened to the sound of his cell phone vibrating on his stand.

"What's up?" he answered in a low tone, so not to awake Shonda.

"Hey, big-big brother!" April beamed. "Did I wake you?"

"I'm good. What's on ya mind?"

"My twin," she answered. "I called him earlier, and some girl told me he was asleep. I just called twice and got no answer. I'm worried."

"Don't be," he told his baby sister. "You gotta look at what he's going through. I'm quite sure he'll call back when he recovers."

"Was it his baby?"

"He thought it was, but I'ma hit him up when I get up."

"Make sure you tell him to call me."

"A'ight."

"Love you, big-big brother!"

"Love you too, baby!"

Concluding the call, James looked over at Shonda. When he called her over last night, his intentions were to fuck her all night, but when they finally got to bed, his *little man* wouldn't even respond to any of Shonda's sexual advances. James knew why, but when Shonda started regarding him with concerned looks as if she was the reason. He went on to explain the reason for the visit to his brother's place and admitted it was still heavy on his mind. She understood.

Now, James eased out of bed and headed for the bathroom. After relieving his bladder, brushing his teeth, and washing his face. He re-entered the bedroom where Shonda was just stirring. The covers had fallen off her, revealing her naked body. His *little man* finally responded! James woke her up with the best oral sex he'd ever performed. After an hour and half of rolling in the hay, they showered, dressed and left the house.

"I guess you're taking me home after we eat, huh?" Shonda asked, once in the car.

"I mean, that was the plan," he said.

"That was *your* plan," she countered. "This is my off day. I don't wanna sit at home all day, doing nothing."

"You gotta check on Sheila," he reminded her.

"That's who I called when we got out of the shower."

"So, you don't wanna go home?"

"Not now."

"Well, where do you wanna go?"

"Wherever you go," she answered. "Unless you gotta check on somma your hoes."

"Don't even go there."

"I'm just saying."

Refusing to respond, James dialed Ray's number. Getting no answer, he called Fred, who was stationed at Eric's house.

"You checked on Ray?" Fred wanted to know.

"I think he got his phone off," James answered. "I'm 'bout to grab me something to eat, then swing by his crib."

"That's what's up."

James called Black.

"Hello?"

"You a'ight?" James asked.

"Yeah, I'm good."

"Connie?"

"I really can't say," Black answered. "She hasn't gotten out of bed yet. That was her best friend, so it might take a while for her to recover."

"True that," James said. "Give her my condolence, and if you need me, you know the number.

James drove to Krystal's, where he and Shonda dined in. Then they rode out to Ray's apartment. James noticed that the Delta Eighty-Eight was gone, but he'd also noticed a dude leaving the door as if he'd just purchased something through the burglar bar door. He remembered Ray saying that he had someone holding down the spot when he's not in, so he pulled up to the door, got out and knocked. The female that was present last night, opened the door.

"He left sometime after eleven," she informed him.

"He didn't say where he was going?"

She just shook her head.

That's when James managed to get a good look at her face. She looked like she'd been crying, and her visage matched the sad tone of her voice.

"Does he have his phone?" James wanted to know.

"And his gun," she answered like she was hinting that Ray had set out to do harm to someone, or himself.

"How was he feeling when he left?" James tested.

She shrugged. "I don't know, he wouldn't talk."

James gave her his number, told her to call if Ray showed up, then left. He was not going to let her make him believe that Ray was going to endeavor a suicidal stunt, and even if that was the case. James wouldn't know the first place to look for his brother. He remembered when they were young, Ray would get upset and disappear for a few hours, or days.

Pondering the situation, James regarded Ray's disappearance as a means of solitary. Keeping that thought in mind, James concentrated on his plans for today. He had to make separate meetings with Moe and Barlow, stop in on Spenz, then meet with the Kingzmen much later. First, he was going to visit his little homie at the Fulton County Jail. Shonda agreed to wait downstairs in the lobby.

"What up lil' homie!" James greeted Boss when he entered the booth, where Boss was already seated.

"I kinda figured it was you," Boss asserted, happy to see James. "I guess Ray didn't wanna come, huh?"

"He's going through some things at the moment," James answered, then explained everything.

"Damn!" Boss expressed. "I saw that shit on the news. If they catch that nigga, and I run into him, I'ma put that tool in his life!"

James didn't doubt that at all.

"You ready for March?" James asked, changing the subject.

"Man, I was ready the moment they told me I was under arrest," Boss answered.

"What about a lawyer?"

"My mama got me our family lawyer," Boss told him. "This'll be his first murder case."

James leaned forward and spoke in a low tone, "Do I need to get rid of anybody?"

Boss looked as if he was considering James' proposal. "Nah," he finally said, shaking his head. "I got who I wanted."

"You sure?"

"I'm positive."

"I can respect that," James told him. "I dropped some money on your books."

"I appreciate that, and you wasn't bullshittin' about that movement! Niggas in here talkin 'bout y'all like some rap stars!"

"We're just trying to get our piece of the pie," James said. "So, how are you living in there?"

"You know I do what I do," Boss boasted. "These fake ass gang members be in here robbing and jumping on niggas. The first nigga that even *look* like he wanna jump, a mission-rescue helicopter gon' land on top of this bitch!"

"I already know," James said, laughing. "You need to be out here with me. I need you on my team."

"As a hitman?"

"Maybe."

They conversated until visitation was called to an end. When James got back down to the lobby, he saw that Shonda was engaged in an exciting conversation with other women.

"You can stay if you want," James interrupted.

When they got back to the car, James told Shonda to drive, and he climbed into the passenger seat, putting his *Kingz* chain back on. After putting on the New Jack City DVD, he gave Shonda directions to Summer Hill. He'd already called Tek and told him to have Barlow at his house. Once Shonda pulled up to Tek's house, James dialed Tek's number.

"Hello?"

"Is he there?"

"Yeah."

"Send him out."

James concluded the call and grabbed the gym bag off the back seat, placing it between his feet. Then, he removed his gun from its holster and placed it in his lap.

"What's about to happen?" Shonda asked, not sounding a bit alarmed.

"Just being careful," he answered, still watching the house.

Seconds later, Barlow emerged from the house in a large over-coat and climbed into the back seat behind James.

"You ready?" James asked.

"Shit, I been ready!"

"You got a number I can reach you at?"

"Yeah." Barlow wrote down his number. "That's my cell number."

James handed him a package from the gym bag. "Can you handle that?"

"Man, they call me, *Trap Star Shawty!*"

"Summer Hill and University Homes?"

"Yeah."

As they exited Summer Hill, James called Moe and asked for a rendezvous spot. Once it was arranged, he told Shonda to stop for gas.

"You got a card?" she asked, once she pulled up to the pump.

"Don't know what one look like," he answered, getting out and donning his trench coat to conceal his shoulder holster, but left his chain visible.

She followed him into the store, and they browsed the aisle for junk food. As they browsed, James was careful to watch his surroundings. Either it was the blunt he and Shonda had smoked on their way to Summer Hill, or the two dudes that entered the store behind them were watching them as they pretended to shop. Not taking any chances, he gave Shonda a fifty-dollar bill and told her to pay for everything, leaving his hands free. Then, he feigned to rub his chest, unlatching his holster.

When he and Shonda reached the counter, the alleged pursuers were still behind them. A dekko showed that their hands were occupied with chips and drinks. When Shonda paid for the gas and items, they exited the store.

To his surprise, she obeyed, putting the food in the car, then tending to the task as James pretended to watch her, but was watching the store from the corner of his eye. Moments later, the two guys exited with bags in their hands. As James had expected, they were headed in his direction. He turned his back to them and rested his hand on his gun, listening to their footsteps. When he felt they were close enough, he drew his gun and turned to face-off with them.

**\*\*\*\***

Black was sitting on the living room sofa being watched by the T.V. it definitely wasn't the other way around when the call came from James. After hanging up, he went to check on Connie, who was still asleep, wrapped in the bedspreads from head to toe. Black didn't think she was asleep. He felt that she was just laying there, awake, silently mourning her friend. Whatever the case was, he was not going to bother her. He didn't like Sylvia for what she'd done to Ray, but he would have never wished death upon her.

Black was about to close the bedroom door when Connie called out to him from underneath the layers of covers.

"Yeah baby?" he answered, not sure if he should approach.

"Come here," she said, sounding weak, pulling the covers from over her head.

Black approached and sat on the edge of the bed, looking down at her. She appeared ten years older, and her hair was severely disheveled.

"That was my best friend," she managed before tears rolled down her face.

All Black could do was hold her hand and kiss her tears away. He didn't love her as much as he loved Nikki, but he loved her. She was there for him when he was going through his ordeal, and he was certain she would be there for many more if they occurred.

Black was kind of glad no one had called a Kingz meeting because he didn't plan to leave Connie's side until he was sure she'd found closure.

**\*\*\*\***

"Why you didn't put me on point?" Shonda asked, driving the BMW along the interstate.

"Cause, I didn't want you to get scared and start looking around," he told her.

James was still tripping on the incident at the gas station. The dudes he thought were going to try something, turned out to be a couple of male *groupies* wanting to meet him, claiming they were at the New Year Eve's party The Kingz threw. He was just glad the gas station wasn't crowded, and the police were nowhere in sight.

"Trust me," Shonda said, casting a glance at him. "I am not that easy to scare."

James just looked at the red bone, whose brown micro-braids were pulled back into a bun. He did notice how extremely calm she'd been both times he'd pulled his gun today.

'*She might be a ride or die, bitch,*' he thought.

They made it to Bolton Road, where Shonda pulled into Pepper Mill Apartments. Moe was already standing by the fenced in pool. Once Shonda parked, Moe climbed in behind James.

"How ya mom's doing?" James asked.

"Man, getting on my damn nerves!" Moe answered.

"You gotta get 'cha own shit," James told him. "It's time to leave the nest."

"I'm trying."

"Here." James handed him a package. "Same as we discussed."

"A'ight."

"You sure it won't be no complications out here?"

"It shouldn't be."

"You did say some Drop Squad niggas be out here, right?"

"Yeah," Moe answered. "I think one of them niggas got a baby mama out here. They don't be out here starting shit, though."

They dapped, and Moe went his way. James already knew that Pepper Mill wasn't doing numbers, being that it was a small community, but Moe swore he was going to be trapping in Bolton Place, Bland Town, and Knight Park, also. He didn't want to rush his young friend, but he had two people he had to pay at a certain time, and he planned on doing just that.

****

Fred was still held up at Eric's house. Eric had called him, earlier, telling him that Kane his cocaine-white Pitbull had, somehow, jumped the fence while he was at the barber shop, and was hit by a car. He wanted Fred to sit with Sharonda and his daughter and hold down the spot while he took Kane to a Veterinary Surgeon.

"I hope they find the nigga that did that to that girl," Sharonda, who was curled up in the recliner, told Fred, who was sitting on the sofa. "He should get the electric chair!"

"They don't use the chair no more," Fred told her. "They use lethal injections."

"Well, he should get both!" She stated, getting up. "I'ma go check on, Erica."

When Sharonda left the room to check on the baby, Fred grabbed the cordless phone off the table and dialed Ray's number. Assuming that if Ray was purposefully dodging his friends, then he would probably answer a number he was not familiar with.

Fred listened to the ringtone for a while. Just as he was about to hang up, the music stopped, indicating that Ray or someone else had answered the phone, but it was quiet on the other end. Fred wanted to say something, but he waited, wanting to hear Ray's voice first. Then the line went dead.

Fred redialed the number, only to get the voicemail. He then dialed James number.

"Yeah?" James answered.

"What's the word on, Ray?"

"He wasn't at the crib when I went by," James told him, then replayed the conversation he'd had with Precious. "She ain't hit me back yet."

"I'm worried about, my nigga."

"Shit so am I," James agreed. "But ain't shit we can do, right now. We gotta wait until he comes out of hiding. It'll be on his own time."

"Yeah, you're right," Fred conceded. "Just let me know when you hear something."

Fred ended the call just as headlights shone through the blinds of the living room window. Peering through the blinds and seeing that it was Eric, he stepped out on the porch, closing the door to keep the cold air from entering the house.

Kane was Eric's favorite dog, so Fred wasn't surprised to hear that Eric immediately left work when Sharonda called and told him what happened.

"I'ma shoot this stupid ass nigga in the head," Eric asserted, letting Kane out of the trunk. "This is the second time his dumb ass done jumped the fence."

Kane stumbled towards the porch with his rear left leg, and whole mid-section bandaged. Fred could tell he was drugged because he wasn't in his normal playful mood.

"You gon' let him sleep in the house?" Fred asked when Eric opened the door to let Kane inside.

"I got to," Eric answered. "If I let him out back, the other dogs are gonna rip the bandages off, and he won't heal."

"He got stitches?"

"Twenty-six. His whole stomach was ripped open."

"Hit and run, huh?"

"Yeah."

Fred could tell his brother was anxious to find out who'd hit his dog, and Lord have mercy on them if he ever did!

"You 'bout to leave?" Eric asked, then, before Fred could answer, insisted he stay for dinner, saying he wanted to talk to Fred about how he and his fellow Kingz had become *above the law*.

Playa Ray

# CHAPTER 17

James returned to his house after dropping Shonda off. He wished he would have called Spenz before they drove to College Park to find out he wasn't home, but when he called Spenz, he agreed to stop by James' place around nine o' clock.

Now, it was almost eight-thirty. He was tempted to call Brenda for some mouth service. Just the thought of releasing in her mouth drove him to a full erection, but James had to fight those thoughts and stay business-minded. At least until after Spenz left.

James grabbed one of the two blunts sitting on the coffee table, sat on the couch and fired it up. He'd never watched the *Chris Rock* narrated sitcom *Everybody Hates Chris*, but that's what was on the tube. Plus, the remote was nowhere in sight, but James couldn't focus on the show due to his thoughts about his brother. He hoped Ray was alright.

"Yeah, mama?" he answered his vibrating cell phone.

"April called and told me what happened to Ray's girlfriend," she said. "And she was pregnant with his child. Why am I just now finding out about all of this?"

"She was not his girlfriend, mama," James contended. "She was pregnant, but nobody knew for sure whose baby it was. I don't know why April took so long to tell you."

"This ain't no time to be funny, James!" she chided. "April said he left home and y'all can't find him."

"April knows a lot to be a million miles away!"

His mother was quiet. James knew if he was in arms reach, she would've taken a swing at him at this moment.

"He's a'ight, mama," James tried to assure her.

"And how would you know?"

"Just trust me," he said, hoping she would, because if she started to worry. Not only would she worry herself, but she would worry him to death, also.

"Well, when you talk to him, tell him to call me and mama."

"You told, grandma?" James asked, already knowing the answer.

"You know I told her!" she stated with attitude. "And she's worried sick about him!"

At that moment the doorbell rang.

"Mama, you know better than to call and get that lady all riled up!" James asserted, getting up and opening the door for Spenz.

"She got the right to know about her grandchildren!"

"I'll make sure I tell him to call y'all," James promised ending the call.

He told Spenz to have a seat and fire up the other blunt, then headed for his bedroom. Moments later, returning with a package similar to the ones he'd given Barlow and Moe. He tossed the package on the table, then took a seat in the recliner.

"So, what's up?" Spenz asked, exhaling weed smoke.

"Shit, you."

"Me?"

"Yeah," James answered. "I know you think we pulled the plug on you on the weed tip, but we didn't. Ray runs that shit independently now. I wanna put you back in the game with a new proposition."

"I'm all ears," Spenz told him. Then, after hearing James' spiel, he said, "I'm not trying to revert back to the white. I fuck with the weed, cause I work at the club. Niggas know I be having it."

James nodded. "Yeah, I know, but why not do both? I'll get you plugged back in with Ray, and you can work for both of us. That's more money."

"What about the other two Kingz?" Spenz inquired. "Y'all don't work as a whole no more?"

"Of course, we do," James answered. "This is just a branch off from the Kingz' tree."

Spenz didn't respond right away, but when he did, he asked. "So, how much are we talking?"

****

Friday came, and no one had heard from Ray. Connie was doing a little better, so she and Black decided to go ahead and move into their house. Black paid two smokers from Capital Homes to help move the furniture, while Connie and Meeka packed their clothes and other belongings in bags and boxes.

Nikki called last night and told him what time they would be in Georgia, so they chose the Publix grocery store in Covington, to rendezvous. Black and Connie grabbed something to eat at a soul food restaurant and made it to Publix, fifteen minutes before the intended time.

"You a'ight?" Black asked Connie, after parking the BMW.

"I'm good," she answered. "What did Felicia say about, Kevin?"

"She said I can get him, but I'ma pick him up after the funeral."

Connie nodded. "And Danielle?"

"That white boy don't want her to come back to Georgia," Black stated, feeling hatred towards Danielle for letting a white man run her life and prevent him from seeing his daughter.

"She shouldn't let him keep you from seeing your daughter," said Connie.

Black didn't want to talk about this. He clearly remembered when Denise was born. He and Danielle had no kind of income. Her dad had died before she'd turned two, and her mother was an abusive alcoholic and drug user. The aunt who raised Black in the Bluff had six other kids of her own.

One day, when Danielle took Denise to one of her check-ups, she met the White guy. Who told her that he was a lawyer. When she told him she wanted to put the baby up for adoption because she couldn't properly take care of it, he offered to take care of them both. Black was vexed when he got a call from her a week later, explaining everything. He was even more vexed when she called him four months later, telling him that her *man* had opened a law firm in Virginia, and they had already moved.

Black had to respect it, though. There was no woman in her right mind, who would have turned down such an offer. Especially if they were in Danielle's predicament.

Now, Black focused his attention on the gray Ford Expedition with chrome wheels, that pulled into the parking lot and slowly drove towards them. The first thing Black noticed was the Florida plate on the front. Then, he could clearly see Nikki through the windshield.

"That's them," he told Connie. "Come on."

Connie looked like she was going to protest but got out and joined him on the driver's side of the car. Black tried his best not to look at Willie through the windshield, lest his visage reveals his contempt.

Nikki and Willie dismounted the truck. He let Nicole out from the rear seat while Nikki got Lil' Keith.

"Hey, Daddy!" Nicole exclaimed, running and jumping into his arms.

"Hey, baby!" Black planted kisses on her cheeks, more than happy to be in the presence of his babies again.

"You gotta save some kisses for Lil' Keith," Nikki asserted, standing in front of the truck beside Willie, holding Lil Keith.

"I got enough to go around," Black stated, putting Nicole down and receiving his son from Nikki before introducing his girl-friend Connie to them.

"You finally moved out of the hood," Nikki commented. "I'm proud of you!"

"You know I try to keep my promises," Black told her. "I'm pretty much-doing good for myself now."

"I heard," she said with a half-smirk. "So, how are the rest of the Kingz?"

**\*\*\*\***

Sylvia's funeral was underway, and everybody was seated after taking turns viewing her body that was resting peacefully in a red oak casket, adorned with gold trimmings. Black was sitting on the second row with Connie who was crying her eyes out, Meeka, Star and some more of their friends. Sylvia's aunt was sitting in front of them with her boyfriend, Sylvia's mother and some other family members who'd driven from Cleveland, Ohio for this purpose.

The Reverend was giving his eulogy on Sylvia, but Black was half-paying attention. He was still thinking about Nikki and the question she'd asked yesterday. *"How are the rest of the Kingz?"*

How the hell did she know about the Kingz, he kept pondering. He had never mentioned anything about their pseudonyms to her. He found it hard to believe that their names were ringing in any parts of Florida, the Drug Capital of The World! Unless there was more to Willie than Nikki had let on.

The abrupt sound of the front double doors opening, cut the Reverend off, causing everybody to look back. The rays from the sun despite the below-thirty-degree weather distorted the features of the person that stood in the doorway in a suit and round-brimmed hat. To Black, it looked like the beginning of *Michael Jackson's Smooth Criminal* video, right before MJ tosses a coin through the air of the pool hall, and right into the jukebox.

The man closed the doors eliminating the sunlight. Then, sauntered down the aisle at a leisurely pace in his dark-blue suit, dress shoes and matching hat. The hat and gold-rimmed sunglasses weren't enough to conceal his face, which Black could have spotted from miles away.

Black along with the whole congregation watched as Ray approached the casket and removed his hat, revealing his neatly kept cornrows. His back was to them, but they could tell that he was talking or praying by the movement of his head. He pinned something to her dress, then to Black's surprise leaned over and kissed Sylvia. Donning his hat, he retraced his steps towards the exit, not looking in Black's or anybody else's direction, but Black saw the tears rolling down his friend's face.

"Was that Ray?" Connie, who Black noticed had stopped crying the moment Ray showed up, asked.

All Black could do was nod.

****

The funeral was over and now, Ray, in his trench coat, was standing several yards away from the plot Sylvia's casket was being lowered into. Ray hated funerals and always said the only funeral he would attend, was his own, but he knew he had to pay his last respects to Sylvia. After all, he did love her, which is why he'd pinned the pendant of a half-heart to her dress. He was wearing the other half. To him, this meant she was taking a part of him with her.

Now, the small crowd of mourners started to disassemble, heading for their respective vehicles. Ray recognized Black, Connie, Meeka and Sylvia's aunt in the crowd. As they parted, Black, Connie, Meeka and a female Ray wasn't familiar with, changed course, and were headed in his direction. Which was unexpected and not a good idea because he was still not in the mood for any kind of company. He wanted to turn and walk away as if he had not seen them, but his feet wouldn't respond.

"How you holding up?" Black asked when they approached.

"I'm good," Ray responded in a raspy voice, then cleared his throat.

Ray could tell Black wanted to say something, or maybe question his disappearance, which Ray really hoped he didn't, but knowing Black, it was inevitable.

"I brought her to see you that night," said the teary-eyed female Ray didn't know.

"What?" Ray asked, not sure of what she was telling him.

"Monday night," she tried again. "I brought Sylvia to see you at Petro. I could see where y'all were sitting from where I was parked."

Ray was looking at her, but his mind had reverted back to Monday night. He remembered exiting Petro and surveying the parking lot, but didn't see her, or any other female sitting in a car.

"Are you sure?" Ray asked, thinking she had the days mixed up.

"I know what I'm talking about!" The girl was mad now. "She was late because I couldn't find the car keys. You had on a gray suit, and you left before she did."

"And you are?" he asked, feeling as if she was trying to insinuate he had something to do with Sylvia's death.

"I'm Star," she answered matter-of-factly. "Sylvia's *girlfriend*."

Although she'd emphasized on girlfriend, it didn't register to Ray what she was saying. All he knew was that he was done talking to her, and ready to get back to his solitude.

"I'ma hit y'all up later," he told Black.

Then, with no dap, hug or high-five, Ray headed for his Oldsmobile that was parked further up the road. At this time, he was in deep thought, absently fingering his half-heart pendant. His memento mori.

****

After leaving the burial site, Black and Connie picked the kids up from one of Connie's friend's apartment in Chapel Forest, then headed for Felicia's house. Black was anticipating this, because the last time Kevin and Nicole played together, was when Nikki was three months pregnant with Lil' Keith. They probably don't even remember each other.

Black parked in front of Felicia's house, being that the turquoise Monte Carlos belonging to Rico of Drop Squad, was parked in the driveway behind Felicia's car.

"I won't be long," he promised Connie.

Before getting out, he looked back at his kids. Nicole was asleep, with her head rested on the soft cushion of the door, and Lil' Keith who was sleep when they picked him up, eyes were wide with excitement.

"Bah?" Lil' Keith managed, offering his half-filled bottle.

"No, thank you, baby." Black smiled at his son, kissed Connie, then exited the car feeling ten times the man he was.

"Come on in," Felicia asserted when she opened the door.

Black's intentions were to pick up his son and leave as quick as possible. He was not in the mood for any of Felicia's shit, but he entered anyway.

"Kevin!" Felicia called out. "Ya daddy's here!"

"He ain't ready?" Black asked, casting a glance at Rico, who was sitting on the sofa with his foot propped up on the coffee table, eyeing him.

"That boy's been ready since yesterday," Felicia answered, taking a seat on the sofa beside Rico. "And you still didn't tell me whose funeral you went to."

"A friend of my girlfriend," he answered, noticing that this was the second time he'd referred to Connie as his *girlfriend*.

"You must really care for her." The envy in her voice was evident.

"Yeah," he answered, silently hoping Kevin would hurry up.

"So, what does your girlfriend do?"

Black wasn't sure about Connie's occupation, but he was not going to disclose that to Felicia. To do so, would boost this bitch's ego, which was already beyond inflation.

Hey, daddy!"

'*Yes*!' Black was so relieved when Kevin entered the living room with his bookbag of clothes on his back, he almost sighed out loud.

"You ready?" Black asked his son.

"Yes."

"Mama can't get a hug before you leave?" Felicia seemed hell-bent on holding them up.

"Yes," Kevin answered and walked over to appease his mother.

Black noticed Rico was still eyeing him. He didn't know what the issue was with this nigga, but, for some reason, Black sensed he was going to end up knocking this nigga off. Fuck Drop Squad!

## CHAPTER 18

'*I knew that shit was gonna get out,*' Fred thought for the hundred-millionth time between last night and now.

According to Eric, word on the street was that The Kingz was holding court for niggas who crossed them, sentencing them to death, killing them execution-style, then chopping up their bodies.

"In other words," Eric said. "Y'all niggas ain't to be fucked with!"

Fred wanted to call James the second those words left Eric's mouth, but decided to sleep on it, and schedule a meeting with him as soon as possible. He figured if this was ringing in the ears of the streets, then it was a matter of time before it was ringing in the ears of authority, which is why he was skeptical about wearing his chain. Which is probably why he'd gotten a call from Yvonne, a girl he had not heard from in over a year. She claimed that she missed him, saying that she'd gotten so caught up in running her salon, she didn't have time to call or spend a respectable amount of time with him.

But now, all of a sudden she'd found the time, which is why he was parked in the parking lot of the plaza, watching her through the large windows of her salon as she gave two of her workers last minute instructions before leaving.

Now, she exited the store, clad in black kitten-heel boots, blue snug-fitted jeans, a white mini fur coat, and carrying a beige make-up bag. For a person that didn't know her, from a distance, they would think she was Asian, with her round face and long, black hair.

Fred had already called and let her know he was in the parking lot. She spotted the Beamer and approached the driver's side, smiling.

"Hey, sexy!" She beamed when Fred let the window down. "You ready?"

"*Hell, yeah!*" he wanted to say but nodded.

He watched as she pivoted and strutted off, tossing her well-rounded ass that perfectly accommodated her 5'4" frame, knowing he was looking.

Yes, he was more than ready! Once she'd climbed into her dark green Isuzu Rodeo, Fred followed her out of the parking lot. She had mentioned that she'd moved into a house in Cobb County. So, she was doing a lot better than the last time he'd seen her. He just hoped that she wasn't on some set-up shit.

****

It had finally gotten dark, Grip had pulled the black Ford Crown Victoria into the parking lot of a small, shack-like, inde-pendent-owned restaurant that had already closed for the day. He parked, facing the gun shop sitting across the street, where the owner seemed to be making last-minute adjustments.

"Do we need to go over the details again?" James, who was sitting on the passenger side, asked.

There was no response from Grip or the three Kingzmen in the back seat.

"Any comments?"

"I think he's gonna buck," said Grip, still watching the store.

"I hope so," James muttered, knowing he had determined the owner's fate the moment the scheme was devised.

As they continued to watch the store, James thought about the call he'd gotten from Black, who was at the time, at Toys-R-Us, buying toys for the kids to play with for the weekend. He told James that Ray showed up at the funeral and burial site.

"What'd he say?" James had asked.

"He just said he was gonna hit us up later," Black told him.

The phone call had eased James' worry about Ray's well-be-ing. He wouldn't allow his mind to adopt the thought of his brother harming himself.

"Fuck!" Grip exclaimed.

James didn't have to inquire, because he was also looking at the police car that pulled into the parking lot of the gun shop. The officer sounded the siren, getting the owner's attention. The owner waved his recognition, then disappeared to the back. Seconds later, the main lights went out, leaving the store dimly-lit. That was the cue that initiated their plan, but the unexpected visitor had just complicated matters. Grip had been casing out the shop for a whole month and, not once, had he mentioned anything about this.

"I think you left this part out, Grip," James said coolly.

"It ain't never happened," Grip answered, now facing him. "I swear!"

"What'd you think we should do?"

"Pull back," Grip responded. "Try it again next week."

James heard Grip's answer, but it wasn't registering as he watched the owner gather his things and move towards the door. Not once did the cop look around for potential danger. Now, the owner was punching in the security code on the pad by the door.

"Do we pull back?" Grip asked.

"We didn't drive out here to pull back," James asserted, watching the owner unlock the door from the inside. "We go to Plan B."

Grip looked confused. "We don't have a Plan B."

"We do now," James told him, watching the owner exit the shop and attempt to lock the door back. "We just add one more body to our list. Let's do it!"

They all exited the car, clad in black cargo pants suits and ski masks as they crossed the narrow, two-lane street that only three cars had traveled since they'd been there. They were all carrying two duffle bags and throwaway Glocks excepts for James who'd brought a .38 Caliber, with the intent to toe tag the shop owner.

They were now crossing the small lot of the shop. The officer was still watching the owner, who'd just locked the door, and was about to head for his black, older-model Ford Bronco. That's when they were spotted, but it didn't matter, because the last thing the cop saw when he finally turned around, was the barrel of Grip's gun, half a second before it flashed. The owner was reaching at his shoulder holster, but James had already quickened his steps, with the .38 aimed at his head.

"Don't do it!" James warned. "You're not, John Wayne!"

"Okay— okay!" The owner raised his hands in surrender.

James pulled the chrome .44 revolver from the owner's holster, with one of his gloved hands.

"Now unlock the door!" James ordered. The owner did as he was told. "Disarm the alarm!"

As soon as the owner disarmed the alarm, James shot him in the back of the head, splattering brain fragments all over the wall and security code box.

"A'ight, y'all know what to do!" James voiced, dropping the .44 beside the corpse. "In and out!"

Each man had their own task. One Kingzman was on ammunition. One was on the handguns. Grip and the other one was on the assault rifles. James was to check the back for the two Tommy guns he'd ordered. The Tommy guns were there.

James carried the rare guns to the exit, while his men were finishing up their chores. At this time, he thought about Fred. He hoped his friend had another plug on the guns because this one had been unplugged.

#### ****

It was 3 p.m., Sunday afternoon and Ray had not called anyone back yet. He knew his people were worried about him especially his mother and grandmother. Truth be told, he was more worried about himself than they were. He couldn't believe that for the first time in his life, he'd actually contemplated suicide. It scared him so bad, he cried himself to sleep, only to have nightmares of Sylvia being gang-raped by a group of men, strangled to death, then taunting him, saying had he never left her, none of this would have happened.

"*This is all your fault, Ray!*" she taunted until Ray was able to force himself awake.

He sat up on the sofa in his still empty living room, panting and perspiring. That's when he realized he was over-hibernated, and it was time to get back to civilization. The first thing he needed to do was call the moving company and have them send some movers to his apartment. Then, while they were moving the furniture, he would go over the number of sales with Precious, and how business would be conducted from here on out.

But, when he entered his apartment, Precious was not there. The first place he checked was the stash room. Everything seemed to be in order. The product had gotten lower, and the money pile had gotten higher. He took out five hundred, which was Precious' weekly pay, and stuffed it in his pocket.

Ray didn't know what time the movers would arrive, so, in lieu of calling everyone to tell them he was okay, he set out to pack the rest of his clothes and other personal things into bags and boxes. The movers showed up after he'd removed his mattresses and began breaking down the frame. He told the two movers to go ahead and move the two dressers since he'd already cleared them.

Apparently, Precious had seen or heard the movers going in and out of the apartment because she showed up while Ray was stripping the bathroom of its toiletries.

"You alright, baby?"

Ray, who was taking down the shower curtain, turned to see Precious standing in the doorway with her arms folded over her chest.

"Yeah, I'm good," he answered, avoiding eye contact as he folded the curtain and placed it in a small box that was marked, *BTRM.*

"Your brotha told me to call him when you came home," she said.

"I'ma call him once I get situated," he told her.

They were both silent as Ray packed the rest of his cosmetics atop the curtain and taped the box shut. Ray knew what he had to tell her, and he knew he had to go ahead and get it out of the way.

"Look, Precious," he started, now regarding her. "We gotta draw the line. From now on, it's strictly business."

"I understand," she said slightly nodding.

"I'ma leave the couch, the kitchen table, and chairs," he told her, handing her week's earnings.

She accepted the money with a nod, then walked away. Ray knew she was hurt. He heard it in her voice. Seen it in her eyes. He wouldn't have dreamed of hurting her, but this was something he had to do.

****

"Can I call you later?" Yvonne asked.

She'd awakened Fred with breakfast in bed, another round of hot, steamy sex, a hot bubble bath, and a full-body massage. After lounging and talking for hours, she cooked him fricassee, some dish she was introduced to while in France.

Now, they were standing in her living room. Fred was fully dressed, ready to make his exit. Yvonne was wearing a pink robe and house shoes, which were the only items of clothing she preferred to wear around the house.

"You got the number," Fred answered her question.

Yvonne wrapped her arms around his neck and stood on her toes to kiss him, inserting her tongue into his mouth. Fred returned the kiss, but when he felt himself getting aroused, he pulled back. She knew what she was doing, and Fred knew he would never leave if he kept giving in to her sexual advances.

Therefore, he made a quick exit. Fred had never been in a relationship, or declared his love for a woman, but, over a year ago, he'd almost given in to Yvonne. Getting to his car, he turned to look back at the beautiful brick house to see Yvonne standing in the window, watching him. He didn't stand there and stare back at her like this was a scene in a love story. He got into his car and pulled out of the driveway. As he drove away, he thought about what Eric told him and quickly dialed James' number.

"What's up, homie?" James answered.

Fred got straight to the point. "We need to talk?"

"Face-to-face?"

"Yeah."

"It'll have to be later," James told him. "I'm having dinner with moms."

"Give me a time," Fred asserted.

"I can't. Is it urgent?"

Fred thought for a second. "Nah," he answered. "But it's important."

"That's good enough," James admitted. "I'll hit you back and let you know what's what."

"That's a bet."

Fred ended the call and, for some reason, felt James was acting strange, but then again, he'd been feeling like that for a while now.

When Fred made it home, he dressed in one of his jean suits. He had forgotten it was his week to take his mother out to Sunday dinner. She was indecisive, so he took her to Houston's in Buckhead.

"I wish you would've told me earlier," Fred's mother was saying. "I would have gone to the funeral."

"Mama, you didn't even know the girl."

"I would have gone on behalf of, Ray," she asserted. "I just hope he's okay."

Fred just sipped his drink and took another glance around the restaurant.

****

Despite the funeral, Black's weekend with his kids was wonderful. Connie, who was still grieving the loss of her best friend, seemed to have had a blast with the kids as they talked, had pillow fights, wrestling matches, and watched movies together. He didn't have to ask Kevin and Nicole if they liked Connie, because it was written all over their happy faces.

Black had always wanted to take his children to Chuck E. Cheese, so, being that it was Sunday, and the kids had to return home, he took the initiative. They were so excited. Lil' Keith couldn't move around and play as much as his older brother and sister, but he was having the time of his life. Well, that was until the guy in the mouse costume approached and scared Lil' Keith to tears. Black found that extremely funny because he thought about how Fred would tease Ray for being scared of rats. He laughed so hard, his ribs felt like they were going to crack.

The kids were all asleep by the time they finally arrived at Publix, where Nikki and Willie were already waiting. They dismounted the truck as soon as Black pulled alongside them. Black got out, unbuckled Lil' Keith and gingerly handed him to Nikki, not waking him.

"I thought you were gonna run off with them," Nikki joked in a hushed tone.

"I thought about it," Black asserted, pulling a still sleeping Nicole from the car.

Willie opened the rear door for Black to place Nicole in the back seat. After buckling her safety belt, he looked over at Nikki, who was strapping his son into the car seat. She seemed much older and mature. He hurriedly straightened himself before she could catch him staring at her. He got the kids' clothes from Connie, who was still sitting in the car and handed them to Willie.

"I wanna take them shopping for some clothes," Black told them. "That way, they'll already have some at my house."

"When?" Nikki asked.

"I'm playing by your rules," Black answered, remembering what Connie had told him. "Next weekend, if you'll let me."

Nikki looked over at Willie. He nodded.

"It's a date," Nikki agreed.

Black was happy with the news. Connie told him, awhile back, to be patient and she'd come around, and she did. Finally! Now, he had to see if Felicia would let him get Kevin next weekend.

"I don't care," Felicia had answered his question.

She was wearing a white robe and black heels with straps that wrapped around her calves. Black had seen the gray Mercedes in the driveway and figured she was entertaining a client before sex until he interrupted her.

Not wanting to hold her up any longer, he kissed his son and was out the door. When he climbed behind the wheel, he was surprised to see that Connie had turned on the radio, being that she hadn't listened to any music since finding out about Sylvia. Hell, they hadn't had sex since that day, either. Black was a firm believer in sexual healing, and that's what he was going to perform on Connie tonight.

Well, he was going to at least try.

****

Ray still hadn't called anyone. After he directed the movers where to put everything, paid them, and sent them on their way. He began unpacking and putting his house in order. He made a mental note to get B.J. to go with him to retrieve his Delta. As he worked around the house, he could not stop thinking about Sylvia. He thought about the dream he'd had prior to her death, where she appeared to be a spirit, which turned out to be a forewarning. He thought about what Star told him. It was evident that she was outside Petro that night, from what she'd told him, but how did he not see her in the parking lot?

Now, Ray was hungry. He went to the kitchen and made it to the refrigerator before realizing there was no food in it, and not once had he went shopping for groceries. So, being that most of his chores were done, he showered, dressed and drove to Wendy's where he used the drive-thru.

While waiting for his food, he thought about Star again. Something about her story wasn't adding up. Unless there was something missing.

'*That's it*!' he thought. '*Something was definitely missing!*'

****

When they arrived home, Black ran a tub full of hot water and bubble bath solutions. Then he and Connie soaked, talked, kissed and washed each other until the water began to get cold. After drying off, Black led Connie to the bed, kissed her some more, then gently laid her on the feather-soft spreads. He looked down at her flawless body as she looked back up at him. He knew she was ready, because her nipples had immediately responded when he was washing her, and they were still hard. Hell, his manhood responded at the same time, and he was throbbing.

As bad as Black wanted to dive on top of her and get straight to it, he knew he couldn't. She was still delicate. Saying nothing, he headed for the living room. After putting on *Keith Sweat's 'Keep It Comin'* CD, he turned the heat down a few notches, then re-entered the bedroom where Connie was still in the same spot, same position.

He climbed atop her and planted his lips on hers, kissing her softly. She moaned when he made it to her neck and arched her body like she always did when he got to her chest. He went to her favorite spot, which was between her breasts. He kissed one breast after the other. Licked one breast after the other. Sucked one nipple after the other. They were only illuminated by the light of the T.V. screen, but he could see she'd turned red from the passion.

Black put his tongue between her breasts and licked all the back up to her mouth. She returned his kiss, gripping his buttocks and grinding her body against his. Yes, she was definitely ready! Black ended the kiss, then worked his mouth down to her stomach, where he circled her navel with his tongue. She moaned, then, came another sound.

His cell phone, but Black didn't budge. He concentrated on what Keith Sweat was saying, and what he was doing. He shifted his body. Now, he had his knees on the floor, and Connie's left leg up, kissing her inner thigh. The ringing stopped but immediately started back up. Black knew he had to answer it because that was the code of an emergency.

"I'm sorry, baby," he apologized, getting up off the floor. "I gotta get that."

She nodded.

The number on the screen was Ray's. "What's up?"

"Ya girl up?" Ray asked.

"Um," Black looked at Connie's naked body and almost said no. "Yeah, she's up."

"Let me speak to her," said Ray. "It won't take long."

"Hold on." Black handed her the phone. "It's, Ray."

"Hey, Ray."

"How you holding up?"

"I'm making it," she answered. "How 'bout you?"

"The same," he told her. "I'm trying to get in touch with Star. It's urgent."

"I can call her and have her call you," Connie insisted.

"Can you do it within a few minutes?"

"Yeah."

"A'ight, thanks."

"No problem."

Ray received his food and found a spot in Wendy's parking lot before calling Black to speak to Connie. Now, ending the call, he drove out of the parking lot, heading home. He really didn't think Star would call him, but, why not? It's not like they had gotten into it at the cemetery. She should know that the call would be about Sylvia. Unless she didn't want to talk about Sylvia, but why not?

Did she have something to hide? Ray pulled into his driveway, cut the engine and gathered his food and drink. Before he could open the driver's door, his phone vibrated in his pocket. Puttin his drink down, he checked it to see an unfamiliar number.

"Yeah?" he answered.

"Connie said you wanted to talk to me."

"Yeah, I do." He sat his food on the passenger's seat. "Are you busy?"

"No."

"It's about, Sylvia."

"I know," she said matter-of-factly. What about her?"

"If you don't mind," Ray said, carefully. "Can you tell me where y'all went, and what happened after y'all left Petro?"

Star sighed, then, after a moment of silence, said, "We didn't leave, together."

Ray did not want to believe what he'd just heard. *They didn't leave together*? Could that mean Sylvia had lied about someone bringing her to Petro? Could she have driven Star's car and filled her in on the date when she returned? Is that how Star was able to describe the date to him at the burial site? From Sylvia's reportage? It had to be because Ray was sure he didn't see her sitting in the parking lot. This shit wasn't adding up at all, but that was the reason for his call, to get her to spill the beans, so he could put everything in proper perspective.

"Y'all didn't leave together?" Ray asked.

"Nope," she answered, flatly. "When you left, she got a call from somebody. All I know is, she came out to the car and told me to go on home because a friend was gonna meet her there."

"How'd you figure she got a call?"

"I was watching her put on her coat," Star answered. "I saw her answer her phone. Anyway, she gave me the money you gave her and told me to put it up. I ain't ask no questions, I just left."

"So, you just left her standing in the parking lot?"

Star didn't answer.

Now, he was expecting her to hang up.

"I, um," she lingered. "I watched her as I drove off. The person who called her was already in the parking lot."

"Were you really in the parking lot?" Ray tested.

"Of course, I was in the parking lot!" she insisted. "Sylvia didn't want you to know about us. So, when I saw you looking around, I ducked.

That's when it dawned on him that Sylvia and Star were lovers.

"How'd you figure the person who'd called her, was already in the parking lot?" Ray went on.

"When I got to the end of the parking lot," she explained. "Before I turned on Bankhead, I looked back and saw her approach the truck."

*The truck*! Ray had definitely seen the truck, and that was not the first time he'd encountered it.

## CHAPTER 19

James wouldn't admit it aloud, but this was the most boring Sunday dinner he'd ever had at his mother's. He wouldn't doubt she was feeling the same. She was missing Ray, too. There had only been small talk. Mary said she was moving in with, Robert. Robert said he would teach her everything about fixing cars. Raymond didn't say much, but James was kind of glad that conversation was to a minimum because his mind was elsewhere. He didn't like Fred's tone when he insisted that they needed to talk, *face to face*!

It was obvious Fred had found out about the demise of his gun plug. Fred had every right to be mad, but reprimanding James for it wasn't going to bring the old, white man back. Unless Fred planned to do more than reprimand him. James' cell phone vibrated atop the table, pulling him from his reverie. It must've done the same to Mary, Robert and Raymond also, because they were all looking at it like it, was about to transform or explode.

James picked it up seeing Ray's number. "Talk to me!" he answered.

"Just listen!" Ray asserted, sternly. "I already know where you are. Don't tell her I'm on the phone."

"Yeah, I had already got that fixed," James said, glancing across the table at his mother, who was watching him. "Right now, I'm at my mom's house."

"Look," Ray went on. "I'm calling an emergency Kingz meeting, right now!"

"Formal or informal?"

"Informal."

"I'm on it."

James excused himself, donned his coat, kissed his mother, and was out the door. As he drove, he called Grip and told him to meet him at The Palace, with two more Kingzmen. He didn't know what Fred had up his sleeves, but he was going to have his Kingzmen on standby.

\*\*\*\*

After calling Fred and Black and informing them of the emergency meeting. Ray pulled out of his driveway and headed for The Palace, playing the conversation with Star over in his head. It still seemed strange to him. He didn't know the dude, but he knew he was fucking Sylvia. So, why, rape and strangle her to death?

He toyed with this until he'd pulled up at The Palace and to his surprise, was greeted by one of the Kingzmen that occupied the security booth. Ray only nodded as he waited for the gate to open wide enough for his car to fit through. Then, he made the seventy-something yard drive to his respectable spot. He was the last to arrive.

Ray was greeted by another KM at the front door, and Grip outside the office. Why would James have them here? Ray wondered as he entered the office, where James, Fred, and Black were already seated. They all stood.

"Welcome back!" James said, being the first to hug, Ray.

After Ray had been embraced by his peers, and they were all seated. He conveyed everything that was on his mind to them, as they listened attentively.

"It makes sense," Fred spoke after a while. "But it doesn't make sense. You summed everything up right, but it's not adding up on his behalf. If he did it, only he and Sylvia knew why. Did they say anything about the autopsy coming back?"

"Not yet," answered Black, who was still in the middle of giving Connie her sexual healing when Ray had called.

•"I know you want this nigga," Fred told Ray. "But at least wait until they plaster his face on the screen as being the one who'd violated her."

"Fuck that!" James finally spoke. "It's K.O.A. Kingz Over Authority! King Ray, if you suspect this nigga, I'll put word out and have his ass brought in! That's what you want?"

Ray just stared at his brother. He knew that all he had to do was give the word, and James was going to make good on his promise. On the other hand, Fred as always was thinking rational, although Ray was not feeling that rational shit at this point.

"We'll wait," Ray finally answered, hating himself the moment he'd said it. "I guess this shit was a waste of time."

"Not really," James asserted. "I think, King Fred, got something to say."

"We're informal," Ray told James, reminding him that they didn't have to refer to each other as, King.

James nodded. "What 'cha got Fred?"

Fred conveyed everything that Eric had told him about the Kingz holding court, executing and chopping niggas up. As he spoke, he focused most of his attention on James, who seemed to relish every word.

"This had to come from one of our workers," Fred continued. "We don't know who it is, but whoever it is, could be detrimental to this operation."

"So, what do you suggest?" asked James, who was doing a good job of hiding his excitement of the revelation.

"I don't have any suggestions right now," Fred admitted.

"Ray?"

Ray shook his head. "None."

"Black?"

"If there was a suggestion," Black answered. "It would be to back out. Pull the plug, but I doubt if any of us would agree to that. I'm in it all the way, however, it plays out."

"I like that," said James. "And I feel the same way. Anybody feel otherwise?"

\*\*\*\*

Fred drove home with a mind full of blank thoughts. He didn't know what kind of results he was going to get by telling his confidants what Eric had told him, but he expected James to, well, be James.

Fred's mother was sitting in her favorite recliner when he entered the house. He couldn't tell if she'd noticed him come in, because her eyes were glued to the T.V. Fred couldn't help but take a look. She was watching the news. A reporter was announcing the death of a gun shop owner and his son, a police officer. Then, they showed the victim's pictures.

Fred almost swore out loud but retained for the presence of his mother. He forced himself to listen as the reporter further explained that the gun shop was stripped of all its guns and ammunition. Even the surveillance tape had been taken.

"According to the local authorities," the reporter continued, "Fifty-two-year-old Jimmy Cambridge, was shot execution-style, with his own gun."

"Now that's bad," Fred's mother said. "You can't even run a decent, legal business, without worrying about becoming a victim."

She looked up as if expecting him to comment, but this just added to the cloud of blank thoughts that already occupied his mind.

"I'm tired," he managed. "You need anything before I turn in?"

"I'm okay. I'ma catch the rest of the news, then take my old self to bed."

Fred kissed his mother, showered, then climbed into bed. He couldn't sleep, so he just stared at the ceiling, mulling over past events. He thought about Tee, who still had not called him back about DNA testing. He thought about what Eric had told him, which prompted him to think about Yvonne. Who still hadn't called him as promised, but the second he'd thought it, his cell phone rang on top of the pillow beside him.

"Yeah?" he answered.

"Hey, baby!" Yvonne beamed on the other end. "Am I calling too late?"

"Nah," he said in his composed tone but was more than happy to hear from her.

"I would've called earlier," she explained. "But I had some business to take care of. It's better late than never, right?"

"Always. So, what's on ya mind?"

"Sucking you off."

"Sounds good!"

"Not as good as it feels."

**** 

James had awakened this morning, feeling like a true King. He'd been anticipating this day so bad, he slept in intervals. What Fred had revealed to them at the Round Table last night, had amplified his ego to the full extent. He was extremely happy to hear that The Kingz was finally respected, but he wanted to see for himself, which was why he was just out cruising, putting his face and freshly-polished *Kingz* medallion on the scene. He had driven through neighborhoods and occasionally stopped at gas stations or mini-marts, just to see how people reacted to his presence as he pretended to browse the aisles. He'd also taken the initiative to not wear a coat over his sweater, so his chain wouldn't be obscured.

To his amusement, people seemed to be regarding him with respect, or, was it, fear? He didn't know which one it was, but people were nodding and moving out of his way as if he owned the world, but this was only the beginning.

**** 

"Don't you ever have your grandma worried about you like that again!"

When Ray had awakened, he knew he had to get back at his people and let them know he was okay. The first person he called was April, who, apparently, was in class, because she didn't answer. Therefore, he left a message. He, then called his mother, who was at work with, Robert. She said she missed him, then hit him with a barrage of questions about Sylvia that he was not in the mood to answer. He promised he would explain it to her some other time.

Now, he was sitting with his grandmother, in her living room, at her house in Decatur. He was going to call her, but he figured he should visit, being that he hadn't seen her in months.

"I was okay, Grandma," Ray now responded.

"Well, did you, at least, go to the funeral?"

"I paid my respects. How's the arthritis?"

"Getting worse and worse," she answered, rubbing her left leg. "I fell down the stairs a couple days ago."

"Where was, Henry?" Ray asked of her boyfriend, who was there for her when their grandfather died a few years ago.

"He was here," she answered, laughing. "He came runnin' like the house was on fire!"

"I'm glad you find that funny!" Ray told her. "It could've been worse."

"But it wasn't," she answered him. "Ya grandma is tougher than you think she is."

Ray left his grandmother's house, making a mental note to periodically call to check on her. He was glad Henry was there for her, but he was also up in age. How long would it be before he would need someone to take care of *him*?

Ray was on his way to check on Precious and decided to kill two birds with one stone. He called B.J. and told him to meet him in Maple Creek, to drive the Delta to his new house. Upon entering the apartment, Ray was engulfed in a cloud of weed smoke. He entered the living room, where Precious was curled up on the sofa talking on the phone and listening to Lisa Fischer's 'How Can I Ease The Pain from a small portable radio that sat on the small table beside the sofa. Seeing him, she quickly concluded her call, shut off the radio, and opened the door to air the apartment out.

"I'm sorry," she apologized. "If I knew you were coming, I would've smoked that blunt outside."

"It's okay," he said, coughing a little. "What we got?"

He followed her to the stash room, trying not to look at how her ass bounced, gracefully in her sweatpants. He also did his best to avoid eye contact while they went over everything.

"Did dude ever come by and pick up those four ounces?' Ray asked, now remembering the order he'd laid out for Joe.

"Short, stocky man with long hair?"

"Yeah."

"He came by," she answered. "He said to call him."

"A'ight." Ray folded the bills from the stash and placed them in the inside pocket of his coat. "I'ma hit my plug up and try to cop a few P's before we run out."

Precious nodded. There was nothing more to say, so Ray went outside and started the Oldsmobile, to let it warm up until B.J. arrived. While he was leaning against the car, his cell phone vibrated.

He removed it from the clip on his hip. "Yeah?"

"How you doing, baby?" Tasha asked.

"I'm decent. What's up wit 'cha?"

"Not much," she answered. "I heard about, Sylvia. It was on the *World News*."

"How's your new place?" Ray intentionally changed subjects.

"It's okay. The condition is not as good as the last one, but it's cheaper. Did you move?"

"Yeah."

"Apartment or house?"

"House," he answered as B.J.'s car pulled into the apartments.

"Have you found somebody to do your hair?"

"Not yet," he told her. "I might cut this shit off."

"Nooo!" Tasha exclaimed. "Don't do that! I'll move back to Georgia before I let you do that!"

"I might not cut it," he said as the Chevy pulled up. "Look, hit me back later."

He ended the call just as B.J. climbed from the passenger side of his car that was driven by, Krystal.

"I hope you didn't call me all the way out here to drive, Miss Daisy!" B.J. joked.

It took a few seconds for Ray to realize he was referring to the Oldsmobile. So, being that he wasn't in a joking mood, he tossed B.J. the keys to the BMW.

"Don't wreck my shit!"

"Don't worry," B.J. said, heading for the BMW. "I need all my limbs!"

It didn't take long for Ray to catch on to *that* statement. He didn't know what to think of the rumor when he'd heard it at the

Round Table last night. He still didn't know what to think of it. To be honest, he really didn't care.

****

After bringing his mother breakfast from McDonald's, Fred was back out the door, en route to Hair Masters, to let Eric cut his hair before it got crowded. While traveling Bankhead Highway, a call came through on his cellular.

"What up?"

"I got all four," Bobby asserted.

"How much?"

"Ten, each."

"Ten what?" Fred asked, hoping he wasn't asking ten thousand, a piece, for some stolen trucks.

"Ten thousand," Bobby answered.

"Forty stacks for some shit that none of us can drive!" Fred asserted, ready to hang up on this nigga.

"Shit, that's way cheaper than what the chop shops get 'em for," Bobby pleaded his case. "Plus, y'all got four trailers. Hell, I'll teach y'all how to drive them bitches for free."

"We ain't trying to drive them muhfuckas!"

"What the hell y'all trying to do wit 'em?"

Fred sighed, "Man, let me get up with the crew and see what they think."

"Okay, well, check this out," Bobby asserted before Fred could hang up. "I gotta fuck with y'all boys, cause y'all from the spot. Just give me fifteen for everything."

"I still gotta run this by the crew," Fred told him.

Fred jotted Bobby's number down in his memory bank and was going to call James but remembered James had said he would be at The Palace all day. So, he figured he would stop by there when he leaves the barbershop.

"What up, Young Blood!" Bear, one of the barbers, who was seated in the chair beside Eric's empty station, greeted Fred.

"I can't call it," Fred asserted. "E' ain't got in yet?"

"He had to run an errand. He told me to line you up if you were in a rush."

"I wish he would've called and told me," Fred said, taking off his coat and laying it on Eric's chair.

\*\*\*\*

"How long do you plan on working there?" Black asked Connie, who was peeling the boiled eggs she was going to add to the tuna fish she was making.

"I guess until I find something better," she answered, keeping her back to Black. Who was perched on a stool on the opposite side of the counter. "Why?"

Connie's boss had given her a week's leave, in which Black planned to use to his advantage. He really wanted her to quit and do something more productive. More professional, more respectable. She was his girl, and he felt that she shouldn't be changing dirty bedspreads for a living. She should be doing better. Better than Danielle, better than Nikki, and definitely better than that high-priced prostitute, Felicia.

"I want you to quit, go to school, and get a degree in business," he prompted with a little more force than intended.

Now she turned to face him with a look on her face that he regarded as disbelief. "You want me to go to school?"

"I do," he admitted. "But it's not about what I want. It's about what *you* want. I'll pay for everything if that's what you choose to do.

She wiped her hands on her apron and stood akimbo. "So, I guess a man of your status can't have a woman who makes beds for a living, huh? That would make you look bad in front of other— um street pharmacists, huh?"

Black was too stunned to answer.

"Well, I guess I have a call to make," she asserted, then marched out of the kitchen.

Now, Black was feeling like he'd stuck his foot in his mouth. He had pissed Connie off. She was still grieving the death of her best friend, then he turns around and applies more pressure with his inconsiderate, and selfish thoughts. He just shook his head.

Moments later, she re-entered the kitchen with a smile on her face and kissed him on the jaw.

"I did it!" she said.

Now Black was confused. "Did what?"

"I quit," she answered. "I told my boss that I wasn't coming back."

"I hope you didn't do it for *me*!" He put an arm around her waist and looked into her eyes.

"I, um—" she started, looking away. "I had already decided not to go back. I didn't know if I could."

Seeing the tears well up in her eyes, Black stood and embraced her. "I understand," he whispered softly, not really knowing what to say.

"I'm okay, baby," she avowed. "Let me finish making our lunch."

"Are you sure you don't want me to finish it?" Black offered.

"Definitely not!" Connie stated, smiling. "When you learn how to boil hot dogs. I'll think about trusting you with our food. Until then, let the housewife do what she's supposed to do."

"Well, gone, wit 'cha bad self!" Black slapped her on the ass when she turned to circle the counter.

She looked back, regarding him with that wide-mouth smile he'd missed for almost a week. Perhaps that sexual healing although interrupted twice had worked.

\*\*\*\*

How are we looking?" James asked Grip when he entered the shooting range, where Grip and four other Kingzmen had set out the guns from the robbery, so they could test them.

"I put the word out to a few of my ex-Navy buddies at the training ground," Grip answered. "But tonight, we're gonna split up and do a good two-hour search, starting at twenty hundred hours."

James had figured Ray would go with Fred's recommendation and wait until the media plastered dude's face on T.V. and broadcast him as the suspect for raping and murdering Sylvia, before going after him. James knew that, once the nigga saw his picture on T.V., he was going to skip town or make it seem as if he did, but he was certainly not going to be driving a white Chevy Tahoe with matching rims.

If the nigga was smart, James thought, he would've skipped town the same night. Either way, James was bound to find out, because he'd already started his own personal dragnet for him.

"Is everything loaded?" James asked, looking around.

"Not everything," answered Grip. "We'll be loading as we go."

"What about the Tommy's?"

"First stall," Grip said, then followed James to the booth, where the guns were leaned against the wall.

James picked them up, then turned to face Grip, with the barrels high. "I feel like a true Mob Boss with these bitches! Fuck Freddy Kruger, with these, I'm a nigga's worst nightmare on whatever street! They loaded?"

Grip nodded.

James thought for a moment, then handed the guns to Grip. "Unload 'em. I'll play wit 'em some other time."

James had wanted a Tommy gun, ever since he'd seen one on an old mobster movie, he'd seen while growing up. Now that he'd gotten one well, two— he was afraid of the power those guns possessed. Yes, the Big Bad Wolf was afraid!

That didn't stop him and the Kingzmen from firing off the other guns like a pack of drunken hillbillies except with accuracy. They had so many guns and ammunition, they ran out of targets before they got halfway through the guns, so they just assaulted the sandbags.

James had just emptied the clip of a .44 Desert Eagle when Grip approached and told him Fred was *seventy-six*, which meant he was en route to the building.

"A'ight," James asserted, relinquishing the .44 to Grip. "Y'all carry on."

James journeyed back to the office, where he flopped down in his chair, propped his feet up on the table, and pulled out his cell phone, toying with it. He was sure Fred had seen, or heard about the gunsmith by now, and had put two and two together. Fred was the quiet type, but he was the toughest and smartest street nigga James had ever encountered.

"What's up, Slick Pimpin'?" James greeted Fred as he entered.

"I can't call it," Fred answered, hanging his coat over the back of his chair before taking a seat. "The KMs in training?"

James listened to the faint sounds of gunfire before answering. "Always. You'll never know when we'll have to go up against one of these fake ass mobs."

"True," Fred answered. He wanted to question James about the demise of his gun plug but put it off. "I got the eighteen wheelers."

"Yeah?"

"Well, Bobby hit me up and told me he got 'em," Fred clarified. "Four trucks and four trailers."

"That nigga don't play!" James exclaimed. "How much he wants?"

"Fifteen, for the whole package."

"Shit, that's not bad," James said. "We gotta call a K—"

He was interrupted by his phone that vibrated in his hand, prompting him to regard the unfamiliar number on the screen.

"Scuse me," he told Fred, then answered his phone. "What up?"

"How's business?" the familiar voice asked.

"Ain't you a lil' too early?" James asked, not trying to hide the anger in his voice.

"I ain't call to hassle you 'bout that lil' paper," The Shark insisted. "We both know what the agreement is. I just called to check on you. You a'ight?"

"Shit, I'm good," James answered, watching Fred leaving the office.

"That's what's up," said The Shark. "My friend is throwing a party on his yacht, down in Fort Lauderdale. I'm quite sure I can obtain an invitation for the Kingz."

"When?"

"This weekend."

"Nah," James answered. "We got some other shit going on."

"That's cool."

James ended the call and wondered what kind of answer The Shark expected to hear when he asked, "How's business?" Did he expect for James to tell him the truth, which was, that everything was moving at a snail's pace and that he would have to knock over a bank to pay him on time?

He probably couldn't handle the truth! James was about to say something to Fred, then remembered Fred had left the office, minutes ago. James lunged from his chair and dashed from the office, knowing Fred had ventured off to the shooting range to apparently see that his assessment ringed true about the gunsmith, and the Kingzmen couldn't stop or question him, because he was a King.

James decreased the momentum of his stride as he reached the door of the shooting range. When he entered, he saw that the KMs were gathered around Fred, who was in the second stall, firing off rounds from a Mac-11. James duly noticed that Grip was standing between stall one and two as if to prevent Fred from seeing the Tommy guns he'd replaced in stall one.

Once Fred had squeezed off the last shot, he turned around with a broad smile on his face. "Boy, I like this muhfucka!"

**\*\*\*\***

Fred left The Palace after receiving a call from Theresa. He had really wanted to get up with Yvonne, ever since the raunchy conversation they'd had last night. Although she could back up everything she said, Fred knew she was just reeling him in for-profit and gain. So, he was kind of glad Theresa had called, insisting that she needed company.

Having no intentions to stay over, they had sex, made small conversations, then Fred migrated from Stone Mountain to Knight Park to get his thoughts together. He half watched T.V. with his mother, took a long shower, then retired to his room, leaving his mother to her nightly sitcoms.

As he laid in bed, staring at the ceiling, he thought about James. He figured James had taken part in the gun heist but couldn't validate it. Well, not until he'd marched into the shooting range to prove his suspicion, and thought he'd walked into an underground terrorist training center. The KMs had all stopped what they were doing, to watch him, resembling deer caught in headlights.

Fred nodded, grabbed the first gun in his reach, the Mac-11 and headed for the next unoccupied booth, which was the second one. Before he could extract the cartridge to see if it was loaded, Grip quickly materialized to his left, with a box of ammunition. Fred could admit Grip was quick, but not quick enough, because he'd already caught a glimpse of the drum of a Tommy gun that was propped against the wall of the first stall before grip attempted to use himself as a buffer. So, it was incontestable to Fred that James had pulled this off with the help of the Kingzmen.

It seemed like, seconds after Fred had closed his eyelids, he heard the sound of the front door being kicked in. His mother screamed, but the report from a gun silenced her. He quickly reached under his pillow for his gun, but it wasn't there.

Fred had never been a victim of a robbery, and he damn sure didn't plan on being a casualty. Not in his own home! However, before he could get out of bed and make a break for his arsenal in the closet, his bedroom door came crashing in, and Grip, followed by the other Kingzmen, surrounded his bed, carrying nothing less than machine guns. He was about to question their intrusion, when James entered, wearing a long trench coat, matching Stetson, and carrying both Tommy guns.

"How ya doin' my friend?" James asked, looking down at him.

"Man, I know you didn't kill, my mama!" Fred spoke with malice.

"I did her a favor," James told him. "Besides, you know we don't leave witnesses at murder scenes."

'*Murder scenes*?' Fred thought. His mother had been having dreams of him getting killed, and he strongly felt that James would be the cause of it if he wasn't the triggerman himself. Now, it had come to pass.

"I just recently realized something," James continued. "One King can run this whole operation, and since I'm the one that put this shit together. I'll take full responsibility. Now, any last words?"

"You just gon' kill me?" Fred asked, trying to buy time as he foolishly sized up the six, highly trained Kingzmen.

"We all pledged Kingz for Life," James answered. "That means until death. So, since you're no longer a King— well, you already know."

James aimed the guns at him. Fred wanted to do or say something— anything! But, before he could come up with an ounce of a plan, James squeezed off both guns in a fusillade of rounds as bullets tore through Fred's torso.

# CHAPTER 20

Black was glad to see that Connie was reemerging. She made breakfast and, after they'd eaten, immediately began tidying up the house, so everything was done when she left for the registration office. Black had planned to accompany her, until James called, informing him of a formal Kingz meeting, at twelve, in full dress.

Being that they'd agreed to trade Connie's car in, she drove off in the Nissan, and Black headed for The Palace in his BMW.

James and Ray were already there. Black parked and carried his plastic-covered robe, crown and treasure box containing his necklace inside.

Ray and James were seated at the Round Table, engaged in conversation when he entered the office. Their robes were draped on the backs of their chairs, crowns on the table, and chains about their necks. Greetings were exchanged, and Black had gotten himself settled in, but the quietness of the room made him uneasy. There was a bad vibe about the atmosphere that gave him chills.

Black checked his watch to see that it was already seven minutes after twelve, which made him wonder where Fred was at. He also wondered what James and Ray had been discussing before he'd arrived.

"This ain't like King Fred to be late," Black said, pretending to check his watch.

"Yeah, you're right," Ray agreed, checking his watch, then looking over at James, who was filing his fingernails with a filer.

"He know the rules like the rest of us," James asserted, not looking up from what he was doing. "If he's not here in ten minutes, we'll go ahead and—"

James words were cut off when the office door open. They all looked up to see Fred, clad in a blue suit and matching dress shoes, with his plastic-covered robe draped over one shoulder, crown in his hand, and chain about his neck.

"Y'all didn't start without me, did ya?" Fred inquired as he entered and proceeded to get himself settled in.

"Nah," James answered. "But, since we're already late, we can go ahead and start. First, what I'm bringing to the Round Table is not a big issue. It's also not a small issue. Anyway, I feel like, as Kingz, as an organization, we should wear our chains at all times, out in public. People already know us, whether they've seen us at clubs, or just heard about us. Now, it's time we put our faces with our fame. That way, people would know who they're dealing with, and how to deal with us. It's like having a vicious dog in the yard, and no *Beware of Dog* sign up. This chain is our *Beware of Dog* sign. Anybody disagree?"

No one disagreed.

"Okay," James continued. "With that settled, I'll turn it over to King Fred."

Fred leaned forward, interlocking his fingers with his hands resting on the table, and said to his comrades that Bobby had obtained the trucks that were to be used as decoys for The Palace, and how much he was asking.

"It's a good deal," Fred told them. "Plus, being on hot-ass Fulton Industrial, we'll need the disguise."

"I agree," said Ray, nodding his head.

"Yeah, me too," came Black.

James said, "King Fred, you can do the honors of setting up the meeting. Anybody else needs to bring anything to the Round Table?"

No one spoke.

"Good," James went on. "Now we can have court."

Before anybody could question him, James grabbed his radio and radioed to Grip that The Kingz would be ready in ten minutes. He then stood and donned his robe as his comrades watched.

'*What is this nigga up to?*' Fred thought to himself. He hadn't mentioned anything about having court over the phone. It was bad enough that last night's dream had already had him on the edge, which is why he was late. He had stopped by the barbershop to confer with Eric about it.

"Shit, I've had dreams of you killing me," Eric told him.

Fred was taken aback by Eric's assertion, but they both knew it would never come to that. By the time Eric had talked some sense back into Fred and eased his fears of James being out to kill him, he had lost track of time, and Eric's customers had started pouring in.

Now, he was back to feeling the same way he was feeling when he'd awakened from the disturbing dream. He'd already conceded that James and the Kingzmen were conducting covert operations. He also felt that, if ordered by James, the KMs wouldn't hesitate to take out the rest of the Kingz.

"What we got—another thief?" Fred asked, hoping to catch some kind of hint.

"I wanna tell y'all," James answered. "But it's a surprise, and I don't wanna spoil it."

Fred didn't pick up any hints, so he didn't know what to think of this. He did try one more question. "How many heads?"

Before James could answer, there was a knock at the door. "It's time fellas," he said. "I'll be outside."

James left the office as Fred, Ray, and Black got themselves together. Black was still trying to figure out what, or, better yet, who this *surprise* was, and he felt if anybody other than James knew who this surprise is, it was Ray, but he knew better than to pry.

"Y'all boys ready?" Ray asked, looking from Fred to Black.

"Let's make it happen," said Black, who couldn't help but notice that Ray hadn't fully recovered from Sylvia's death.

Fred, Ray, and Black exited the office to see James talking with Grip and three other Kingzmen, who were all armed with shoulder-strapped submachine guns. Seeing them, James handed Grip a folded newspaper, then led the way to the courtroom. Once the Kingz had settled onto their thrones, James ordered Grip to bring in the prisoner.

"We'll be doing this without the audience from now on," James asserted, once the Kingzmen had left the room. "Unless requested by a King."

No one said a word. Perhaps, James thought, they were still trying to figure out who their surprise guest was.

At that moment, a man clad in a black jean suit, shackled and handcuffed to the back, with a pillowcase over his head, was ushered into the room. James took a quick glance at his comrades and could tell they were all sizing the guy up to see if they could tell who it was before he was revealed, but little did they know, only one of them could actually do that because only one of them knew him.

"Thank you, gentlemen," James said, once the man was brought forth. "Please, unveil the criminal."

The pillowcase was removed. The guy's mouth was smeared with dry blood, and his left eye was swollen.

"King Fred, do you know this criminal?" James asked.

"Nah," Fred answered slowly, still not sure.

"King Black?"

"Nope."

"King Ray?" James looked over at his brother, who was looking at the guy like he was ready to pounce on him. "King Ray?"

Ray heard his brother calling him, but his jaws were set, which made it hard for him to respond. He couldn't believe that this nigga was actually standing before him. He reached to make sure he didn't leave his gun in the car, this time. No, he was definitely armed— *and dangerous*!

## CHAPTER 21

"King Ray, James tried again. "Can you tell us who this criminal is— a name at least?"

"Corey," Ray managed, maintaining eye contact with the man, who was now returning his stare.

"Negative!" James prompted. "This criminal's name is Keyonne Sharpe. He's brought up on charges of rape, and two counts of murder that involved Sylvia Baker and her unborn child."

Keyonne began to protest, "Man, I didn't rape—"

"Silence!" James shouted, and one of the Kingzmen delivered a stiff jab to Keyonne's ribs, causing him to cry out in pain.

"We can't really say he did it," Ray said, hating every word.

"I agree," Fred chimed in. "We can't prove that."

"Is someone requesting evidence?" James asked.

"I am," Fred quickly spoke up.

"Me too," said Black.

"KM-One," James called out. "Could you, please, present evidence?"

Grip approached with the folded newspaper and passed it around. The paper, that was published this morning, was folded to the page where Keyonne's picture appeared, and the reporter alleging that he was wanted for the rape and murder of Sylvia Baker, being that his semen was extracted from her body.

Ray was so heated he almost drew his gun and emptied the whole clip on this nigga. '*This nigga is surely going to breath his last breath*,' Ray thought.

"King Ray, I believe this is your case," James stated, anxious to see how his brother was going to handle himself.

Ray sat there for a few seconds, not knowing what to say or do. The evidence was there, this nigga was as good as dead. Making that assessment, Ray slowly rose to his feet and descended the two steps that elevated their thrones, getting into Keyonne's face.

"Nigga, you don't know half the pain you've caused me!" Ray vented through clenched teeth.

"Man, I swear—" Keyonne tried to protest again.

"Shut up!"

This time, Ray delivered the blow, punching Keyonne in the chin, causing him to buckle and drop to his knees. Ray returned to his throne as James watched with admiration.

"What'd you find out about this nigga?" Ray asked James.

"He has a wife and three kids," James answered.

"You know where they are?"

"Yep."

"I want him and that bitch dead, as soon as possible!"

"What about the kids?"

"No kids."

"Not even the firstborn?" James prodded.

While Ray was looking like he was considering this. Fred was silently hoping he wouldn't agree to it, knowing how much Ray loved kids.

"No kids," Ray reiterate. "Just him and the bitch."

"Ray, please hear me out," Keyonne tried again with tears rolling down his face. "If you gon' kill me, kill me. Just leave my wife out of it. I swear to God I didn't violate Sylvia like that! I picked her up at Petro, that night. We had sex in my truck, and I dropped her off at the entrance of Dogwood. Sylvia was a prostitute. Plus, she told me the baby she was carrying, was mine."

This revelation struck Ray like a slap in the face. He was not hearing this shit! Ain't no way this nigga just told him some shit like this!

"Man, off this nigga!" Ray spat.

James quickly took the initiative. "Keyonne, we, The Kingz, find you guilty of rape and two counts of murder. For that, we sentence you and your wife to death. Any King, disagrees?"

No one answered.

James nodded to Grip.

"KM-Six!" Grip barked. "Execute!"

The appointed Kingzman pulled out something that resembled a black rubber belt and in a lightning-like motion, wrapped it around Keyonne's neck. Using the other end wrapped around his hand, he pulled, causing the device to tighten and cut off Keyonne's circulation as the Kingz impassively looked on, but Ray, James noticed, had the visage of a stone-cold killer.

'*Damn!*' James thought. '*Had I known that Sylvia's death would've brought this out of him, I would've done it myself, months ago!*'

**** 

Saturday rolled around, and the Kingz were all in the office, doing inventory on their money and product. Plus, they had put aside the fifteen thousand for Bobby, who'd already shown up in one truck and was riding back and forth with his fiancée to get the rest.

"We'll be out before Saturday," Fred announced, looking up from his notes. "Way before Saturday."

"Either way," James responded. "We still have to wait. We won't miss out on any money or lose any customers."

James had gotten a call from Grip, this morning, informing him in code that they had finally killed Keyonne's wife last night. It took a couple of days because her house was being watched by the authorities, in case Keyonne was stupid enough to show up. His body still hadn't surfaced.

There was a knock at the door.

"Yeah?" Fred answered.

"Bobby just pulled up with the last truck," Grip informed through the door.

"We'll be out," Fred told him, then began packing the fifteen thousand into a paper bag.

"Everybody got their paperwork?" James asked.

"I'm decent," Ray answered.

Black nodded.

"Good!" James said, standing. "Let's get this deal over with, so we can retire to our respective homes and rest.

"That's the move," Black said, anxious to get back to Connie and the kids, who he'd spent all morning shopping with.

James began removing the stacked bills from the table and placing them back into the safe. Once he placed the record book on top of the money, he closed the steel door and slid his key into the top lock, connecting the bolt. The others followed suit, donned their coats, and exited the office.

"Y'all go ahead," Ray told them. "I'ma catch this bathroom."

Ray headed for the bathroom as the others exited the building. It was after seven, and the sun had already set for tonight, but it was not quite dark yet. They saw that Bobby had backed all four trucks into the loading docks, giving the warehouse the look of a legit-functioning business. He was leaned against a blue Mazda Protégé, with his fiancée cradled in his arms. Grip and two other Kingzmen were standing off to the side, holding the dogs at bay.

As The Kingz approached the Mazda, Bobby and his wife-to-be, turned to face them. That's when they all recognized her. As if they were thinking the same thing, they exchanged quick glances and simultaneously glanced back at the entrance.

Fred didn't waste time. He thanked Bobby and handed him the money, as Bobby handed him four sets of keys and tried to explain which set belonged to which truck.

"We'll sort it out," Black cut in, taking another glance at the entrance.

"I wanna introduce y'all to my fiancée, Trina," Bobby said proudly.

'*Is this nigga serious!*' Fred thought. '*Did he forget that they were highly familiar with this bitch? That Ray used to so-call date this slut? Or, did he not know that Ray was a part of this organization?*' Perhaps he did and intentionally brought her by to rub it in, which was extremely dangerous, considering the state Ray had been in since Sylvia's death.

The faint click of the entrance door got everyone's attention. When Ray emerged, it seemed like the whole world stopped, and he was the only person moving as he made it to the rear of his BMW and leaned against the trunk, looking out at them. His facial expression was unreadable.

\*\*\*\*

James had already told Shonda he was going to pick her up after he left his first meeting, so she was ready when he arrived. After taking her to get something to eat, he dropped her off at his house and headed for Knight Park, where he met Grip and two other Kingzmen on a deserted road. There was a blue Ford Mustang, and a gray Chevy Celebrity, parked, with the engines running. Once James gave them their instructions, he climbed behind the wheel of the Mustang and headed for Hollywood Courts to meet with Carlos.

"Come on in, my nigga," Carlos said, letting James in. "I didn't think a man of your status would even travel to the hood at night."

"I can't fear something I helped build," James stated, taking offense, but not letting it show.

"I like that!" Carlos said, smiling. "Have a seat. "You want a beer?"

"Yeah."

Carlos headed for the kitchen, and James took a seat in the living room, wondering where Carlos' pit bull was. Carlos returned with two beers, handed one to James, and copped a seat on the sofa.

"Where the dog at?" James inquired.

"Shit, I left that bitch at my sista's crib," Carlos answered. "She does the breeding. So, if y'all want some pits, get at me."

"I'll remember that," James said, pulling a small paper bag from his inner coat pocket and handing it to him. "I appreciate the business."

"Glad I could help," Carlos placed the package on the table. "I hope y'all got everything straightened out."

"Yeah, we good."

They conversed for another fifteen minutes, or so until they suddenly heard a loud crash come from next door. They exchanged glances before Carlos quickly pulled a pistol-grip pump from under the sofa, keeping a wary eye on James, who maintained a puzzled look. Convinced James wasn't part of this sudden intrusion, he cocked the gun and moved towards the secret door that led to the adjacent apartment. James made his move. He was out of his seat in no time, clutching a Glock. Carlos must've sensed his proximity, but it was too late. Before he could turn the pump on James, he caught two slugs in the head and slumped to the floor.

James already knew that his men were next door, raiding Carlos' stash spot, so he reholstered the Glock, grabbed the bag of money and his beer off the table, then exited the apartment, being careful not to touch the doorknob with his bare hands.

****

The next morning, James couldn't wait to drop Shonda off and take his share of last night's heist to Kado, who was going to cook and at the same time, teach him how to cook the cocaine, in which he should've learned from Fred, a long time ago.

Carlos' stash only consisted of seven keys that were split between him and his accomplices. There was no money, which made James wish that he'd searched the main apartment, but anything was better than nothing.

"What 'cha got?" Kado asked once they entered his kitchen.

"You know I charge extra for *Glass Pot One-o-One*,' right?"

"You already told me that," said James, dumping the product on the table.

Three hours later, James was leaving Herndon Homes, and on his way to University Homes to meet with Barlow at his sister's apartment, with a package he'd prepared at Kado's. James knew his mother was upset about him canceling Sunday dinner, but he had something planned for his fellow Kingz tonight.

****

Ray could not figure out why, or how he still let Trina get to him, after all this time. Probably because he still loves her, which he would never admit. Which is why he hadn't ordered the Kingzmen to take her ass out. *Her and Bobby*!

'*The type of women niggas would pledge their troth to*,' Ray thought as he exited the highway, remembering Joe's instructions on how to get to his house.

He'd never been to Douglasville, but he'd heard constant rumors of how quick the police were to get behind anybody that resembled a drug dealer, which is why he sagely pushed the Oldsmobile through Douglas County until he came upon Joe's house. The house looked quite expensive, but it was the kind of house Ray expected Joe to dwell in. He exuded the ambiance of a nigga that was faring well.

Ray pulled into the driveway and parked alongside the Infiniti truck that sat outside the two-car garage that was closed. He'd counted, at least six kids running around, playing in the yard before he exited the car. They all stopped to see if they knew him.

"Stop being nosey!"

Ray looked up to see Joe standing in the front door, smiling at the kids, who laughed at his joke and continued playing.

"You gotta excuse my nosey kids," Joe told Ray when he approached the door. "Come on in."

Ray followed Joe into the living room, where Valerie and two other females were engaged in conversation.

"Hey, Ray!" Valerie beamed, then introduced the two women as her sister and friend.

"We'll be in the garage," Joe told his wife.

"Should I bring y'all some beer?" she asked.

"I don't think Ray—" Joe started, looking at Ray, who was already shaking his head. "I'll grab one on the way out."

Joe did just that, and they made it to the garage, where a gray Chevy Lumina and a bowling ball-orange-colored Ford Crown Victoria on chrome wheels sat. Ray figured the Lumina was Joe's low-key car, being that it had no special effects.

"Have a seat Pimpin'," said Joe, taking a seat in one of the four lawn chairs.

The atmosphere was warm, so Ray shed his light jacket, and took a seat.

"I know those pieces cost a grip!" Joe asserted, eyeing Ray's chain.

"Pretty much," Ray answered, absently fingering it. "So, what kind of numbers your trap be doing?"

"I ain't really got no trap," Joe answered. "I just know a lot of niggas in the South who smokes. That's how I get off."

"But you only fuck with it every now and then," Ray said, more of a statement than a question.

"Yeah." Joe took a sip of his beer. "For some extra cash."

"Why not make it consistent?" Ray asked. "We can put our bread together and cop a bell."

"Shit, I'm quite sure y'all can do that without me."

"Ain't no 'y'all,'" Ray rectified, then explained to Joe how he'd been running his own business before *The Kingz* came about. "Those are my niggaz," he continued. "But I'd rather keep my shit independent."

"I feel that," Joe said, looking as if he was considering Ray's proposal.

****

Black's plan was to spend all day with his kids, have dinner as a family and meet Nikki at Publix to relinquish Lil' Keith and Nicole. Then drop Kevin off, return home and hit Connie off with some good lovemaking. Well, that was until James called and informed him of a Kingz Dinner, tonight. Connie was a bit upset because she was also looking forward to having dinner with the kids, who she'd already grown attached to. But as always, she was empathetic to his organization and their line of work. Black didn't want to strip her of that, so he told her to go ahead and have dinner with the kids, meet with Nikki to turn Lil' Keith and Nicole over to her, then he would take Kevin home.

"I'll take him home," Connie had insisted.

"Nah, baby," he told her, knowing Felicia would raise hell, and bring down heaven if he permitted such a feat, but he did call Felicia and informed her of the change of plans.

Black kissed Connie and the kids and was out the door. He couldn't imagine how, or what kind of dinner they would have at The Palace, but as James instructed, he pulled into the parking lot around 6:30 p.m. To his surprise, there was a black, stretched Cadillac Escalade parked in front of the building.

Fred, James, and Ray, who were all dressed in suit and tie, and adorned with their chains were standing near the truck, conversing with the Kingzmen. Grip, along with three others, was clad in black dress suits, so Black assumed they were the ones who were going to accompany them, trailing them to the mid-size SUV.

Almost an hour later, The Kingz entered an exquisite restaurant out in Rome, Georgia where upper class predominately White people were dining as soft, barely audible, jazz music played in the background. They had never been to anything like this, so they including James, who'd made the arrangements were impressed.

"May I have your names, gentlemen?" asked the frail-looking, older White male who met them at the entrance.

"Kingz," James answered with much authority.

The man stared at James for a moment as if he hadn't heard a thing, before donning his extremely small reading glasses and checking the logbook.

"Ah!" the old man exclaimed. "The Kingz, and you will be dining with The Queenz, who, I'm afraid, hasn't arrived yet, but your table is ready."

He flagged down a waiter, a young White guy by the name of Edward, who showed them to their table, where there were eight chairs, and cards on the table that indicated where each King was to sit, which left an empty chair between each of them.

The waiter disappeared with the promise of bringing breadsticks, and their pre-ordered champagne as The Kingz took their seats, surveying the restaurant to see that most of the small crowd were actually watching them.

"They act like they ain't never seen four men have dinner before," James joked, getting a laugh from Fred and Black. Ray, James noticed, just toyed with his cell phone.

Two bottles of champagne on ice and breadsticks arrived. Once the waiter poured four glasses and left, The Kingz enjoyed the champagne, bread, and indulged in small conversation, but no one asked about *The Queenz* who were supposed to be dining with them. Hell, knowing James, he'd probably called an escort service and ordered four Asian women for the evening.

"Kingz," the old man interrupted them. "May I present your Queenz!"

The old man left, and there stood Shonda, Theresa, Ebony and yes, you guessed it Sheila, casually dressed for the occasion, wearing heels and posing like they were at a grown and sexy photo shoot. James stood, prompting his comrades to follow suit.

"Y'all look good!" James complimented, pulling out a chair for Shonda. "Now, can we eat?"

Everybody followed suit, except Ray, who just watched Sheila as she pulled out her own chair and sat down like she wasn't expecting Ray to be a gentleman. He didn't know if this was a front, or a clone, because this was definitely not the same chick, he'd encountered at the New Year Eve's party. But Ray didn't care, because he wasn't in the mood for none of her shit. So, whatever tricks she and James had up their sleeves, was going to backfire in their faces. Straight up!

"Hey, y'all!" Sheila spoke, pushing one of her long, brown curls out of her face. "I wanna apologize for the way I was acting on the night we met. I was just going through something at the time."

The Kingz all exchanged glances, but everyone's gaze seemed to automatically land on Ray like he was the one who held the power to forgive her. But Ray rejected them, took a sip of his beverage, and pretended to take interest in the chandelier above their table. Seeing this, James immediately looked around for Edward, who was already en route to their table.

"May I pour The Queenz a glass of champagne?" Edward asked, passing out menus.

"Yes, you may," Shonda answered, obviously relishing the title James had fabricated for the girls to use as a means of identification upon entering the restaurant. "Thank you, ah—"

"Edward, Your Majesty," Edward answered, refilling The Kingz glasses, also.

"Yes, thank you, Edward," Shonda said, slapping James on the thigh. "Baby give the man a tip!"

James glowered at her, then looked up at the waiter, who was standing there as if he was actually anticipating a tip.

"Shit don't drink and drive!" James spat, prompting laughter from everyone around the table except Ray.

"James!" Shonda exclaimed, now punching James in his thigh.

"Here you go, Edward." Sheila handed him a five-dollar bill.

"Thank you, Your Highness."

Sheila nodded.

"When you all are ready to order, give me a holler," Edward said, then walked away, five dollars richer.

"So, how have you been, Ray?" Sheila asked, looking into Ray's face like the answer to her question would magically appear.

"I've been a'ight," he answered, scanning his menu to avoid eye contact. '*I can do this shit all night,*' he thought.

Dinner was going well with the help of the champagne, which had loosened everybody up, causing conversation to come with ease. All the while, James had been subtly keeping an eye on Ray, who still seemed to be mourning Sylvia. Sheila, who'd proven to be the silliest one out of the four girls, had periodically tried to get Ray's attention, to no avail.

Just as James had been watching Ray, Shonda had also been watching her silly-ass cousin make a fool of herself. She had been asking about Ray, ever since she'd heard of Sylvia's passing. When Shonda told Sheila about tonight's dinner, and that James wanted her to come along, the first thing she asked was, "Is Ray gonna be there?" Now, Shonda was feeling sorry for her cousin, because she knew Sheila really liked Ray, but the nigga was treating her like she was a groupie, when she was far from that.

This made her wish that she hadn't brought Sheila, but she still didn't feel right about leaving her at home alone. She'd been feeling that way ever since they were kids. What happened to Sheila, was all her fault, and she was going to carry that guilt to her grave.

Dessert had arrived and, while they ate, James announced that they had one more spot to hit up. So, after they'd eaten, everyone headed for the restroom to relieve themselves, and to freshen up.

Being that the girls' limousine was to just drop them off at the restaurant, they all piled into the stretched Escalade and headed out, with only James and the driver knowing the destination. It didn't take long for Fred to discern where they were going when the truck exited off at the East Point exit.

'*This is just like James,*' Fred thought when the truck pulled into the parking lot of the bowling alley. Now, he wished he'd brought his gun.

It was just after ten o'clock, and the place was pretty much packed. They all dismounted the truck, looking around at the onlookers who'd stopped what they were doing to see who was stunting so hard at a low-budget, run-down bowling alley.

"Why'd we come to some bullshit like this?" Ebony, who'd been making sexual advances at Black, all night, asked in disgust.

"To bowl," James answered, leading the way.

A gang of men wearing Drop Squad chains was standing by the entrance, looking like they were there to prevent anyone not affiliated with them, from entering.

"What y'all niggas ain't gon move?" James asked, visibly sizing them up.

For a moment, they looked as if they were going to put up a fight, so automatically, Fred, Black, and Ray stepped forward, putting the girls behind them. James already knew Grip and another Kingzman was standing in the midst. Plus, the two

Kingzmen who were driving the limousine and SUV, were heavily armed.

But the kids didn't want any problems. They reluctantly stepped aside, allowing them entrance. Being that this was one of the Drop Squad's regular hang out spots, there were Drop Squad chains all over the place. Some even stopped to gander at the new arrivals.

*'That's right, the Kingz are in this bitch!'* James thought as he led the way to the counter, where they were to exchange their shoes for bowling shoes.

After a moment of protesting from the women, they gave in, and everybody headed for the two lanes at the far end that seemed to be out of order.

"We can't play here," Sheila asserted. "They don't even—"

At that instance, the lights and monitor came alive at the end lane, leaving the other one dark, where Grip and the other Kingzman would stand guard.

"I hope y'all ready," said James, rubbing his palms together. "It's The Kingz against The Queenz!"

Yes, it was the battle of the sexes, and they were already three games in, with the men in the lead. They were having so much fun, they had managed to draw a small crowd, with the men cheering the men, and the women cheering the women on. On several occasions, when it was Ray's turn, Sheila would hand him his bowling ball, sparking an *aww* from the crowd, in which she would blushingly smile, and take her seat.

Each time, Fred would find himself smiling, because, although Ray would slight her when she did this, they actually seemed like the perfect couple. They shared the same characteristics when it came to sense of humor. Perhaps she would be the one to pull Ray out of the stupor he was in.

Black checked his watch to see that it was almost twelve o'clock. Ebony wanted him to spend the night with her, but he declined, telling her he would have to get up with her later, in the week. Right now, his mind was on getting home, so he could get Kevin home and spend some make-up time with Connie. He conveyed this to James, so when the fourth game was over, with the girls tying the score. James announced that it was time to go, but the girls were not hearing it. They felt they were on the brink of winning and wanted to break the tie. So, once everyone concurred with the girls including the crowd the tie-breaking game began. The Kingz won.

## CHAPTER 22

Wednesday rolled around and Black had been quite busy. Connie had been accepted at Atlanta Tech, where she'd be taking Business and Cosmetology classes. Black sold her car to a used car dealership and bought her a Range Rover. He also took her shopping for a new wardrobe.

"Are you trying to change my mind?" she asked while they were shopping.

"Nah," he lied. "Why would you ask me that?"

"Because it seems like you're picking out everything."

Black didn't know what to say, he was guilty. Everything he'd picked out for her had no similarity to anything she already had at home. It was all casual and costly. She was his girl and she represented him. So, he was going to make sure she represented him right. Especially in front of that bitch, Felicia!

"Baby, you're going to be taking business classes," he finally managed. "You should, at least, look like a businesswoman."

****

Ray was sitting in his Delta Eighty-Eight, parked in Kroger's parking lot with the engine running listening to *T.I.'s Trap Muzik*. The Kingz was out of cocaine, but this visit with Poppo was different, in which Poppo had insisted they go to his place. When the white Lexus pulled into the parking lot, and they flashed their lights at each other, the Lexus made a U-turn, and Ray followed. But upon leaving the parking lot, the Lexus went the opposite way of the apartments Poppo claimed he stayed in. Then, it turned down a street Ray didn't bother to catch the name of because he was too busy trying to figure out what was going on. Poppo didn't seem like the type that would pull a set-up stunt. Plus, Ray didn't have a bad feeling about this at all.

After a couple more turns, the Lexus pulled into the driveway of a white house, parking behind a burgundy Lexus truck. Ray parked in front of the house. He waited until Poppo got out before dismounting and following him to the front door.

"This must be your girl's crib?" Ray inquired.

"Yeah, she *wish*!" Poppo answered, laughing. "You didn't think I would invite a King to the projects, did you?"

Ray didn't respond. Poppo opened the door, and they entered. The house resembled a family home, more than it did a drug dealer's, being that there were toys, stuffed animals and family pictures here and there.

"I got some Heineken in the fridge if you—"

"I'm decent," Ray cut him off, ready to get down to business.

"You hollered at 'cha folks up top?"

"Yeah," Poppo answered. "Have a seat." Once they were seated in the living room, he went on. "They won't just trust anybody, but they've heard of The Kingz. Plus, they'll do it on the strength of me, but it won't be coming from New York. They're connected with some dread nigga in Miami, who does all the trafficking."

"I really don't care where it comes from," Ray said. "I wanna know when I make the transaction."

"They already know what you want," Poppo told him. "As soon as I hit them back, they'll get at Thang, and set it up."

"And Thang is supposed to be the dread nigga?"

"Yeah."

"Is he trustworthy?"

\*\*\*\*

"Shit, you're doing good for a nigga who don't sell white," James told Spenz.

James was sitting on the living room sofa, counting out bills on the coffee table. Spenz was, indeed, doing a good job of getting off the cocaine, although Barlow had surpassed him and Moe, all together. The nigga said he was a trap star, and proved it, which is why, on the next package, Barlow would be on his own two feet.

"I'd rather sell weed at the club," Spenz responded. "And niggas been asking for that shit too."

"I don't know why Ray ain't hit you up on that," said James. "But give me a few days, I'll have you back in there."

"That's what's up," Spenz said, receiving the new package, and walking James to the door. "You know they got that Battle of the DJs coming up this year?"

"Oh, yeah?" James was not interested.

"Hell yeah!" Spenz exclaimed. "All the DJs are gonna be there! DJ Snake, DJ Red Alert, DJ Clue, DJ Drama, DJ Goldfinger, me, that fine ass DJ Diamond Kuts, and some other local niggas. That shit's gonna be off the chain!"

"My nigga Goldfinger won that shit last year didn't he?"

"Oh, you just gon' rub that shit in, huh?"

James laughed knowing Spenz hated when he spoke of DJ Goldfinger, who'd grown up in Bland Town with him and Ray.

"You know they be looking for celebrity judges," Spenz told him. "Hood-rich niggas 'N shit. Niggas like y'all."

Now, James was interested. "How do they determine who judge the event?"

"I don't know, but I can find out."

"Yeah, do that, I'ma get up wit' 'cha."

They dapped, and James made his exit. He hadn't gotten ten feet, when he spotted Spenz's younger cousin, J-Bo, and another young dude, headed in his direction with book bags on their backs.

"What up, King James!" J-Bo greeted.

"What it do lil' homie!" James gave him dap.

"I can't call it," J-Bo replied. "I'm still waiting on y'all to put some money behind me, so I can take the rap game by a storm."

James laughed. "You're an arrogant lil nigga! I like that, but we ain't messing with that music shit, right now."

"Well, if you help me make the money, I'll do it myself."

James already knew what the young nigga was insinuating and being that he was always looking for a few good men. He told J-Bo to give him a few days and he would put him and his friend whose name was Mat on, so they could lock Banneker High down together.

**\*\*\*\***

Ray and Precious hadn't done much talking since they'd ended their sexual relationship and agreed to resume with strictly business. They definitely weren't doing much talking now as they sat at the kitchen table, counting the money from the stash, and the money he'd brought from his personal stash at home to put with Joe's half when he arrived.

After leaving Poppo's house yesterday, Ray didn't expect to hear from him for a few days, but Poppo had called him at ten, this morning to inform him that Thang would meet him in Cordele, Georgia, around ten tonight.

"He wants five for the drive," Poppo told him.

"Five stacks!" Ray exclaimed. "Shit, I might as well drive to Miami and get my own shit!"

But Poppo had convinced him that the trafficker was worth it, which is why he was now waiting on Joe to come through with his half, and the rental car. Being that this was Ray's first-time purchasing weight without his fellow Kingz being present, he felt skeptical. James wanted to send the Kingzmen with him, but Ray declined. Instead, he called on B.J. and T-Roc, who would tail him and Joe, and watch the transaction from a distance.

Someone knocked on the door. Sensing it was a customer, Precious answered it. It was Joe, he entered, carrying a large, brown paper bag. By the time they were half-way through counting Joe's half, B.J. and T-Roc had shown up. Ray's plan was to get to Cordele, at least, an hour early, to check out the drop area, and map an escape route, just in case shit went sour.

Once they decided everything was everything and was ready to go, Ray entered his old bedroom and closed the door. Hanging in the closet was a black trench coat. Before putting it on, he grabbed the Mac-11 from the top shelf, tested the strap attached to it, then threw the strap over his head, letting the gun hang at his left side. He grabbed his coat, but before he could put it on, Precious tapped on the door and entered. She looked like she was about to say something, but stood there with her mouth agape, and her eyes transfixed on the sub-machine gun.

"What's up?" Ray asked, donning the trench.

"Um, nothing." She placed a hand over her chest.

They locked eyes as she backed out, closing the door back. Ray noticed that her hazel always seductive eyes didn't convey their usual sexiness. This time, they had a look that sent chills up his spine.

**\*\*\*\***

It had taken almost forty minutes to case out Crisp County and map an escape route. Now, Ray and Joe were back at the drop spot, which was the parking lot of a Chinese restaurant, called Chong Yong. Since they had time to spare, he and Joe managed to grab a bite to eat from the restaurant that to their surprise also sold soul food.

"Man, where this nigga at?" Ray looked at his watch to see that it was twelve minutes after ten.

He was sitting on the passenger side of the rented Dodge Charger, with the Mac-11 Fred gave him, resting in his lap.

"Shit, it's about an eight-hour drive from that muhfucka!" Joe explained. "Hell, he probably—"

His words were cut short when the headlights of a dark-colored SUV shone through the windshield as it entered the parking lot. The three occupants sported dreadlocks.

"These niggas look like somma them *real* Jamaican niggas!" Joe joked as the truck parked directly across from them, cutting the lights.

"This better be the drop," said Ray, now thinking of the look Precious had given him that sent chills up his spine. Now, he was experiencing those chills again.

"Do we get out first?" Joe asked, seeing that the dreads didn't budge.

Ray was ready to get this over with. "Blink the lights!"

Joe flashed the headlights and got the same response.

"Let's do this!" Ray said, exiting the Dodge, letting the Mac-11 hang inside his trench, and turning his *Kingz* medallion over, so they'd know who they were dealing with.

Joe grabbed the large paper bag from the back seat, and they approached the truck as the dreads were dismounting.

"Pat dem down!" the passenger commanded the other two.

"No need to," Ray asserted, holding a hand up. "We're strapped."

"Me need your guns," the passenger insisted.

"You must be Thang?" Ray asked him.

"Yar mon, I'm T'ing," he answered. "Da' original Don Dotta!"

"And I'm King Ray. The one and only!" Ray felt he had to rep his own title. "Now that that's outta the way, let's do business. Can we see the product?"

****

I hope these dread-head muhfuckas don't pull no bullshit, James thought as he, Fred, Black, and the Kingzmen watched from some woods, opposite from where B.J. and T-Roc were. They were all dressed in black and carrying nothing less than sub-machine guns.

When Ray had told him of the transaction, he offered to send the Kingzmen. Ray declined, but James had already made up in his mind that he was not going to let his little brother make this trip without proper protection. Fred and Black felt the same way, which is why they'd chosen to tag along.

They had inconspicuously trailed B.J. and T-Roc, in two rental cars, as they drove around the small town, presumably planning an escape route, in case something jumped off, but truth be told, if something jumped off, Ray wouldn't be the one needing an escape route.

Now, they watched as Ray conversed with one of the men. Minutes later, they approached the rear of the truck.

"We lost our targets," one of the Kingzmen said. He was laying on the ground, looking through a night vision scope attached to a rifle.

"Just maintain your positions!" Grip commanded.

James really wanted to rob these niggas but didn't want to bring heat on Ray, or whoever he was dealing through. Besides, he already had some other shit planned.

Playa Ray

## CHAPTER 23

James had promised Spenz and J-Bo that he would have them some weed in a few days, but the only people he knew he could cop a couple of pounds from were Eric and Ray. He didn't know if Ray had planned on getting back at Spenz after copping that shipment last night. He didn't want to cop any from Ray and raise suspicion, just in case. So, he chose to indirectly deal with Eric, telling him he knew somebody who wanted to cop a couple of pounds.

"Shit, why you ain't holla at, Ray?" Eric asked while cutting James' hair. "He got the lowest prices in Georgia."

"Bullshit!" James eyed Eric through the huge mirror to see if he was serious.

"Nah, straight up," Eric said, spinning James back around to face Shonda, who was seated in the waiting area. "He hit me up earlier and put me on point."

"Won't that affect you in a way?" James asked, trying to see what kind of vibe he'd get from Eric.

"It could in the long run," Eric responded. "But that's part of the game. If you ask me, he's doing the right thing. Plus, I salute him for giving me heads up."

"Yeah, that was some real shit," said James, glad to see that Eric was taking it well. "So, you gon' turn down this business I'm trying to bring to you?"

"These some people you deal with on the regular?"

"Of course," James answered winking at Shonda, who he was going to use to purchase the product.

\*\*\*\*

Ray, Joe, and Precious spent all day Thursday, breaking the bell down half in pounds, half in ounces. Joe had taken his half back to Douglasville, and Ray's half remained in Maple Creek.

After calling Eric and informing him on his product and low competitive prices, Ray called Spenz and told him he was pushing nothing less than an ounce.

"Shit, I'm with that!" Spenz agreed. "Count me back in!"

"That's a bet," Ray said. "Can't say too much on the phone, so I'll swing by tomorrow, and let you know what's what."

"A'ight."

Well, tomorrow had finally arrived and Ray was ready to get down to business. He'd made calls to some of his regular customers, last night, giving them the good news and for the ones whose numbers he didn't know, Precious would inform them whenever they drop into the shop. Thinking of Precious, Ray wanted to get her something for being understanding and staying down with his movement. Even if it was for her own benefit, so he stopped by a jewelry store and had her a platinum ring made with the letter 'P' encrusted in diamonds, in which the jeweler placed in a small, black box with a red ribbon tied around it into a bow.

Ray was going to present the ring to her right before he made his exit, so when he pulled into Maple Creek, parked the Delta and dismounted, he tucked the small box into the inner pocket of his black leather coat. This made him feel like he was going to propose to Precious, which made him think of that slut, Trina, and pussy whipped Bobby.

He expeditiously pushed those thoughts out of his mind as he entered the all too quiet apartment. Before he could make any assumptions as to where, or what Precious could be doing. He spotted a yellow letter envelope on the kitchen table, standing erect between the salt and pepper shakers.

"Now, what?" he mumbled as he grabbed the envelope that had '*To Ray*' in blue ink. Preparing for the inevitable, he tore open the envelope and read the enclosed letter.

*Dear Ray,*

*I'm sorry we didn't work out. I guess I wasn't the one for you. Or, perhaps you're looking for something more. Anyway, I've decided to move in with Bree. I moved the rest of my things to storage this morning. Well, I guess this is goodbye. Thanks for everything!*

*~Precious~*

Ray read the contents two more times to make sure he hadn't missed anything. Then, as if it was a subliminal message, he reverted back to the last three words— *Thanks for everything!*

"I know this bitch didn't!" he spoke through clenched teeth as he rushed towards his stash room, where everything seemed to be in order, but he still took the initiative and the fifteen minutes to make assessments. Everything was in order, she hadn't taken anything. Not even her week's pay.

**** 

The Kingz had run out of product a couple of days ago, but James was still good on his personal stash. He was waiting on Barlow to hit him up any minute to collect and serve him with his own order. He was losing a worker but gaining a customer because Barlow had agreed to shop with him, but James knew he had to accumulate more workers. Therefore, he was going to wait until after they'd copped the fifty kilos from Franco, tomorrow, then put forward the part of his plan that he'd been anticipating since the day he'd come up with the movement.

Now, he was pulling his BMW into College Park Projects, but quickly made a U-turn when he spotted Ray's Delta, already parked.

"What's wrong?" Shonda asked from the passenger's seat.

James didn't answer her as he exited the apartments, dialing Spenz's cell phone.

"This Spenz," he answered.

"Call me when he leaves," James told him.

Minutes later, James pulled into a gas station and parked by the pay phones, leaving the engine running.

"Is everything alright?" Shonda tried again.

"Just a minor delay."

He looked over at Shonda, who was clad in blue, snug-fitted jeans, a red, light-weight jacket, with her brown micro-braids pulled back into a ponytail. She didn't know anything about the drug game until James taught her how to cook cocaine, and how to use a scale.

He like her and had no intentions of getting her involved in the game, but she was so thorough and attentive. He offered her the position of being his assistant, in which she immediately accepted, and quit her job at a fast foods joint in Stone Mountain, Georgia, but for some reason, she always seemed worried about being away from Sheila for a long period of time, which was a bit too odd to him.

James was just about to question her insecurity when his phone rang. It was Spenz, informing him that Ray had just left. His mind back on business, he pulled out of the gas station and headed back to Spenz's place.

"Do I stay in the car?" Shonda asked once James had parked.

"I don't pay you to stay in the car," he answered. "Where the package at?"

"In my pocketbook."

He didn't tell her to stuff the package into her pocketbook, but he sure as hell wasn't about to reprimand her for it. Instead, he got out and headed for Spenz's apartment, with Shonda on his heels. Spenz already had the door open.

"What's the word?" James asked as they entered.

"Nothing but ounces," Spenz answered.

"Damn!" James exclaimed. "A nigga can't get a half ounce— a quarter?"

"Man, ya boy ain't bullshittin'!" Spenz told him. "He's about to step on a lot of niggas toes with them low-ass prices! Niggas will fuck around and have to switch to Geico!"

'Spenz is right,' James thought, but what Ray was doing, had been going on for centuries. The drug game had always been competitive. Niggas did what they had to do to eat and survive. It'll be that way until the world ends.

James conversed with Spenz for a few more minutes, dropped the package off, then had Shonda drive to Banneker High, to unexpectedly meet with J-Bo and Mat. He just hoped he would catch them before they boarded the school bus. Therefore, he had Shonda park close to the entrance, and got out, leaning against the car, looking around at the school buses that were only occupied by the drivers.

Minutes later, the last bell of the day rang, and the kids came pouring out of the building, most of them thanking God it was Friday as they made for their buses or vehicles of their awaiting parents. Surely, J-Bo and Mat could not miss him, when his car and unsubtle Kingz medallion had captured the attention of the students passing by, or just standing around.

After ten minutes of waiting, James had begun to think the youngsters had probably skipped school. So, after a few more minutes, James gave up, but as he was about to climb back into the car, someone called his name. He turned to see J-Bo, Mat and a young girl approaching.

"You looking for me?" J-Bo asked.

"Both of y'all," James opened the rear passenger door. "Hop in!"

J-Bo didn't hesitate. Mat was about to let the girl climb in behind J-Bo.

"Who is this?" James asked, causing her to stop in her tracks.

"Shonte," Mat answered. "My girlfriend."

"She'll have to miss this ride," James told him.

Shonte looked at Mat like she was expecting him to fend for her. Instead, he pulled her off to the side to talk to her, but the girl appeared to be putting up a fight. She was feisty, but Mat, who appeared to be a young Casanova, subdued her within seconds.

The scene reminded him of how he and Kim were back when they were high school sweethearts. Now, he was wondering what she was doing, and if she'd had the baby yet, being that she was expecting to deliver in February.

**** 

The Kingz were ready to re-up, which is why they were on their way to Lithonia, Georgia, in a rented Cadillac CTS. To their surprise, Franco had chosen the exact same spot to meet up. Plus, he was more than happy to supply them with the fifty kilos they'd asked for, when, in the beginning, he would only supply ten to the newcomers.

Black pulled the Cadillac onto the deserted dirt road and parked, leaving the engine running, but the Kingz didn't have to wait long, because, before they could start to relax, the same two white Cadillac Escalades pulled in, parking at the same distance.

The Kingz got out and gathered on the right side of the car, with James holding the briefcase. Then, Franco and his seven soldiers dismounted. Franco flashed some kind of hand gesture to his armed men, then stepped forward with three of them in tow.

"The Kingz!" Franco exclaimed, shaking their hands. "You guys have proven yourselves worthy of my respect. I hope to continue doing business with you all." He looked at James. "Shall we?"

James followed Franco to the truck as the three guards backed away with their guns still trained on Fred, Ray, and Black. Once again, James was frisked, but he wasn't armed this time. Then, instead of getting into the back seat of the first truck, they went to the rear of it, where Franco opened the compartment, and James laid the briefcase beside a large, black gym bag.

"I don't feel like I need to count the money," said Franco, unzipping the gym bag. "But if you wanna test the product, I'm cool with that."

"It's the same shit, right?" James asked, examining one of the neatly wrapped kilos.

'*Something about this shit don't feel right,*' Fred thought as he watched the scene.

It wasn't the fact that he didn't like being held at gunpoint by apparently U.S. soldiers, because he definitely didn't like that, but there was something very uncanny about the whole scene.

Then Fred's suspicion was confirmed.

James did some kind of swift gesture with his right hand, then came the sound of firecrackers in a distance, causing everyone to recoil, except for Franco and three of his men, who had actually fallen to the ground with blood oozing from their heads. These were not firecrackers!

Playa Ray

# CHAPTER 24

It didn't take long for Fred to discern what was transpiring. The shots had come from the wooded area to the right of them. He did a quick sweep of the area but didn't see anyone, although it was still daytime. Then he looked at Ray and Black, who had equally stunned looks on their faces. More gunshots rang out.

The remaining troops being the trained soldiers they were were returning fire, ducking behind the second truck for cover. Fred noticed that James had grabbed a black gym bag and the briefcase from the back of the first truck, and walked around the other side, moving as if none of this was taking place. Like he was incapable of being hit by stray bullets.

Before James could circle the truck, Fred saw that one of the troops had turned his AK-47 on them. Fred didn't know at what part of the ordeal he'd drawn his Beretta, but it was in his hand, and now aimed at the soldier. They let off shots, simultaneously, as Black dove across the hood of the CTS, but Fred had to actually push Ray to the other side of the car, as he returned fire and caught slugs to the upper body. He screamed out in pain as he and Ray collapsed to the ground.

James rounded the truck in time to see one of the troops gun Ray and Fred down, which was something he did not intend to happen. In a towering rage, he dropped the bag and briefcase, walked over to one of the deceased soldiers a black female relieved her of her AK-47, and emptied the clip on the remaining soldiers, leaving them for dead.

Dropping the gun, James checked his watch. He then, retrieved the bag and briefcase, and moved briskly towards the car, he saw that Fred was sitting with his back against the left front tire, and Ray, who appeared to be unharmed, was helping him out of his blazer. Black was leaned against the rear tire, holding his gun and sweating profusely.

"Everything's clear," James told them. "Fred, where are you hit?"

Before Fred could answer, a black GMC van pulled in, moving at a fast pace, startling Ray and Black, who were now standing with their guns aimed at the unfamiliar vehicle.

"They're with us," James asserted, moving towards the van as it came to a halt.

Grip and one of the Kingzmen got out, received instructions from James, then rushed over to help Fred to the van's cargo area that was carpeted. Before James, Ray, and Black got into the van, they watched the Kingzmen pour gas all over the CTS and set it on fire.

\*\*\*\*

Fred was glad he'd worn a bullet-proof vest on the day they'd met with Franco. He was even more relieved when Sharonda who happens to be a nurse at Grady Memorial Hospital informed him that the hit he'd taken was only a flesh wound. He was still furious at James for the asinine stunt he'd pulled, that could have gotten them all killed, which is why he'd declared the Kingz take two weeks off, followed by a Kingz meeting. Well, those two weeks were up, and Fred was ready to be heard.

"This meeting is informal," Fred told his comrades, who had still taken the initiative to don suits and ties. "James, you should already know why I called this meeting. A King is never wrong in another Kingz eyes, but when it comes to reckless, suicidal stunts like the one you pulled two weeks ago. I disagree! Does any other King agree with me on that?"

"I do," said Black, who'd spent the last two weeks with Connie, and weekends with her and the kids.

"Yeah, me too," said Ray, who'd spent the last two weeks in Maple Creek, holding down the trap spot, being that Precious had gotten ghost on him.

"Hell, I agree myself," added James, who'd still been active these past two weeks. Hiring new workers, claiming new territory and putting the word out that the Kingz had the kilos, ounces, and half ounces for the low, which is why he already had a few customers on standby, ready to switch to Geico.

"I know I put y'all lives in danger," James continued. "And I accept whatever punishment y'all impose on me. But y'all know I had y'all covered. My Kingzmen are trained marksmen."

"So were Franco's men," Fred asserted, noticing James said *my*, instead of *our* Kingzmen.

"Franco's men are deceased!" James spat. "The Kingzmen came out unscathed! The Kingz came out with one wounded! Come on, y'all! This is the same shit we did to come up in the first place!"

"But everybody knew what was, what," Fred countered. "We mapped shit out. Now, suppose I didn't wear a vest?"

"But you did."

"But suppose I didn't?"

"I can't say what the outcome would've been," James admitted truthfully. "But I'm glad you did. Now, what's my punishment?"

Fred pondered this for a while, then asked Ray and Black if they had any suggestions. They didn't, and Fred really didn't know what to do with James. Who he should have expected that kind of behavior from. Perhaps he did, which is why he'd worn the vest.

"I can't think of anything, right now," Fred admitted. "But that doesn't mean you're off the hook. The next time you plan on pulling some shit like that, make sure we know what's up!"

"I'll do that," James avowed. "Now can we get back to the money?"

****

The Kingz were back on their grind, and the money was coming in like never before. Now that they had runners, they didn't have to make any drops, which gave them ample free time. Ray was concentrating his time and energy on his weed trap, with his rapidly-growing clientele. By this time, he and Joe had grown real close, visiting each other's homes, and hanging out together. Ray had even introduced Joe to Poppo. Now, the three of them were talking about putting their money together and opening a rim shop.

Black was still being the family guy. Connie had adapted to her new businesswoman look, and Black had practically taken her with him everywhere, showing her off. Especially to Nikki's, and Felicia's, whenever he picked the kids up, although he could only see Nicole and Lil' Keith every other weekend, considering the distance.

Fred was still trying to get his mother to consider moving out of her old, run-down house, into something better, but she remained adamant. He was still dallying with Yvonne and Theresa well, whenever he wasn't held up with his new girl toy, Cherry, who'd recently started dancing at Club Strokers.

James, who had been the locomotive of the operation, had been extremely busy rubbing elbows with the right people to expand the Kingz Distribution. Now, they were supplying dealers in Rome, Georgia, Savannah, Georgia, Waycross, Georgia, Dalton, Georgia, Athens, Georgia; Columbus, Georgia, Albany, Georgia and Griffin, Georgia. He'd even managed to secure another plug for their next re-up, but for now, their product was plentiful, and business was running smooth.

Well, that was until one of their workers informed them that some Muslim's had confronted him about selling drugs in their community. After a Kingz meeting was held, the Kingz had all decided to use the worker as bait to lure the opposers in, so they could confront them.

Now, The Kingz was sitting in a black Cadillac Escalade the company's truck watching their worker from across the street as he proceeded with his daily routine. It was after 6 p.m., and they along with the Kingzmen, who was parked behind them in a similar truck had been staked out for over four hours and hadn't encountered any negative activity.

"I think we should pull him out and try again tomorrow," Fred suggested from the rear passenger seat.

"Yeah, don't they have Jumah or some shit like that?" Black, who was seated beside Fred, asked.

"They have Jumah, tomorrow," James asserted from the front passenger seat. "They'll spend all day getting ready for that. If y'all wanna pull back, we can. But if we do, and they come by and not see our worker, they'll think we backed down. Then, they won't have a reason to come by. I say let's handle the beef while it's hot!"

"That sounds about right," Fred agreed. "I'm in for another—"

"This might be them," Ray, who was sitting behind the wheel, announced, cutting Fred off.

They all looked to see two black Lincoln Town cars pull to the curb in front of their worker, who seemed to sweat bullets, instantly. He had a reason to, because eight, religiously-dressed Muslims, emerged from the vehicles and seven of them were carrying AK-47s— *in broad daylight*!

Playa Ray

# CHAPTER 25

James had done his homework on the one who wasn't carrying. His name was Akbar, one of the high-ranking figures in the Nation of Islam. Word is, he was taking up the slack for Abdullah, who he'd once been a right-hand man too, before the shooting went down in the West End that involved the Fulton County Sheriff's Department, a few years ago.

'*Whoever, or whatever the nigga is, he's not going to back The Kingz into no corner,*' James thought as he dismounted, followed by the Kingz and Kingzmen.

They were all wearing vests and carrying AK-47s, Mac-11s and Carbon 15 rifles as they crossed the street and approached the opposing clan. Of course, Akbar didn't have to ask '*who*' because The Kingz were all sporting their chains over their visible vests.

"What's the problem?" James asked as he stood before Akbar, who was of similar height and size.

"I'm Akbar," he asserted in a composed tone, extending his hand.

"Don't ring a bell!" James came off rude, disregarding Akbar's hand. "What's the problem with you and my worker?"

Akbar withdrew his unshaken hand. "Well, my brotha, this is a drug-free community, and we intend to keep it that way."

"And who declared this a drug-free community?" James inquired.

"The community and we're just here to enforce it, in the name of, Allah."

"Man miss me with that *Malcolm X* shit!" James spat. "We declared this Kingz territory! If y'all don't like it, we can shoot this shit out, right now!"

Akbar looked as if he was considering it, but his disciples looked like they were liable to run than participate in anything brutal.

"You make the call," James prompted, knowing that if Akbar chose to shoot it out. He and his men would be dead before they could get the barrels of their guns high enough to squeeze off a shot.

Akbar must've realized the same thing, because he nodded, turned, then he and his men retreated to their cars.

**** 

Getting home, James parked in front of the red Ford Mustang convertible he'd bought for Shonda, who'd pretty much moved in with him.

"You got some mail from the courthouse," Shonda said sitting on the living room sofa, applying nail polish to her toenails and talking on the phone. "Boss called, I accepted the call and told him you were out on business. Your lawyer called, too. He said to call him back as soon as you get in."

James grabbed the letter from the courthouse off the coffee table, opened it and read the contents that informed him that his court date was in two weeks.

He immediately called Attorney Paul Scott.

"Hello?" the attorney answered.

"James Young," James asserted. "I got the letter from the courthouse about the court date in two weeks."

Paul explained to James that the state was offering twenty years for the assault, gun and drug charge altogether. If he takes it to trial and loses, he would have to serve thirty-five years.

"But they didn't find that shit on me!" James protested.

"I know that," Paul stated. "That's why I'll be pushing for them to place the case on dead docket."

James got off the phone with the attorney, telling himself there was no way he was going to take twenty years. He definitely wasn't going to let them White folks lure him into the courtroom to give him thirty-five. Fuck that!

While he was pondering this, his cell phone rang. He checked the caller I.D. before answering. "What up, Tek?"

"Man, you heard about, Barlow?" Tek asked.

"Nah," James answered, realizing he hadn't heard from *Trap Star Shawty* in a while. "What happened?"

"Some niggas tried to rob him last night," Tek answered. "He bucked and blasted on 'em. Killed one, damn-neared the other one. Marissa just called and told me that shit."

"Where this happened at?"

"University Homes."

James was not hearing this. Not only did he have two weeks until his court date. He also had two weeks to pay Vincent one hundred and fifty thousand dollars, in which he didn't have half of, being that he couldn't touch the Kingz Account without tipping his comrades off that he'd dealt with the loan shark.

****

"Baby?"

Fred roused from his sleep to see Cherry, who was still laying beside him, holding his cell phone out to him. After leaving the West End and parting ways with his comrades. He grabbed his mother some dinner from a soul food restaurant, showered, and went out to Club Strokers. Where he paid for several dances while waiting for Cherry to get off.

"I thought you cut this off," she stated with attitude. "Somebody done called you three times!"

"Did they wake you?" Fred was smiling.

"Yes!"

She shoved the still vibrating phone into his hand, then slid her naked, 5'7", 34-26-42 frame out of bed, with her dark-red hair in disarray from their sexcapade. She didn't bother to cover herself as she sauntered out of the room. Fred loved the way her ass cheeks bounced, but there was something about the dripping cherries she had tattooed on her lower back, that just did something to him.

"Yeah?" Fred answered his phone.

"He's a legit player," James asserted on the other end. "But he has one penalty."

"What's that?"

"He plays for the opposing team."

"What about the other refs?" Fred questioned. "They know?"

"Yep."

"Any flags on the play?"

"Not yet. You throwing one?"

Fred had to think about this for a moment. One of their workers had informed them, a couple of days ago, that some dude wanted to cop five keys from them. Now, James was saying that the nigga was legit, but he was affiliated with Drop Squad. Ray and Black let James tell it were aware of it but were willing to conduct business with him.

"We need to huddle," Fred finally spoke.

"We can do that," James said. "But the play has already been called.

Nothing James did ever seem to surprise Fred anymore. Hell, it seemed like he was running this whole operation by himself. It didn't matter to Fred, because he got into the game to get his paper right, and he was doing just that.

To save time, Fred showered at Cherry's apartment, rushed home to change into a suit, then made it to The Palace in time enough to have a fifteen-minute huddle, in which he requested.

"Y'all don't find it strange that these niggas are calling us all of a sudden?" Fred asked, looking around the table at his comrades.

"Look at how cheap our shit is!" James asserted. "I wouldn't be surprised if God hit us up for a couple of bricks! We got this shit on lock!"

"That's my point!" Fred confirmed. "They had this shit on lock. Now, we done took over. I mean, do I have to paint the whole picture?"

"Nope," answered James. "That's why I picked the location myself. Our Kingzmen are all certified sharpshooters, and they should already be in position. So, if these niggas can't respect the game— well, you get the picture." James looked at his watch. "It's about that time. Anything else?"

"Any surprises?" Fred asked, looking directly at James.

"Not that I know of," James answered. "As far as we know, it's all business, but we won't know until we get there."

**** 

The meeting was in Marietta, Georgia. Black pulled the Escalade into the parking lot of a small plaza and quickly spotted their customer. Who was sitting in a black, four-door, 76 Chevy Impala, with the windows rolled down. He was accompanied by three more guys, who were all sporting Drop Squad chains over their coats.

"Park over there!" James said, pointing to a spot directly across from the Chevy.

Once Black backed the truck into the parking slot, and both parties blinked their lights for recognition. The driver and front-seat passenger got out and walked into the laundromat, with the driver carrying a gym bag.

"We got two minutes," James told Black, who was to accompany him. "Ray and Fred, y'all keep these niggas in sight. They move, y'all move."

He dialed Grip's number.

"Everything's still neutral," Grip answered. "The score is still tied up in the sixth inning. No sign of foul play."

James ended the call, then looked over at Black. "You ready?"

"Let's do it!"

James and Black, who dressed in street attire for the occasion, dismounted the truck and headed for the laundromat. James looked around to see if he could spot any of their Kingzmen in the forest-like setting across the street but couldn't. That made him smile to himself because he had something the rest of the big-time drug dealers didn't. His own militia!

James and Black entered the not so crowded laundromat, where the customer and his partner were pretending to read the instructions on how to actuate the washing machines. James approached and lifted the lid of the washer beside theirs, while Black pretended to get change from the change machine.

Being that the negotiations were already made over the phone, there was no need for talk. They both dropped their bags into the two washers. Then, after looking to see if anyone was watching, they swiftly switched sides. The customer reached inside, opened the bag, did a quick count, lifted the bag, then headed for the door with his friend in tow. James knew there was no way he could count the money inside the store without being seen, so he just grabbed the bag, and he and Black exited.

****

After Jamal scored the keys from The Kingz, he dropped his friends off and headed for Kado's apartment in Herdon Homes. He would usually buy his product from Kenny, to keep it in the family, but when he heard of The Kingz low prices, he couldn't resist. It wasn't like he just said, *Fuck Drop Squad*! He would never do that. He just saw an opportunity to get out of the game quicker, being that he didn't plan on making it a career.

Jamal didn't want Kenny to know that he'd shopped else-where, so, instead of getting Jerry of Drop Squad to cook his dope, as always. He made an appointment with Kado, who he was intro-duced to through one of his Drop Squad affiliates. It took several hours, but the product was done, and Jamal was headed for the Impala that had no hubcaps and was in dire need of a paint job, *his trap car*. He casually looked around for any potential threat, though niggas wouldn't dare cross paths with Drop Squad. Even the Kingz, despite what the streets were saying about them, wouldn't cross paths with Drop Squad. Hell, there was only four of them.

Jamal climbed into the Chevy, tossed the bag on the passenger seat, and started the engine, but before he could put the car into reverse, a black SUV pulled up to his bumper, preventing any movement.

"What the—"

Jamal didn't bother pulling his gun from under his seat as he got out to confront the intruder. Who obviously didn't know who, or what they were dealing with. At the same time, he dismounted, two masked men emerged from the rear of the truck with AKs and immediately fired upon him, leaving him slumped between the hinges of the driver's door of his car. One of the men grabbed the gym bag from the Chevy before they climbed back into the truck and rode off.

**** 

After departing from his comrades, Ray drove to Bland Town, where he dropped off two ounces to Twon. His mother had moved in with Robert, so, in lieu of driving home, he chilled on the Rocky Road, and kicked it with Twon.

"Who is this?" Ray asked, spotting a black four-door Mercedes Benz on chrome wheels, approaching at a turtle-like pace.

"Shit, that's ya big homie," Twon answered, smiling.

Just as Twon said it, Ray was looking at the plate on the front of the car that read: *NORRIS*.

"Y'all step on a nigga's toes and don't even say excuse me," Norris, who was seated in the passenger seat, stated when he let the window down. "But I respect the game. I'm glad to see my lil' homies doing their thang."

"Shit, if I owned half the shit you owned, I wouldn't be fucking with none of this shit," Ray admitted. "Plus, you got a Mercedes, *and* a Lexus dealership. Just one of those would be enough for me."

"Damn, boy, who you got wit 'cha?" Twon asked Norris.

Ray hadn't paid any attention to the driver, until then. She had to be the finest Asian chick he'd ever seen! Norris used to fuck with some scraggly-looking bitches back in the day, but when he got his money right. A nigga couldn't catch him with anything less than a dime, and the bitch that was with him now was a certified twenty!

"This is my fiancée, Sue Lin," Norris answered, then spoke something in Chinese to her that caused her to blush and hold her left hand out, showing them the large diamond ring on her ring finger.

"She don't speak English?" Ray asked, silently commending the dude he'd always looked up to with great respect.

"Nah," Norris answered, looking at his gold watch. "I'm 'bout to get up outta here. Y'all boys hold it down."

"Always!" Twon spoke.

Ray nodded.

Norris said something in Chinese, and his wife drove on, but the look he gave Ray as the car moved on, was lethal. At least Ray thought so.

****

It had gotten dark. The Jumah service was over, and Muslims were exiting the Mosque, some heading for their vehicles, and some standing around out front, conversating. It was clear that Akbar had taken Abdullah's place, as others respectfully acknowledged his presence when he exited the building like he was God, with his seven, ever-present disciples, who accompanied him with the zeal of bodyguards.

Akbar was all smiles as he shook hands with men, hugged women, and kissed kids on their foreheads, but no one seemed to notice the old, dark-colored, four-door Cadillac that approached at a slow pace. Nor, had anyone noticed the barrel of the Tech-9 that hung out the rear window, until it erupted, sending a barrage of slugs through the crowd. Smiles became frowns, talking became screaming, and laughter became crying as bodies fell to the pavement.

One of Akbar's men dove in front of him, taking the slugs that were meant for the Caliph as the others pulled him back into the building, saving his, as well as their own lives.

218

# CHAPTER 26

It was Sunday and Mary had begged her sons to come out to the house she now shared with Robert, being that they'd prepared a big dinner. Ray wasn't really up for it, but he made the drive out to Smyrna anyway. He was surprised to see April, who no one had mentioned anything about.

"Why you ain't tell nobody you were coming down?" Ray asked her over dinner.

"I told mama," April, who was seated extremely close to Raymond, claimed. "I thought she told y'all."

"I thought *you* told them," Mary countered.

Ray looked from them to James, who was tending to his dinner like he hadn't heard a thing. Now, he was aware that he was the only person in the room who didn't know of his sister's arrival.

"When did you get here?" Ray asked her.

"Yesterday."

"Who picked you up from the airport?"

"Raymond," she answered, then quickly added. "Mama was busy, so—"

"Where'd you spend the night at?" He cut her off, already sensing she'd spent the night with, Raymond.

As far as he knew, April had never lied to him. They'd always had the tendency to be truthful with each other. No matter what, but for some strange reason, at this moment, she was retaining the answer to his question.

"Ray?" their mother intervened. "Can we please have a peaceful dinner?"

"Of course."

Ray got up from the table, found his light jacket and left the house. At first, he didn't have a problem with Raymond dating April, but now, suddenly he found himself vexed just over the thought of it.

No, that couldn't be it. He couldn't attribute their relationship to how he'd been feeling, lately. He didn't know what had come over him, but it seemed like the small things, that had never bothered him before, had become prominent issues, and gradually increased by the day.

Without any destination in mind, Ray just drove, trying to sort out the jumble of issues that had seemed to cloud his mind. When he finally realized he'd come to a stop, he was standing on the burial ground where Sylvia was buried. *Standing?* He didn't remember pulling into the cemetery. He definitely didn't remember getting out of the car in the drizzle of rain that he now noticed coming down. He must've been standing in the rain for quite some time because his clothes were soaked and his hair that Joe's wife, Valerie had braided two days ago, was loose. Plus, it was getting dark, and he saw that he was the only person in the cemetery. When he finally fixed his eyes on the grave he was standing in front of, he realized that the tombstone didn't say Sylvia Baker, but—*Keyonne Sharpe?*

Bile rose in his throat. He couldn't block it, and he wasn't quick enough to turn aside to prevent his Sunday dinner from spewing over the grave. His whole body quivered and, as if pushed from behind, he fell to his knees, extending his arms to keep from falling on his face. Then, after another vomiting spell, he looked up at the tombstone for a better confirmation, but his vision was blurry, and the damn tombstone wouldn't stop moving. It took a while, but when he regained focus and reread:

*In Loving Memories of Keyonne Sharpe, 1977-2003*, it was confirmed.

They'd killed the wrong person!

# CHAPTER 27

Everything was dark, but Ray could hear distinctive chatter. He tried to open his eyes, but his eyelids were heavy. He tried again and succeeded, but his vision was blurry. He would've wiped his eyes, but his limbs weren't responding to his brain's command.

"He's awake!" someone exclaimed.

"You alright, baby?" came Mary's voice.

"Man, the doctor said something about food poisoning," James said.

'*Food poisoning*!' Ray's botched mind tried to compute. His limbs were still uncooperative, so he tried to blink the filmy curtains from his eyes to no avail.

"That damn doctor don't know what she's talking about!" Mary protested. "I cooked that food myself! If it was some damn poison in the food, then why the hell—"

Her words faded as he suddenly lost consciousness. When he finally regained consciousness, his vision was clear. The recovery room was clear, except for some female who was balled up in some chair with a coat thrown over her, leaving only her brown microbraids revealed. Ray's head was hurting too bad to play guess who. Plus, his mouth was dry, and he was in dire need of some pain pills. He pressed the *Nurse Call* button.

It seemed as if the nurse was right outside the door because, seconds after he'd pressed the button. The nurse, a middle-aged White woman, rushed into the room and stood on the left side of the bed.

"Hi, Mr. Young!" she spoke in a hushed tone. "What can I do for you?"

"My head," he managed, not really knowing if she'd heard him.

"I have something for that."

She pulled a small, balled up paper cup from her pocket and poured two pills into his hand. Then, instead of walking around the bed to the small bedside table, she leaned over him to pour him a small cup of water, with her breasts resting on his manhood.

"Oh!" she exclaimed, jerking back, spilling some of the water on him. "My God! At least we know *something* still works!"

She was all smiles. That's when Ray realized his *little man* was standing at attention. Plus, he realized he was naked, so his rod was exposing its full length beneath the thin white sheet. Ray was so embarrassed, he quickly threw the pills into his mouth, and snatched the cup from the nurse. Who looked as if she was ready to strip the sheet off and dive on top of him.

"Well, I guess I'll inform the doctor of your condition," she said, still smiling. Then, when she rounded the bed, she stopped, taking another look. "Well, I won't tell her *everything*."

She winked, then made her exit. Ray downed the water, placed the cup on the table, and closed his eyes. Then, his eyes snapped back open. He'd forgotten about the girl. He looked over at the chair, she was gone. He hadn't seen her leave, but he knew she couldn't have gone far, because her coat was laying across the arm of the chair, and her pocketbook was sitting on the counter.

He still couldn't figure out who she was. Then, when he heard the toilet flush, he knew he was about to find out. Whoever it was, he didn't want her to see him with his dick standing up like this, so he tried to think of all kinds of platonic shit to make it go down. It wasn't working. Besides, he was too late, because the bathroom door opened, and his erection was the first thing the girl noticed. She gasped, blushed, and tried her best not to look at it as she slowly approached the bed.

To say that Ray was disconcerted, would be an understatement. Now, he was pissed off. Out of all people in the world, he didn't expect to get caught with his pants down by Sheila.

'*What the hell is she doing here, anyway?*' he thought.

"The doctor ran everybody off, so you could get some rest," she explained, still trying her best to ignore his erection, but failing. "I told her, I was your girlfriend, and she let me stay."

Ray just stared at her, but he couldn't help but get a glimpse of her figure. He would have never denied that she was cute, but he didn't know she was this damn fine! Her C-cups sat perfectly in her green turtle-neck sweater, and her curvaceous hips and thighs that threatened to burst through her green, snug-fitted jeans, left nothing to the imagination. *This was not working!*

It seemed as if his headache was subsiding as his penis escalated, so he closed his eyes as he spoke to her. "What did they say happened?" he asked. "Did somebody find me or something?"

"They said a groundskeeper at the cemetery found you," she answered. "He thought you were drunk and called the police. Oh, the doctor gave me this. She said you had it in your hand when you were brought in."

He opened his eyes to see her with her hand held out, containing the half-heart pendant. His memento mori.

\*\*\*\*

Two weeks had gone by, and it was time for James to face the *White folks* although the judge and DA were Black. All Kingz were present, plus Mary and Shonda, who were all seated on the same row, while James sat beside Attorney Paul Scott at the defense table.

At the same time, in another courtroom, a jury selection was being conducted for Boss' trial, in which the Kingz had all agreed to attend, and show their support.

James' proceeding didn't last long. The DA called out the charges and announced the State's offer, which was twenty years. Paul Scott contended that the gun and drugs were not found on his client, who was not interested in the State's offer, and that they would take their chances at trial if the judge didn't see fit to place the case on dead docket. The judge didn't find Paul's argument justifying and said that James would remain out on bond until a trial date was set. Court adjourned.

Boss' trial was already in motion when the bailiff let them into the half-crowded courtroom. Boss, who was seated at the defense table with his attorney, spotted James and despite the situation regarded him with a wholehearted smile. James couldn't help but smile and nod at his little homie as he and his crew took seats on the back row.

As the trial went on, James could see why Boss said they were going to find him guilty. Hell, they found the gun on him. Plus, he'd murdered the dude in front of several people. Including the man's mother.

So, it happened, the jury found him guilty of first-degree murder. The judge sentenced him to life without parole and, as deputies were escorting him out of the courtroom. He looked back at the victim's mother and said, "Go and dig ya son up, bitch!"

****

"That's half," James told the burly man seated behind the oak wood desk, who just stared at the paper bag James sat before him. "That's all I have, right now."

Truth was, James had more than half. It was just that he had to build his stash back up. Plus, he had bills and a handful of people on his payroll. His personal venture wasn't doing as good as he wanted it to, but after knocking off Franco. He, along with the other Kingz was able to add a good twenty thousand to their personal stash spots, which did him a bit of good. Plus, he'd sold more than half of the guns from the gun shop heist.

"That's not what we agreed to," the loan shark now asserted.

"I know what we agreed to," James said, taking a seat in one of the guest chairs. "I just needed more time than I thought I did."

"I knew you couldn't meet the deadline with that much money," Vincent told him.

"You did?" James sat up in his seat. "And you still gave me the money?"

"You just seemed so determined at the time," Vincent said with a chuckle. "To be honest, I thought you and your men were going to knock over a bank. Or skip town."

"And you still gave me the money?" James reiterated, not feeling how this conversation was going.

"Money means nothing to me," asserted Vincent, leaning back in his chair. "I live by principles and morals. I believe in letting people hang themselves. I just supply the rope."

It didn't take long for James to access that statement. He'd always wondered why Vincent would loan that kind of money to someone he knew nothing about. Now, he'd just revealed his ulterior motive. If James failed to deliver, it would give him a damn good reason to knock The Kingz off.

"But I'll give you more time," Vincent continued, leaning forward. "Just know this, I see, know and hear things people don't think I see, know or hear."

*Bingo*!

Playa Ray

# CHAPTER 28

It was the Fourth of July, and these past months had been quite sensational for The Kingz. They had managed to connect with other drug dealers in Florida, New York, and Virginia, transporting merchandise on Greyhound. They'd also opened a car dealership *Kingz BMWs* and were thinking of trying their hands at real estate.

Ray and Joe were still dealing with Poppo's people in New York, and receiving the product from Miami, and instead of a rim ship, they, Ray, Joe, and Poppo opened a customs shop, where they installed tint, sound systems, rims, T.Vs and body kits. At RJP Customs, they'd done work for people such as Michael Vick, Shaquille O'Neal, T.I., Jermaine Dupree, Ludacris, and Evander Holyfield.

Now, The Kingz were enjoying themselves at the huge, Fourth of July barbeque they'd thrown at Grant Park, where they'd paid Fulton County Deputies to patrol the entrance and forbid passage to those who didn't have invitations. There were three catering services, and a DJ stand, where DJ Spenz and some guy named DJ Mike Fresh, from Savannah, took turns mixing it up.

"Y'all boys know how to throw a barbeque!" Norris said when he approached Black, who was talking with three of their workers.

"Damn, what's up, Big Money?" Black dapped Norris and nodded at the tall blonde White woman who flanked him.

"Man, I'm small-time compared to y'all," Norris contended. "Four heads are always better than one."

"Sometimes," Black replied. "I know you gon' be at the Battle of The DJ's, next month."

"Yeah, you know I gotta support, lil' bruh. Hell, I guess I'll be supporting y'all too since y'all gon' be judging it. I just hope y'all play fair."

"Don't worry," said Black. "We're gonna let the crowd judge."

"Baby?" Connie had approached, holding Lil' Keith. "I gotta take Lil' Keith to the truck and change his diaper. Ain't no more diapers in the bag."

"You need me to walk wit 'cha?" Black offered.

"I got it."

"Boy, you should have a whole football team by now!" Norris stated once Connie departed.

"That's just number four."

"Shit, I can't see how you let Nikki breeze like that," Said Norris. "That nigga she's with ain't no better, but that's not my business. Anyway, I'ma mingle with a few more kats, get my grub on, and head up outta here."

Norris walked off, leaving Black to ponder what he'd said about Nikki and her current boyfriend. As he thought about it, he realized that when Nikki dropped the kids off to him yesterday, she was wearing large, dark, sunglasses, and refused to look in his face. Plus, she was wearing make-up. Nikki had never worn make-up.

\*\*\*\*

Later that night, James took The Kingz to a small club in Buckhead to relax. Well, that was what he'd told them. Truth was, he was there on business. Once he spotted Milton, his ex-cellmate from the Pretrial Detention Center, he excused himself from the table and approached the bar.

"What can I get 'cha, sir?" Milton asked, not looking up as he wiped the bar.

"Nice place you got here," James asserted.

Milton looked up. "Goddamn!" He smiled and shook James' hand. Then noticing the *Kingz* medallion, he said, "Man, I didn't know you were a part of that."

"Yeah," James replied. "I was hoping you could plug me in with the X-Man."

"Well, you're in luck," Milton told him. "Because the guy I was telling you about is sitting right over there."

James looked in the direction of where Milton was pointing. Just two tables away from their table, in the back of the club, sat a well-dressed, full-bearded White guy, who was accompanied by three White women.

"What's his name?" James asked.

"Jack," Milton answered. "But watch out, he's on his high-horse."

James nodded, then made for Jack's table.

"Jack!" James approached with arms extended. "How's it going, my friend?"

Jack regarded him with suspicion. "Surely you have the wrong Jack," he asserted. "But if you step into the men's room, spit into the palm of your hand, and apply it to your crotch, you may find this *Jack* that you seek."

This corny-ass joke prompted hysterical laughter from the three dim-witted bimbos, who, apparently were on ecstasy.

"Ladies!" James maintained his anger. "Could y'all excuse us?"

The women looked at James as if he'd disrespected them by referring to them as *ladies*, then looked at Jack as if to ask, "Are you just going to sit there and let him disrespect us like that?"

James was through being nice. "Are y'all bitches deaf!" he hissed. "Get the fuck up!"

Their eyes widened with apprehension, but they grabbed drinks, pocketbooks and cell phones, and got their asses up. Perhaps they figured that a mad Black man was more dangerous than a mad White man.

"Hey, man!" Jack protested. "You can't just—"

"Shut up!" James cut him off, taking a seat across from him. "I wanna talk business. That's if you don't mind doing business with, The Kingz."

"*The Kingz*!" Jack leaned forward, now interested. "Of course, I'll deal with The Kingz!"

\*\*\*\*

Black ventured off to the restroom, minutes after James had left the table. He had drunk so much beer at the barbecue, it was finally starting to run through him. While he was waiting on a stall, he decided to call home and check on Connie and the kids.

"Everything's okay," she told him. "We were watching a movie, and the kids fell asleep in our bed."

Black laughed.

"Are you coming home tonight?' she asked.

"Of course."

"Okay, I'll wait up."

Black had finally gotten to a stall to drain his aching bladder. Once he'd washed his hands, he exited the restroom.

"Hello sexy, remember us?"

For a moment, Black just stared at the two White women who apparently, were waiting for him outside the restroom, but he remembered them very well. They were the women who'd given him a ride on the night the undercover cops initiated that foot chase in Bland Town. The same night James was arrested.

"How could a man forget *Thelma and Louise*?" Black was now smiling at the two women who looked to be in their late-thirties.

"See, Becky!" the brunette, who was the passenger that night, said to her blonde friend. "I told you he'd remember us."

"We saw you come in," said Becky. "But we didn't want to approach you while you were with your friends."

"And we were already looking for some action tonight," the brunette stated, looking down at his crotch. "Some *big* action!"

Black was already turned on. He'd let these two freaky-ass bitches out of his hands, once. He was not about to make that mistake again. Not tonight!

"Y'all wanna get a room?" he asked.

"That's only if you can handle two cougars in heat," the brunette replied. "And anal sex is still out of the question for you!"

"I don't know, Megan," Becky intervened. "I think I've reconsidered."

**\*\*\*\***

The next day, Black awakened to Becky and Megan, both licking and taking turns filling their mouths with his dick as they'd done the night before. He moaned, wishing this could go on forever, but he knew he had to get home to get the kids, so Connie could leave for school. He looked at his watch. It was already seventeen minutes after nine, and he knew he was not going to make it home on time, but he had to try.

After fighting off the cougars who were still begging for him to fuck them in their asses. He grabbed his cell phone and rushed into the bathroom, locking the door.

'*Those bitches are really in heat*,' he thought.

He was still feeling the effect from the Stamina – Rx pills he'd purchased while purchasing the condoms which he'd never used. He called the front desk and told them to call him a cab. Then, he took a brief shower. Once the girls had collected themselves, they all exited the Ritz Hotel and parted ways. A taxi was already waiting on Black, so he gave the driver a fifty-dollar bill and told him to break all traffic laws.

Connie had to be in class at ten, and it was forty-five minutes after ten when the taxi pulled up in front of his house, making Black wish for the millionth time he'd driven his car to Buckhead, instead of riding in the company's truck with his friends, but hell, he didn't know he would run into *America's Next Porn Stars* again.

Well, there was no need to prolong or reprimand himself for it now. He was sure Connie was going to give him the business as soon as he walked through the door, but he was wrong. As soon as he entered the house, Connie was approaching the door with her pocketbook in one hand, and keys in the other.

"Where the kids at?" he asked as she brushed past him.

"Watching cartoons," she said, not looking back as she headed for her truck.

Black couldn't help but watch her leave. Just then, he knew he had a lot of making up to do. He'd already lost one good girl.

He couldn't stand to lose another, and everyone knows that, once a good girl goes bad, she's gone forever.

**\*\*\*\***

Ray was awakened by the sounds of his doorbell. He didn't have company often, so it startled him a bit. When he peered through the transom, he saw some teenaged White kid standing on his porch.

He opened the door. "What's up?"

"Hi, I'm Ben," the kid said, proudly. "I was wondering if you needed someone to mow your lawn. I only charge ten bucks, front and back."

Ray looked at his lawn he'd been meaning to tend to but had been too busy to do so.

"Are you any good?" Ray asked.

"Of course, I'm good!" the kid boasted. "This is what I do every summer. Plus, I have my own lawn mower, John Deere."

'Well, let me know when you're done."

Ray was hungry but didn't feel like cooking, so he opted for Pop Tarts and orange juice. He'd been eating light, ever since he'd gotten sick at the cemetery, and awakened at the hospital. The doctor had assumed food poisoning, but the tests had confirmed it was a stomach virus. What happened at the cemetery that day, still remained mysterious to him.

Kingz BMWs would not be open today, but RJP Customs was. Therefore, Ray just donned some shorts, a Polo shirt, and a pair of Nikes he'd never worn. Topping his gear off with a Kangol hat, mirror-tinted sunglasses, his *Kingz* chain, and half-heart pendant, and was out the door.

He saw that Ben had done a good job with the front yard and was still cutting the back. Not wanting to disturb the kid, Ray placed a twenty-dollar bill under the gas can that sat on the porch, got into his BMW, and drove off.

For some reason, he could not stop thinking about Sheila. Yesterday was the first time he'd seen her since that day at the hospital, and he'd done a great job of dodging her all day. Fred and James kept telling him that she was a good girl and that he should give her a chance. Plus, on several occasions, they'd even tried to set up dates for the two of them, in which Ray had always declined, claiming to be busy. It's not that Ray didn't like her, it was just that— okay, he didn't know what it was. Perhaps he hadn't gotten over Sylvia yet.

Before going to the shop, Ray stopped in Maple Creek to check on his trap he'd hired B.J. and T-Roc to maintain, while he flew from Kingz BMWs to RJP Customs. He knew one day, he was going to regret making that decision, but, until he found someone more trustworthy, they'd have to suffice.

Ray used his key to let himself in and was instantly angered by the sight of various fast food bags, cups, and wrappers on the kitchen table, counter and living room, where T-Roc was asleep on the sofa, and B.J. was curled up on the floor.

"I'm finna fire both of y'all niggas!"

They both stirred from their sleep. B.J. grabbed his gun off the floor beside him and pointed it at Ray. "That's how niggas get shot, creeping up on niggas like that!"

"The next time I come in here and see this place like this," Ray responded. "*I'll* be the one doing the shooting! Now clean this shit up!"

Ray left the apartment, already regretting his decision. He really missed Precious. To be honest, he was really tired of the drug game. He just wanted a decent, profitable business, so he could sit back, relax and let the money pile up.

Ray pulled into the shop's parking lot on Browns Mill Road, parking beside Joe's Crown Victoria. He looked at the car and shook his head, seeing that Joe had changed rims again. Since they'd opened RJP Customs, Joe had been like a kid in a candy store. He switched rims twice a week, installed T.Vs all over his car and truck, PlayStation Twos, and probably had the best sound system in town.

Poppo had only installed three screens in his Lexus, and a nice pair of rims on the BMW convertible he'd bought from The Kingz. Ray had only upgraded the rims on his BMW.

"Hey, Ray!" Brittany, their secretary, beamed when he entered.

"What up, Brit?"

"Nothing much," she answered. "Some girl came looking for you, 'bout twenty minutes ago."

"Are you sure she was looking for me?" Ray asked, trying to figure out what female he'd told about the shop.

"She asked if Ray was here," Brittany told him. "I said, not yet and she left."

"She didn't leave her name?"

"Nope."

"What'd she look like?"

"Brown-skinned," she answered. "'Bout my height, had her hair pulled back into a rabbit's tail."

"Rabbit's tail?"

"It was too short to be a ponytail," said Brittany, smiling. "But she didn't look like the type of female *you* would mess with."

Ray almost questioned that statement. Instead, he asked, "Did you see what kind of car she was in?"

"She was on the passenger side of a beat-up car," Brittany answered, making a face. "It had the whole shop smelling like burnt oil!"

Ray had the feeling he knew who it was, but he was about to make sure before he made assumptions. He entered the office, where Joe was, apparently, talking to an unsatisfied customer.

"Somebody's always complaining about something!" Joe said, hanging up the phone. "Tell 'em sum', Ray!"

Ray was supposed to respond with, '*Tell 'em sum', Joe!*' a joke they'd gotten from *Martin Lawrence*, in the movie *Bad Boys*, when *Will Smith* was threatening to shoot Joe-Joe the Tire Man. Instead, Ray told him to run the surveillance tape back for him.

"Right there!" he said when he'd spotted the female that fit Brittany's description. "Play it from there."

Ray didn't need any zoom-in technology to identify the girl who was talking to Brittany at the counter. He definitely didn't need it to identify that raggedy ass Chevy Celebrity, but how did she know about RJP Customs?

What did she want?

**\*\*\*\***

"Hit Campbellton Road," James told Shonda.

They had just left Spenz's place, where they'd found out J-Bo had gotten caught this morning, at school, with a bookbag full of weed, and a gun in his locker. He was hauled off to Metro Youth Detention Center, but James saw it coming because the young nigga had gotten careless, splurging, flashing money and buying gold teeth and jewelry. James hadn't told Spenz that J-Bo was selling for him, but he pretty much knew Spenz was suspicious of it. He just hoped that the lil' nigga was trill enough to keep his mouth shut.

Speaking of *jailbirds*, Barlow was still being held with no bond, and Boss was shipped off to prison, immediately after he was sentenced. He hadn't written, or called, James figured he was probably going through a faze, after being told he was going to spend the rest of his life in prison.

Now, Shonda pulled the BMW into Deerfield Apartments and drove around to where Steve was posted with three other men. At first, Steve appeared surprised, then he looked both ways before approaching the passenger side of the car, but James' eyes were locked on the *Kingz* chain Steve had around his neck as he rolled the window down.

"What up, babes!" Steve greeted, giving James dap.

"I can't call it," James replied, flashing a wide smile. "You done got blinged-out on them folks, ain't 'cha?"

"Oh, yeah." Steve playfully struck a few poses. "You know ya boy King Steve just done took over Campbellton Road."

"Yeah?"

"Hell, yeah!"

"Let me see that shit."

"It ain't real gold," Steve admitted as he leaned forward to allow James to inspect his medallion.

James held the plastic, light-weight piece in his hand. Steve was so caught up in his ego. He didn't notice James was no longer smiling until the chain was abruptly snatched from around his neck.

"Damn, man!" Steve cried out. "What the—"

"Don't ever disrespect us like that again!" James vented. "You ain't no fucking King! That's false-claiming! That type of shit'll get 'cha whole family knocked off! Now get the fuck away from my car before I consider it!"

Steve backed away from the care with apprehension in his eyes. He knew James would make good on his word.

"Let's go, shawty!" James told Shonda.

James broke the plastic medallion and, when they got halfway up Campbellton Road threw it in the dumpster of a fast food restaurant. Then, they journeyed off, checking on other spots, but when they got to Carver Homes and didn't see Killah in his usual spot. James instantly felt that something was amiss.

"Where the hell this nigga at?" James said almost to himself, pulling out his cell phone to dial Killah's number.

Shonda pointed. "There he is!"

James looked to see Killah coming from his apartment, looking around, with his hand under his shirt as if he was about to draw his pistol.

"What the fuck you got going on?" James asked, wary of this gesture.

"Man, niggas out here trippin'!" Killah asserted, looking around once more.

"Who's out here trippin?"

## CHAPTER 29

Black was exhausted when he'd returned home this morning and wanted to hop into bed, but it was his turn to watch the kids while Connie was at school. So, he watched cartoons with them, until they complained of being hungry. Then, he took them to McDonald's. While Kevin and Nicole played on the McDonald's playground, he tended to Lil' Keith, thinking about what Norris had said about Nikki and Willie. Now, he was wondering how did, Norris know about Willie? He didn't want to think that Norris was speaking out of hatred, envious of what they'd established. That couldn't be true, because The Kingz was small time compared to Norris, who'd established and accomplished way more than they have, all by himself.

Well, whatever was going on with the three of them, Black knew he couldn't dwell on it too long. Now, Connie and the kids were his only concern. As long as Willie didn't harm his kids, or try to keep him from seeing them, he was doing nothing wrong. Thinking of Connie, Black looked at his watch and figured she should be home by now. When he pulled up to the house, he saw that her truck was not in the driveway. Instead of waiting for her, he decided to go ahead and take Kevin home. Connie would always come straight home after school, so, by the time he gets back, she should be there.

"Hey, big head!" Felicia exclaimed when she opened the door, hugging Kevin. "You had fun?"

"Yes," Kevin answered. "Me and my sister, Nicole, had a lot of fun! Lil' Keith be falling, trying to keep up with us."

"Well, he's still a baby," she told him. "Go on in and feed the fish."

"Okay," Kevin said, then hugged his dad. "I love you, daddy!"

"Love you too, baby! Be good!"

"Okay."

"You wanna come in and feed the fish, too?" Felicia asked, seductively eyeing him.

"Yeah, right!" Black turned and headed for his car he'd left running.

"It's still yours," she said to his back.

Black didn't respond. Right now, Connie was on his mind, and God must've known, because when he got into his car, Jaheem was on the radio, crooning:

*'When she starts bringing up old dirt/And the fights keep getting worse/Finding numbers in her purse/You better put that woman first/When you notice she ain't wearing her ring/And she starts playing little games/Comin' in late from work/You better put that woman first.'*

Black did not need to hear this! He immediately turned the radio off.

"Daddy, I like that song!"

He looked over at his daughter, who was seated in the passenger seat, regarding him with that same mean but cute look Nikki would hit him with. Being that he could never resist that look, and he would do anything for his children. He turned the radio back on and silently prayed that God was not using that song as a sign to him.

By the time he made it back to Covington, Nikki had called his cell, telling him that they were on their way to Publix. Now, all he had to do was swing by the house and pick Connie up to accompany him, but she still hadn't made it home. Black was pissed, and wanted to call her cell phone, but thought against it. He knew she had to be upset about him staying out all night when he'd told her he was coming home.

Nikki and Willie were already in the Publix parking lot when Black pulled in. Before he could park, Willie was already out of the truck, approaching the passenger side of the BMW.

"We're in a hurry," Willie said, unbuckling Nicole's seatbelt and helping her out.

"What's wrong with, Nikki?" Black asked Willie, who was now unstrapping Lil' Keith.

"Headache," Willie answered, slamming the rear door.

Black watched as he and the kids approached the truck, where Nikki, with those same sunglasses on, sat in the passenger seat, holding her head. He couldn't really see her face from how the sun was glaring off the windshield of the truck, but he could tell something was wrong.

When he arrived home, he was a bit relieved to see that Connie was there. Now, he was going to have to get his Keith Sweat/James Brown on, because he knew he'd messed up, and he was not trying to lose another good thing.

He entered the house and heard sounds coming from the kitchen. So, that's where he headed. Connie was sitting at the table, looking over a newspaper. Curious, Black stood behind her to see that she was reading the Classifieds.

"You a'ight, baby?" he asked, softly massaging her shoulders.

"Mmm-hmm," she responded, not regarding him.

Black struggled to find something to say, but his mind was blank. As if matters couldn't get any worse, his cell phone rang. It was James calling an emergency meeting.

"Right now?" Black asked, not believing his luck.

"Like yesterday!" James answered.

****

Fred knew it was too good to be true. The Kingz had all decided to take the day off, and he was going to spend it with Cherry until she had to go to work. Then, he was going to head home and spend the rest of the evening with his mother, but while he was receiving a private dance from Cherry, before sex, James called to report an emergency meeting, raining on his parade.

Fred pulled into The Palace, seeing that he was the last one to show. There were no Kingzmen. Shonda was at the front desk. One of their workers, Killah, was waiting outside the office. The rest of The Kingz were at the Round Table.

"What we got?" Fred asked, taking a seat.

"Some interference on Kingz territory," James answered. "Ray, would you let, Killah, in?"

Ray did so and retook his seat.

"Killah," James proceeded. "Tell them what you told me."

"Some Crips in my hood started bugging yesterday," Killah asserted. "They're on some extortion shit, saying niggas can't trap in Carver Homes unless they get half."

"Crips?" Ray asked. "As in the gang?"

Killah nodded.

"Man, niggas ain't gang banging in the South!" Fred stated. "Especially in Atlanta! Where they from—L.A.?"

"Nah," Killah answered. "Half of them niggas grew up in Carver Homes."

"So, what're we gonna do about these wannabes?" Fred wanted to know.

"I'm asking y'all for permission to handle this myself," said James.

"You sure?" asked Black.

"I'm positive."

"I don't know," came Fred. "If you're talking gunplay, I want in!"

"Me too!" said Black.

"Nah," James answered. "At least, not on my first visit, but if it comes down to that. I promise I'll let you in on it. That's on the crown!"

Ray, Fred, and Black agreed, giving James their permission to do whatever he'd planned to do. Once the meeting was over, Fred, Black, and Killah exited. Ray had informed James that he needed to speak to him once everyone had left.

"What's on ya mind, lil' bruh?" James asked once they were alone.

"I don't know why, or how she found out about it," Ray started. "But Kim came by the shop today."

**\*\*\*\***

The Kingzmen showed up at The Palace minutes after Ray had left. James sent Shonda home, telling her he would see her later. Once the KMs were in full gear, they all climbed into the two company trucks and headed for Carver Homes.

It was not dark yet when they'd arrived. Plus, it was not hard to spot the blue-bandanna-wearing wannabes. Who were all posted on the block, looking like a group of extras for a segment of a film. James was expecting to encounter more than six of them. He and the Kingzmen pulled up and jumped out on them with assault rifles.

"Don't get scared now!" James told the group that looked as if they were about to make a break for it. "Somebody told me y'all run Carver Homes. Is that true?"

No one answered.

"Who's the leader?" James asked.

"I'm over the Crips in Carver Homes," a short, stocky dude, admitted.

"And you are?"

"I'm Gutta-Loc!" the man answered. "And yeah, we run Carver Homes! Can't nobody get money out here, unless we're getting half!"

"Do you stand firm on your word?"

"Hell yeah!"

"Die for what you believe in?"

"Damn right!"

"Well, believe this, I now declare Carver Homes a no-Crips zone! Get caught out here after today, we gon' fire y'all asses up! And I stand firm on my word with all ten toes!"

"My big homie ain't gonna go for that shit!" said Gutta-Loc.

"Well, tell your big homie to have his ass standing out here the next time we roll through!" James told him.

\*\*\*\*

Black had returned home from the meeting with the intent to make things right with Connie, but it wasn't as easy as he thought it would be. She had cooked, ate and was already in bed, leaving his plate in the microwave. So, he consumed his dinner, showered and decided he would put the moves on her, giving her a mouth-to-body massage, being that she always slept naked whenever the kids weren't staying over. But when he climbed into bed, he saw that she had on a pair of pajama pants and a tank top.

This upset Black, because he had nothing else to come up with. He knew he had to do something but trying to force her to talk while she was playing sleep, could spark an ugly confrontation, which he was attentively trying to avoid.

The best thing to do now was to give Connie her space. Therefore, Black just rolled over and tried his best to lure himself into la-la land. It wasn't happening, now, his mind had switched from Connie to Nikki. He immediately changed the channel, forcing her to the back of his mind. Then, he started thinking about the orgy he'd had with Megan and Becky which sparked an instant erection.

This was a good and a bad thing. It was good because he was no longer thinking about Nikki. It was bad because he was not getting any pussy tonight, but somehow, he'd managed to fall asleep, only to be awakened by his cell phone he'd forgotten to put on vibrate. He glimpsed at the clock on the stand as he reached for the phone. It was 10:41 p.m. Nikki's number was showing on the screen.

"Yeah?" he answered in a low tone, easing out of bed and leaving the room.

"I can't take this anymore!" Nikki asserted, crying. "I haven't done anything to deserve this!"

"What's wrong?" Black asked, already pissed that she was crying.

"Willie put his hands on me!" she sobbed. "Nicole tried to help me and he pushed her down."

"*He did what*!" Black was already picturing himself choking this nigga out.

"I didn't do anything, Keith. I swear I don't know what to do."

"Where that nigga at?" Black asked, ready to jump in his car and drive to Miami.

"He left."

"Nikki, get the kids and go to your parents' house, *now!*"

"He knows where they stay," she told him. "He'll just come and get me like he did the last time."

'*The last time?*' he thought. '*So, this nigga had been beating on Nikki?* "Well, go and check into a hotel," he told her.

"I don't have any money."

"Do you have anywhere you can go until tomorrow?"

"I have a friend," she answered. "She'll let us spend the night."

"You sure?"

"Yes."

"Well, go there," he told her. "I'll call you in the morning."

"Black, I love you!" she broke into an uncontrollable sob.

"Nikki, would you please get the kids and leave before that nigga gets back?" Black asserted, trying to fight back the tears that welled up in his eyes.

****

It was 12:27 a.m. and the Kingz were all assembled in the parking lot of an abandoned warehouse, at Black's behest, after getting off the phone with Nikki. Since then, he'd run through a blunt and thirteen cigarettes.

"You don't wanna let the Kingzmen handle this?" James now asked.

"Nah," Black answered, firing up his fourteenth cigarette. "This some personal shit. Y'all ain't gotta be in on it if y'all don't want to."

"You sound ridiculous, right now!" Fred asserted. "That nigga violated the family. You know we don't play 'bout family!"

"You already know we're in," Ray spoke. "But we can't just drive to Miami without a plan."

"I got a plan," said Black. "I'ma kill that nigga and bring my family back!"

"We already know that," Fred voiced. "We still need to map that shit out. How much do you trust, Nikki?"

Black just looked at him.

"When this nigga come up dead," Fred continued. "She's gonna know you had something to do with it. How much do you trust her?"

"Here's the plan," James spoke before Black could. "We'll go as five, all of us and Grip. Black, you call Nikki and find out where her friend stays. Tell her that somebody's coming to pick her and the kids up. That'll be Grip, he'll bring them back and drop them off at a hotel, while we handle Ike Turner. Good enough?"

"Maybe we should let Black bring them back," said Ray. "Then—"

"Nah," Black cut him off. "I want that nigga myself!"

"I know that," Ray acknowledged. "That's why we're gonna kidnap his ass and bring him to you. Then, you can take him to court."

"That's a good ass plan!" Fred announced. Then, to Black, he said, "It's on you, I'm down for either one."

"Plan A," Black chose. "I wanna hold court in Miami!"

"Good!" said James. "Everybody go home and strap up. I'll call Grip, then swing through to pick y'all up in the company's truck. Nobody is to know about this trip. Any questions?"

"Black, do you know where the nigga stay?" Ray inquired.

"Fuck!" Black exclaimed, knowing he'd forgotten something.

"We'll find that out," James interceded. "Right now, we need to move. We got a long ride."

The Kingz branched off. On his way home, James called Grip and gave him the run-down. Once he'd gotten home and geared up without waking Shonda. He headed for The Palace, where Grip and another Kingzman were already waiting. He climbed into one of the Escalades, and they followed him as he picked up his fellow Kingz and began their journey to the Orange State.

# CHAPTER 30

It was well after 10 p.m. when The Kingz finally made it to Miami. Fred used his fake I.D. to get a room at a hotel. Black had called Nikki, earlier, acquired her friend's address and told her that someone was coming to pick her and the kids up. He relayed the information to James, who relayed it to Grip.

"So, how do we find out where he stay?" Black asked once they'd made it to their room.

"I'm on it," James answered. "Right now, we need to get some sleep."

While they were pulling out extra blankets and sheets to make pallets on the floor for a night's rest. Nikki called Black's cell to let him know that his friend had arrived and that she and the kids were on their way back to Georgia.

"Did you get the money?" he asked of the envelope he'd given Grip to give to her, which contained twenty-five hundred dollars.

"I got it," she answered. "When will we see you?"

"As soon as I can make arrangements."

"Arrangements?"

"The room is paid up for a week," he said, disregarding her inquiry. "Stay there until I find a better and safe place for y'all. Is that nigga still calling you?"

"Yeah," she answered. "He's called and been to my parents' house, too."

"Did he threaten them?"

"No." She sighed. "They're crazy about him. They said I need to go back home and stop acting childish. They don't know what he's been doing to me."

"Baby call me when y'all get to the hotel." Black was too exhausted to go through the emotions, right now.

Fred, Ray, and Black were awakened by the sound of the door opening and closing. James, who'd eased out while they were still asleep, entered, carrying bags from a fast food restaurant.

"Man, what you got going on?" Fred asked, shielding his eyes from the bright sunlight that beamed through the thin curtains hanging over the large window of the balcony.

"Food," James announced, placing the bags on the only bed, which Fred occupied. "Plus, I got the address. So, the quicker y'all eat, the quicker we can get at this nigga and head back to the city."

"You got the address?" Black asked, getting up off the pallet he'd made on the floor.

"Fred, I'ma take you to rent a car," James continued as if he hadn't heard Black. "Ray and Black, y'all wipe the room down and be ready to roll out when we get back."

No one argued. After they'd eaten, everyone set out to perform their duty. It had taken Fred and James almost thirty minutes to return with the rental, which was a blue, four-door Ford F-150. Once Ray and Black joined them, James gave Fred the directions, and thirty minutes later, they pulled up, parking across the street from Willie's house.

"Yeah, that's it!" Black exclaimed, recognizing the Ford Expedition that sat in the driveway. "Jay, how the hell you find out?"

"I asked around," James answered, not willing to reveal that he'd memorized Nikki's friend's address, drove to her place, threatened the information out of her at gunpoint, then drowned her in her bathtub, so she couldn't alarm Willie or the police. "You think he's here?" he asked Black.

"I can't say," Black answered, eyeing the convertible Benz beside the Ford truck. "I don't know how many cars he got. I just know the truck."

They all watched the house in silence. The only sound that could be heard, was the hum of the F-150's engine, and the periodic clicking sound that signified the air conditioner was activated. Although they were wearing bullet-proof vests under dark clothing, they had all opted for short pants, considering the weather in Florida.

In the moment of silence, James thought about Kim, wondering how she'd found out about Ray's shop, and why all of a sudden, she'd go by there. Perhaps she was doing bad and needed

246

money. She knew Ray was pissed at her for her betrayal, but she also knew he was kind and understanding, and if she was really in need of some cash, he would give it to her. But Ray didn't know that James had tracked her down, months ago. He knew she was staying with Patrice, and still seeing Mark.

"There he is!" Black exclaimed, seeing Willie exit the house, carrying a gym bag and climbed into the Expedition.

"So, what'd we do, follow him?" Fred asked.

"Fuck no!" James answered. "Block his ass in!"

Fred didn't hesitate. He pulled the truck into Willie's driveway and blocked him in. Immediately, gloves and ball caps were donned, and The Kingz quickly dismounted. Black being the first to approach the driver's side, snatched the door open, punched Willie in the face, then pulled him out of the truck. Before he could hit the ground, they were all punching, kicking, and pistol-whipping him. He pleaded for his life as they beat him for over a minute.

"I'll take it from here," Black told his comrades as they stood over a battered and bloody Willie, who was now regarding Black as if he was a ghost.

"Go ahead and sentence that nigga!" James said, taking the gym bag from the truck.

"I find you guilty of putting your hands on something that never belonged to you!" Black spoke with his gun aimed at Willie's face. "I sentence you to death! Any objections?"

No one objected. Black squeezed the trigger, sending all fourteen slugs through Willie's skull.

"Now that's some real closed-casket type of shit, right there!" James marveled. "Let's get back to the city!"

They climbed back into the truck, and Fred casually backed out of the driveway, headed for the hotel. James opened the gym bag in his lap to see three kilos of cocaine, but it struck him as odd. Not the drugs, but the way they were wrapped. He only knew one person who wrapped their bricks this way— *Franco!*

# CHAPTER 31

It's been a week, and Miami officials were still in helter-skelter about Willie's, and some White woman's untimely deaths. Nikka was aware of it, but hadn't indicated, or intimated that Black had anything to do with it. He'd moved her and the kids into some apartments in Avondale Estates, for the time being.

Everything was back to normal with Black and Connie, but, since she'd started her new job at Home Depot, they rarely spent time together. Now, it was after seven, and Black was leaving Nikki's place, after having dinner with her and the kids. She wanted him to stay longer, but he couldn't, because the more he looked at her, the more he wanted to make love to her. Plus, the more he wanted to ask her if she knew Willie was a drug dealer, but he had to squash both thoughts, and the best way he knew how to do that was to run!

As he drove, he thought about the success he and his friends had accomplished. They were huge in the drug game. Now, some of his DJ affiliates were pushing at clubs and parties they'd DJ'd at. Plus, Kingz BMWs was bringing in a nice piece of change. As Black got onto the expressway, he peered into his rearview mirror and caught a glimpse of a black H-2 Hummer, two cars back. It was the same truck he thought was following him, yesterday. He darted his eyes from the road to the mirror and, seconds later, it was confirmed. The truck had turned onto the expressway.

His pistol was already in his lap as Black accelerated a bit, to put a little more distance between them, but the H-2 kept up, casually switching lanes, maintaining a good four-car-length distance. The sun was doing its reflector's trick off the vehicles, making it hard to see any kind of features of any occupants, and Black knew the only way to see who his pursuers were, he had to slow down. Therefore, he eased off the gas pedal, but it seemed as if the driver of the Hummer was doing the same. The truck was dropping back now. Black maintained a steady 54 mph, but the H-2 dropped back, until it with the ray of the sun's reflector's trick disappeared.

\*\*\*\*

Gutta-Loc had phoned his big homie in California and told him about The Kingz' threat. The big homie told him they'd better let *nobody* run them off their turf, which is why they continued what they were doing, but remained strapped, and vigilant. Obviously, they were bluffing, because it had been a week, and they hadn't been back.

"Say, cuz, ain't this them?" one of the gang members asked as a black H-2 approached at a slow pace.

"Nah," Gutta answered giving the truck a once over. "That's that lame-ass nigga, Rodney."

"I thought Rodney had rims on his shit," another member voiced.

That's when Gutta-Loc took another look. By the time he'd realized it was not Rodney's truck, it was too late. The front and rear-passenger windows rolled down, and two handguns appeared. The gang tried to run for cover while reaching for their weapons, but the handguns went off with accuracy, pinning fatal upper body and headshots.

\*\*\*\*

Kingz BMWs opens at 9 a.m. and closes at 5 p.m., Monday through Saturday, but James was always the last to leave. Shonda, who was their secretary, left shortly after Fred leaving him alone. Ray was pretty much part-time, being that he had RJP Customs to help out with. He said Kim hadn't been back to the shop, which didn't surprise James, who was still fighting the urge to send the Kingzmen to off her, Mark, and their son. That's what distinguished him from Ray because he cared nothing about taking a child's life.

Now, it was almost eight o'clock, and James had been making calls, checking on their customers and workers. He'd even called Vincent, to let him know he was still alive and kicking, and that he would have everything for him on the day they were supposed to meet, which was the day after the DJ tournament. Moe was the last person he had to call, then he was going to see what to do about some pussy since Shonda had moved back home complaining that Sheila started having those nightmares again.

"Hello?" some female answered Moe's phone.

"Where Moe at?" James asked, not sure if he'd dialed the right number.

"He's at Grady Hospital," she responded.

"For what?"

"Somebody shot him, last night,"

James locked up the dealership and drove to the hospital determined to find out who'd capped his little homie. The girl that answered Moe's phone, was the one who was pregnant by him. She told James it happened in Pepper Mill Apartments, and that she was on her way back to the hospital to see him. She was there when James arrived, sitting beside Moe's bed, looking like she was ready to go into labor at any minute, and speaking of looks. Moe didn't look like he'd been a victim of gunplay, but he was. He told James that the three Drop Squad members who hung out in Pepper Mill, robbed and shot him in the stomach.

Now, James was highly pissed off. These niggas really think they can just fuck with anybody and get away with it. Apparently, they didn't know that if The Kingz were pushed, they would push back! James left the hospital, met up with Grip and three other Kingzmen, and drove out to Pepper Mill in a stolen car. He parked it a few apartment buildings away from their target spot, where the three culprits stood on a porch with two females. One of the guys was holding a child.

These niggas are bold, James thought as he and the KMs, all clad in black fatigue and strapped with machine guns, watched them from the corner of another building.

"Kill everything in the vicinity!" James commanded, and they all came from behind the building, briskly approaching their targets.

When they got within twenty feet, all guns went up, and simultaneously exploded. The man with the child tried to use the child as a shield, but slugs tore through the baby like a stuffed animal. There were no survivors.

****

James felt as if he'd just fallen asleep when he was awakened by the constant ringing of his phone, 1:51 was showing on the clock.

"Yeah, bruh?" he answered, seeing Fred's number on the screen.

"Man, somebody done set our shit on fire!" Fred asserted with anger in his voice.

James sat up. "What shit?"

"The fuckin' dealership!" Fred voiced, furiously. "The Fire Department called Sharonda a few minutes ago. I'm on the way there."

"Does Ray and Black know?" James asked, getting out of bed.

"Not yet."

"We gotta tell 'em. You call Black and I'll call Ray."

"A'ight."

James called Ray, and delivered the news, telling him that he didn't have to drive out to Marietta, but he insisted, and was there with Eric, Sharonda, Black, Connie, Fred, and Yvonne, when James finally arrived on the chaotic scene, where the building looked as if it had been bombed by a fighter jet. Although the fire had been extinguished, and firefighters and inspectors were assessing the damage. Other officials were talking to Sharonda, being that the dealership was in her name.

No one spoke as they all stood around, watching the scene, and waiting for Sharonda to return and tell them what they had already figured out. Minutes later, she approached and confirmed their thoughts. It was arson.

****

Fred couldn't believe he was finally able to fall asleep, after leaving the dreadful scene of the dealership this morning, but when he awakened, he saw that it was after twelve, and Yvonne had already left for the salon. He didn't have an appetite, so he showered, donned the suit he was going to wear to work at Kingz BMWs, activated Yvonne's house alarm and used the key she'd given him to lock the place up.

As Fred drove from Cobb County, he thought about all the things that were suddenly transpiring. He knew they'd stepped on a lot of toes when they reduced the prices of their product. So, anybody could've been behind the dealership's arson. Especially Drop Squad and even Akbar wasn't *too holier than thou* to attempt such a feat, considering the confrontation they had, and the cabalistic shooting that supervened in the West End that injured and claimed the lives of a few of his people. Also, Fred couldn't help but add Norris to the list for the comment he'd made two days ago, at Eric's barber shop.

"Y'all got the rest of us at a stand-still," he'd said. "Hell, if I don't hurry up and knock y'all off. I'll fuck around have to sell the mansion!"

It was said in a joking matter, but Fred had never known Norris to joke like that. Plus, Norris had been under investigation for the death of a notorious drug dealer that was rumored to be a murder-for-hire, three years ago, but somehow, managed to shake the allegation.

So, yes, Fred was going to bring his name up at the Kingz meeting later.

"Look who finally made it!" Fred's mother greeted him when he entered the house.

"I brought you lunch," he said, handing her a Burger King's bag.

"What happened to breakfast?"

"I overslept," he answered, flopping down on the sofa. "Somebody burned down our car dealership."

"That was y'all's car place?" Her eyes were wide with apprehension. "I just saw that on the news. They said the name, but I wasn't familiar with it."

"I guess it was the top story, huh?"

"No," she answered. "The top story was the massacre that took place in Pepper Mill Apartments last night. Five adults, and a two-year-old. They say it was the second shooting in two nights."

****

"So, that's Drop Squad, Akbar, and Norris," James read from the small tablet."

The Kingz had been at the Round Table for thirty minutes. First, going over all the events that had taken place. Now, they were trying to put together a list of potential enemies.

"Have anybody gotten into it with anybody lately?" Fred asked, looking around the table at his comrades. "This is the moment of truth. Right now, we need everything out on the table."

James hesitated before asserting, "Three members of Drop Squad had robbed and shot Moe in the stomach, night before last."

"Moe?" Ray inquired.

"And you and the Kingzmen retaliated last night," Fred summarized.

"What about the Crips?"

"I ain't have shit to do with that," James answered.

Fred shot him a skeptical look.

"That's on my crown!" James protested. "Ain't no telling who them niggas done pissed off. They weren't getting no money. They were just making noise, but I had nothing to do with that."

"What about, Akbar?" Fred asked, still skeptical. "The West End shooting?"

****

As always, Yvonne was the last to leave her salon. She activated the alarm and was headed out the door when four, masked men rushed her, forcing her back into the store. She screamed and put up a fight as she tried to get a grip on her pepper spray on her keychain, but they wrested her keys and purse from her and thrust her into one of the stylist chairs. One placed tape over her mouth, two used handcuffs to cuff her arms and legs to the chair and the fourth man was pouring gasoline all over the place, including her. Once complete, they all rushed for the door. The last man looked at her for a second, struck a match, then dropped it to the floor, watching the store and Yvonne go up in flames.

"Fuck that!" James exclaimed. "Whoever the muhfucka is, is trying to make us fold by coming at us indirect! Now, I don't know about y'all, but I'ma King til' the death of me! They buried Tupac a G.' They gon' bury me a King!"

"I feel that," Ray asserted. "Ain't no need of laying down now. We done came this far."

"Yeah," Fred spoke. "We can't let these niggas back us into a corner, but we gotta be careful. Just because these niggas ain't brought it to our front porch, doesn't mean they won't!"

"I just wish we knew where the heat was coming from," said Black, thinking about Kevin. Since Felicia was dealing with Rico, a member of Drop Squad, but she was a prostitute. So, there was no telling what other potential enemies she was sucking off.

"I think we should call the Kingzmen," James said. "Strap up, and just go down the list. We got two weeks before the DJ battle. I believe the ten of us can clear the list by then. Starting with Drop Squad."

"I disagree," said Fred. "The heat could be coming from anywhere. We don't wanna hit the wrong people. That's a good plan, but I think we should hold off on it."

All Kingz agreed, then decided to retire to their homes, with no one mentioning anything about a mysterious, black Hummer. James stayed back gathering up a few things. Plus, he was waiting on Raymond to stop by and pick up a key that he was going to traffic to Savannah. Being that Raymond and April had declared and admitted their relationship over a month ago. James was going to let this be Raymond's last run, for the sake of his sister. If Raymond was to get caught up in some bullshit, April would never forgive him.

James was sitting on the trunk of his car when Raymond pulled the wrecker through the opened gate of The Palace. The dogs barked and chased the truck all the way to the building.

"What's up, bruh-in-law!" Raymond greeted, stepping down from the cab.

"Shit, you." James dapped him, then handed him a plastic bag containing a brick. "Veezy already know you'll be a lil late."

"A'ight."

Raymond planted the bag in the wrecked car on the bed of the truck, then rode off. James locked the gate, and hit the expressway, listening to *C-Bo's 'Straight Killah'* from the classical Boss Ballin' soundtrack. The next exit was MLK, his exit, but after checking his rearview. He decided to take the following exit. He was expecting his anonymous guest. It was not yet dark, so the black H-2 that was four car-links back was quite conspicuous.

James didn't tell his crew about the truck, because he didn't want them to worry. He knew they were after him for something he'd done. Although he didn't know what, or who these people were, whoever they were, if they thought he was going to be an easy target, they were dead-ass wrong! James made the next exit, starting *'Straight Killah'* back over, and pressing repeat. He kept at a casual pace, being careful not to make any indications he'd spotted them. This was good, because they stayed with him, this time, three car-links back as he cruised the main street.

After passing two traffic lights, James decided it was time to get this shit over with. He initiated a right turn down a residential street. Then, immediately and quickly, he slammed on the brakes, threw the car in park, pressed the trunk button on his keychain, and lunged from the car. The first car rode by before he got to the trunk. His target was next, but he was already feeling like a Mob Boss from one of those old mob movies, holding the Tommy guns waist high as '*Straight Killah*' played in the background. He was definitely not going to be an easy target!

# CHAPTER 32

James' palms were already sweaty as he held the fully loaded Tommy gun with his finger rested on the trigger. He'd forgotten all about his fear of the weapon. He knew that the weapon couldn't harm him as long as he was on the opposite side of the barrel. But he was about to make sure the powerful gun did more than harm somebody, tonight!

Just then, the H-2 came into view. James tightened his grip. All the driver had to do, was make the turn and James was going to turn the H-2 into an H-Zero, but the dark-tinted SUV drove on by with no indication that it was ever going to make the turn.

This pissed James off because he was ready to get this shit over with, but this didn't stop him. He felt he knew where, and who the heat was coming from. Slamming the trunk, climbing behind the wheel, and placing the gun on the passenger seat, James drove off, dialing Grip's number.

It took over an hour for he, Grip, and three other Kingzmen to gear up and move out. Now, in the black GMC van, they were on their way to East Point. James, Grip and two KMs were ducked off in the cargo area, as one drove. Getting to East Point, the driver entered the bowling alley's parking lot and circled once, so everyone could get a fair look at the Friday-night crowd.

"It's a green light, fellas!" James said, seeing that most of the crowd were members of Drop Squad.

As planned, the driver circled the lot again and stopped ten feet away from the entrance, with the rear of the van facing the building. Once all ski masks were on, Grip counted to three and simultaneously, Grip and James popped out of the rear, both with Tommy guns, and the two Kingzmen were out the side, with AK-47s. All guns went off and bullets pierced through flesh, glass, wooden pool tables and more flesh. The KMs with the AKs had expertly gone through two cartridges before the drums of the Tommy guns went dry.

Once all guns were empty, James and the KMs were back in the van, leaving the place looking like a scene from an old slasher film.

****

*Two weeks later*

It was Sylvia's birthday, and Ray who'd come down with a cold the night before, had bought her some flowers, but when he'd gotten to her grave. He was surprised to see there was already a variety of flowers left for her. He let out a series of coughs and spit out a blob of cold. This flustered him because it was the middle of August, and he'd already come down with a cold. Plus, this was the night of the DJ battle. He'd already laid out his suit and robe. It seemed like it was all everyone talked about, as if the boost in Georgia's crime rate over the past two weeks, didn't matter.

Fred's friend, Yvonne, was found dead and handcuffed to a chair inside her salon that was set on fire. A fatal shooting at the East Point bowling alley that left sixteen people dead, and nine in critical condition, was said to be the initiation of the sequence of deadly shootings in the projects. Even some of the Kingz' workers had gotten caught up in the rapture, but still, everyone was carrying on like the Battle of the DJ's was all that mattered.

"Maybe you *are* in a better place," Ray said to Sylvia's grave, before going into another coughing fit. Happy Birthday!"

He kneeled down, placing his flowers with the rest. As he stood, he heard the sound of a passing vehicle and looked back to see a black H-2 Hummer slowly riding through the cemetery. He'd been seeing this truck, lately, and he knew there weren't too many people in the same area, with black H-2 Hummers, but the truck moved on. Ray didn't feel threatened by its presence as he made for his Delta Eighty-Eight and drove to Maple Creek. Where he checked on B.J. and T-Roc and collected the money from the ecstasy pills sales that went to The Kingz Account.

He kicked it with them until eight, then headed home to get ready for the D.J. battle, in which The Kingz were supposed to be at the club around nine-thirty, being that the battle kicked off at ten. On the expressway, Ray was halfway home, when his Service Engine light came on, and the engine died. Being that he was in the middle of light traffic, in lieu of attempting to pull to the shoulder, he threw the gear into neutral, restarted the car, then shifted back to drive. This happened again and Ray reworked the same maneuver, this time moving to the far-right, lest the Delta decides to call it quits, and, just so happen, it did.

"I know damn well you ain't gon' act up on me now?" Ray exclaimed, pulling over, attempting to restart the car to no avail.

He called James.

"What up, lil bruh?" James answered.

"Man, my car cut off on the expressway," Ray told him.

"I don't know why you're still riding around in that raggedy-ass Delta, anyway!" James chided. "Hell, I can't pick you up no how. We're still waiting on this nigga with the limo. Then, Fred wanna stop by The Palace."

"He wanna stop by The Palace?"

"Yeah," James answered. "He didn't say why. You know what, Ray just pulled up. Let me see if he'll scoop you up." James spoke to Raymond in the background, then, "Where you at?"

It took less than thirty minutes for Raymond to locate him. Once Raymond pulled his convertible BMW in front of the Delta, Ray dismounted and climbed in beside Raymond.

"I got a cold," Ray warned, cracking the window a bit.

"In August?" Raymond inquired, pulling off.

"Yeah."

"You want me to pick your car up tomorrow?"

"Hell yeah!" Ray answered. "I gotta give you my spare keys. They're at the house.

"When they pulled up to Ray's house," Raymond asked, "You want me to wait out here?"

"Hell nah!" Ray answered. "You're family now. My house is your house. Just don't use my toothbrush!"

Raymond laughed, causing Ray to laugh a little. That's when he realized his sense of humor was returning.

"It's some drinks in the fridge," Ray said, once they'd entered the house.

Ray went straight for his bedroom for the spare keys, but another coughing spell directed his attention to the Dayquil bottle on the dresser. He took a swig from the bottle just as Raymond entered with a Sprite in his hand.

Are you sure you gonna make it?" he asked.

"I'm a King!" Ray answered, looking at his red, watery eyes in the dresser's mirror. "They'll just think I'm high. White people might think I'm stoned."

Raymond laughed. "Yeah, that'll be after you pass out."

The doorbell rang, Ray checked his watch. "Damn, that's the Calvary. Let 'em in!"

Raymond left the room, and Ray began undressing. He was down to his boxer shorts when James, Fred, and Black came to the door, all dressed in suits, and wearing their chains. He assumed they'd left their robes and crowns in the limousine.

"Come on Christmas!" said James. "We already might be a lil' late."

**** 

In full Royal Fashion, The Kingz were on their way to the much-anticipated Battle of The DJs, with Grip and three other Kingzmen trailing the stretch Escalade, in the company's Escalade. Although he was affected by Yvonne's death, Fred had done his best not to show it. He hadn't told his comrades yet, but after tonight, he wanted to go with James' plan, and bust on every nigga they'd pinned as a potential. He believed James had something to do with the bowling alley shooting and was glad he'd popped it off. Fuck Drop Squad!

B.J. didn't tell Ray that he was going to the DJ event, but he'd already left to beat the crowd. Ray was not going to miss out on any money because he left T-Roc to hold down the spot, and T-Roc wasn't tripping. He had some twenty-three-year-old chick coming through. He was playing the Play Station 2 when someone knocked on the door. He figured it had to be her, but when he opened the door, there were two men on a motorcycle, with their helmets still on, just looking at him.

"What y'all want?" he asked.

Saying nothing, the passenger pulled an Uzi from inside his jacket, and fired upon T-Roc through the screen of the burglar bar door, with a burst of rounds, leaving him dead on the kitchen floor.

\*\*\*\*

It was a bit too quiet in the limousine, but James knew his trues were thinking like he was thinking. He was really just hoping they could get through the night with no drama. He was also wishing he'd went ahead and knocked Akbar and Norris off. That way, he wouldn't be worrying about anything jumping off, tonight. Drop Squad had pretty much tucked their tails after that East Point shooting.

"Black, you aight?" James asked.

"Yeah, I'm good."

"Fred?"

"Yeah."

"Ray?"

"I'm straight."

\*\*\*\*

Shonda, Sheila, Ebony, and Theresa were already outside the club, amongst the large group of people that were waiting to get in. They were not going to stand out there for long, because, as soon as The Kingz pull up, they were going to accompany them. Tonight, Sheila was determined to show Ray she was not like those other women he'd been messing with who'd broken his heart. He was going to hear her out, tonight, even if she had to stage a spectacle!

\*\*\*\*

The Kingz had pretty much loosened up and were engaged in a casual conversation. They were so caught up in the conversation, they hadn't noticed that the driver had run a red light, leaving the Kingzmen stuck at the intersection.

The driver passed two more lights, then stopped at one that had not yet turned red. Suddenly, four black H-2 Hummers pulled up, two on each side of the limousine. Tinted windows rolled down, and the barrels of assault rifles stuck out. Instantaneously, the guns erupted, sending slugs through fiberglass, windows, and flesh.

*The saga continues in*
*Queenz of the Game*
*Coming Soon*

# Submission Guideline

Submit the first three chapters of your completed manuscript to ldpsubmissions@gmail.com, subject line: Your book's title. The manuscript must be in a .doc file and sent as an attachment. Document should be in Times New Roman, double spaced and in size 12 font. Also, provide your synopsis and full contact information. If sending multiple submissions, they must each be in a separate email.

Have a story but no way to send it electronically? You can still submit to LDP/Ca$h Presents. Send in the first three chapters, written or typed, of your completed manuscript to:

**LDP: Submissions Dept**
**Po Box 870494**
**Mesquite, Tx 75187**

*DO NOT send original manuscript. Must be a duplicate.*

Provide your synopsis and a cover letter containing your full contact information.

Thanks for considering LDP and Ca$h Presents.

A HUSTLER'S DECEIT 3

KILL ZONE **II**

BAE BELONGS TO ME III

By **Aryanna**

THE COST OF LOYALTY **III**

By **Kweli**

SHE FELL IN LOVE WITH A REAL ONE **II**

By **Tamara Butler**

RENEGADE BOYS **III**

By **Meesha**

CORRUPTED BY A GANGSTA **IV**

By **Destiny Skai**

A GANGSTER'S CODE **III**

By **J-Blunt**

KING OF NEW YORK V

RISE TO POWER III

COKE KINGS II

By **T.J. Edwards**

GORILLAZ IN THE BAY III

**De'Kari**

THE STREETS ARE CALLING II

**Duquie Wilson**

KINGPIN KILLAZ IV

STREET KINGS 2

PAID IN BLOOD 2

**Hood Rich**

STEADY MOBBIN' **III**

**Marcellus Allen**

SINS OF A HUSTLA II

**ASAD**

TRIGGADALE II

**Elijah R. Freeman**

MARRIED TO A BOSS III

**By Destiny Skai & Chris Green**

KINGS OF THE GAME III

**Playa Ray**

**<u>Available Now</u>**

<u>RESTRAINING ORDER</u> **I & II**

By **CA$H & Coffee**

<u>LOVE KNOWS NO BOUNDARIES</u> **I II & III**

By **Coffee**

<u>RAISED AS A GOON I, II, III & IV</u>

<u>BRED BY THE SLUMS I, II, III</u>

<u>BLAST FOR ME I & II</u>

<u>ROTTEN TO THE CORE I III</u>

<u>A BRONX TALE I, II, III</u>

<u>DUFFEL BAG CARTEL I II</u>

By **Ghost**

<u>LAY IT DOWN</u> **I & II**

<u>LAST OF A DYING BREED</u>

<u>BLOOD STAINS OF A SHOTTA I & II</u>

By **Jamaica**

<u>LOYAL TO THE GAME</u>

<u>LOYAL TO THE GAME II</u>

<u>LOYAL TO THE GAME III</u>

<u>LIFE OF SIN</u>

By **TJ & Jelissa**

<u>BLOODY COMMAS I & II</u>

SKI MASK CARTEL I  II & III

KING OF NEW YORK I II,III IV

RISE TO POWER I II

COKE KINGS

By **T.J. Edwards**

IF LOVING HIM IS WRONG…I & II

LOVE ME EVEN WHEN IT HURTS I II

By **Jelissa**

WHEN THE STREETS CLAP BACK I & II III

By **Jibril Williams**

A DISTINGUISHED THUG STOLE MY HEART I II & III

LOVE SHOULDN'T HURT I II III

RENEGADE BOYS I & II

By **Meesha**

A GANGSTER'S CODE I &, II III

By **J-Blunt**

PUSH IT TO THE LIMIT

By **Bre' Hayes**

BLOOD OF A BOSS **I, II, III,  IV, V**

By **Askari**

THE STREETS BLEED MURDER **I, II & III**

THE HEART OF A GANGSTA I II& III

By **Jerry Jackson**

CUM FOR ME

CUM FOR ME 2

CUM FOR ME 3

CUM FOR ME 4

An **LDP Erotica Collaboration**

BRIDE OF A HUSTLA **I  II & II**

THE FETTI GIRLS **I, II& III**

CORRUPTED BY A GANGSTA I, II & III

By **Destiny Skai**

WHEN A GOOD GIRL GOES BAD

By **Adrienne**

THE COST OF LOYALTY

**By Kweli**

A GANGSTER'S REVENGE **I II III & IV**

THE BOSS MAN'S DAUGHTERS

THE BOSS MAN'S DAUGHTERS II

THE BOSSMAN'S DAUGHTERS III

THE BOSSMAN'S DAUGHTERS IV

THE BOSS MAN'S DAUGHTERS **V**

A SAVAGE LOVE **I & II**

BAE BELONGS TO ME I II

A HUSTLER'S DECEIT I, II, III

WHAT BAD BITCHES DO I, II, III

By **Aryanna**

A KINGPIN'S AMBITON

A KINGPIN'S AMBITION **II**

I MURDER FOR THE DOUGH

By **Ambitious**

TRUE SAVAGE

TRUE SAVAGE II

TRUE SAVAGE **III**

TRUE SAVAGE **IV**

TRUE SAVAGE **V**

TRUE SAVAGE **VI**

By **Chris Green**

A DOPEBOY'S PRAYER

By **Eddie "Wolf" Lee**

THE KING CARTEL **I, II & III**

By **Frank Gresham**

THESE NIGGAS AIN'T LOYAL **I, II & III**

By **Nikki Tee**

GANGSTA SHYT **I II &III**

By **CATO**

THE ULTIMATE BETRAYAL

By **Phoenix**

BOSS'N UP **I , II & III**

By **Royal Nicole**

I LOVE YOU TO DEATH

**By Destiny J**

I RIDE FOR MY HITTA

I STILL RIDE FOR MY HITTA

By **Misty Holt**

LOVE & CHASIN' PAPER

By **Qay Crockett**

TO DIE IN VAIN

SINS OF A HUSTLA

By **ASAD**

BROOKLYN HUSTLAZ

By **Boogsy Morina**

BROOKLYN ON LOCK I & II

By **Sonovia**

GANGSTA CITY

By **Teddy Duke**

A DRUG KING AND HIS DIAMOND I & II III

A DOPEMAN'S RICHES

HER MAN, MINE'S TOO I, II

CASH MONEY HO'S

**By Nicole Goosby**

TRAPHOUSE KING **I II & III**

KINGPIN KILLAZ I II III

STREET KINGS

PAID IN BLOOD

By **Hood Rich**

LIPSTICK KILLAH **I, II**

CRIME OF PASSION I & II

By **Mimi**

STEADY MOBBN' **I, II**

By **Marcellus Allen**

WHO SHOT YA **I, II**

**Renta**

GORILLAZ IN THE BAY **I II**

**DE'KARI**

TRIGGADALE

**Elijah R. Freeman**

GOD BLESS THE TRAPPERS I, II, III

THESE SCANDALOUS STREETS I, II, III

FEAR MY GANGSTA I, II, III

THESE STREETS DON'T LOVE NOBODY I, II

BURY ME A G I, II, III, IV, V

A GANGSTA'S EMPIRE I, II, III

**Tranay Adams**

THE STREETS ARE CALLING

**Duquie Wilson**

MARRIED TO A BOSS... I II

**By Destiny Skai & Chris Green**

KINGS OF THE GAME I II

**Playa Ray**

**<u>BOOKS BY LDP'S CEO, CA$H</u>**

<u>TRUST IN NO MAN</u>
<u>TRUST IN NO MAN 2</u>
<u>TRUST IN NO MAN 3</u>
<u>BONDED BY BLOOD</u>
<u>SHORTY GOT A THUG</u>
<u>THUGS CRY</u>
<u>THUGS CRY 2</u>
<u>THUGS CRY 3</u>
<u>TRUST NO BITCH</u>
<u>TRUST NO BITCH 2</u>
<u>TRUST NO BITCH 3</u>
<u>TIL MY CASKET DROPS</u>
<u>RESTRAINING ORDER</u>
<u>RESTRAINING ORDER 2</u>
<u>IN LOVE WITH A CONVICT</u>

**<u>Coming Soon</u>**
BONDED BY BLOOD 2
BOW DOWN TO MY GANGSTA

Playa Ray

CPSIA information can be obtained
at www.ICGtesting.com
Printed in the USA
LVHW051546201220
674691LV00012B/1036